PRAISE FOR THOMAS M. DISCH

"When it comes to Thomas Discl This literary chameleon redefined scie com-pared to the best from Orwell to Huxley, wrote bestselling children's books about talking kitchen appliances, earned censure from the Catholic Church for an off-Broadway play, published light verse, twisted the pulp conventions of gothic fiction, experimented with interactive software, and demolished the American poetry establishment, UFO cults, and other sacred cows in brilliant critical essays."

– THE MINNEAPOLIS STAR-TRIBUNE

"One of the most remarkably talented writers around."

– THE WASHINGTON POST BOOK WORLD

"Diversely gifted... entirely original... joyously versatile... a unique talent."

– NEWSWEEK

"Novelist, poet, and critic, he has become a most significant literary presence."

– THE AMERICAN ACADEMY OF ARTS AND LETTERS

PRAISE FOR *The Word of God*

"Thomas M. Disch isn't afraid of backlash for what some might consider the writing of a heretic. The author is known for both his science fiction and incisive literary criticism. His latest, *The Word of God*, a first person 'memoir' written as if he were God, will no doubt push literary buttons – and boundaries. Regardless of a reader's religious persuasion, there is no denying one fact – Disch is extraordinarily funny."

– KIRKUS

"The god Disch is brilliant, startling, playful, vengeful, poetic, and kind of scary. As gods go, we could do worse. The writer Disch is brilliant, startling, playful, vengeful, poetic, and kind of scary. As writers go, there is no one better."

– KAREN JOY FOWLER, AUTHOR OF *The Jane Austen Book Club*

"Tom Disch is the Devil! He says he's God, but he's not. Read this book against my warning, and at your peril. Every page you turn will send you deeper into the abyss. Tom Disch is America's own Mephistopheles!"

–ALICE K. TURNER, AUTHOR OF *The History of Hell*

"Of course, Tom has always been Jovial... but an actual divinity? Only now must I relinquish my birthright atheism, in recognition of the presence of a literary god. An obscure Vietnamese cult worshipped Victor Hugo, and I was tempted, but that was long ago, and they have passed from the scene."

–NORMAN RUSH, AUTHOR OF *Mating* AND *Mortals*

"I first came to believe in God when he successfully cured my cancer in 1969. A few years later he again answered my prayers by laying his hands on my first wife's belly and ensuring that our child would be a son. On almost every occasion when I have prayed sincerely and selfishly to God in whatever country I have been in he has answered me with his generous blessings, most recently when he cured my diabetes in what I call the Miracle of the I-35 Dairy Queen. I cannot worship nor give my heart to a more beneficent or loving God than He. I have thanked God on every occasion I have been presented with a major literary prize or when those I consider my literary rivals and enemies have been denied awards or been struck with deadly diseases."

–MICHAEL MOORCOCK, AUTHOR OF *Stealer of Souls* AND *Behold the Man*

"A lovely, funny, interesting, incisive, and wonderfully blasphemous novel."

–JEFF VANDERMEER, AUTHOR OF *City of Saints and Madmen* AND *Shriek*

"I had never thought of Tom as stooping to God before, but it turns out to have been a good idea. It's good to hear from a Voice up there that knows the score, knows how to share His laughter with those who are mostly victims of His terrible laugh, knows that He too is art of the Joke. So please stay on high. Do us all Worlds of good."

–JOHN CLUTE

"It has been the happy fate of myself, my twin brother Greg, and our two younger sibs, Gary and Nancy, to have grown up with a god for an older brother. Sometimes it has been difficult to get along with such a perfect know-it-all, but didn't Jesus's siblings have the same blessed problem? What can I say? We adore him."

—JEFFREY JAMES DISCH

BOOKS BY THOMAS M. DISCH

FICTION

The Genocides (1965)
Mankind Under the Leash (1966)
The House that Fear Built [WITH JOHN T. SLADEK] AS BY "CASSANDRA KNYE" (1966)
One Hundred and Two H-Bombs (1966)
Echo Round His Bones (1967)
Black Alice [WITH JOHN T. SLADEK] AS BY "THOM DEMIJOHN" (1968)
Camp Concentration (1968)
Under Compulsion (1968)
Alfred the Great AS BY "VICTOR HASTINGS" (1969)
The Prisoner (1969)
334 (1972)
Getting Into Death and Other Stories (1973)
Clara Reeve AS BY "LEONIE HARGRAVE" (1975)
The Early Science Fiction Stories of Thomas M. Disch (1977)
On Wings of Song (1979)
Fundamental Disch (1980)
Neighboring Lives [WITH CHARLES NAYLOR] (1981)
The Man Who Had No Idea (1982)
The Businessman: A Tale of Terror (1984)
Torturing Mr. Amberwell (1985)
The Silver Pillow: A Tale of Witchcraft (1987)
The M.D.: A Horror Story (1992)
The Priest: A Gothic Romance (1994)
The Sub: A Study in Witchcraft (1999)
The Voyage of the Proteus: An Eyewitness Account of the End of the World (2008)
The Word of God: Or, Holy Writ Rewritten (TACHYON, 2008)

NON-FICTION

The Castle of Indolence: On Poetry, Poets, and Poetasters (1995)
The Dreams Our Stuff Is Made Of: How Science Fiction Conquered the World (1998)
The Castle of Perseverance: Job Opportunities in Contemporary Poetry (2002)
On SF (2005)

POETRY

Highway Sandwiches [WITH CHARLES PLATT AND MARILYN HACKER] (1970)
The Right Way to Figure Plumbing (1972)
ABCDEFG HIJKLM NPOQRST UVWXYZ (1981)
Burn This (1982)
Orders of the Retina (1982)
Here I Am, There You Are, Where Were We (1984)
Yes, Let's: New and Selected Poems (1989)
Dark Verses and Light (1991)
Haikus of an AmPart (1991)
The Dark Old House (1996)
A Child's Garden of Grammar (1997)
About the Size of It (2007)

AS EDITOR

Alfred Hitchcock's Stories That Scared Even Me [WITH ROBERT ARTHUR] (1967)
The Ruins of Earth: An Anthology of Stories of the Immediate Future (1971)
Bad Moon Rising: An Anthology of Political Forebodings (1973)
The New Improved Sun: An Anthology of Utopian S-F (1975)
New Constellations: An Anthology of Tomorrow's Mythologies [WITH CHARLES NAYLOR] (1976)
Strangeness: A Collection of Curious Tales [WITH CHARLES NAYLOR] (1977)

CHILDREN'S BOOKS

The Brave Little Toaster (1986)
The Tale of Dan De Lion (1986)
The Brave Little Toaster Goes to Mars (1988)

THE WALL OF AMERICA

THOMAS M. DISCH

The Wall of America

TACHYON PUBLICATIONS | SAN FRANCISCO

The Wall of America

Cover design by Ann Monn
Interior design & composition by John D. Berry
The typeface is Kingfisher, designed by Jeremy Tankard

Tachyon Publications
1459 18th Street #139
San Francisco, CA 94107
(415) 285-5615
www.tachyonpublications.com

Series editor: Jacob Weisman

ISBN 10: 1-892391-82-1
ISBN 13: 978-1-892391-82-7

Printed in the United States of America
by Worzalla

First Edition: 2008

9 8 7 6 5 4 3 2 1

Contents

THE WALL OF AMERICA

The White Man

> "If human testimony, taken with every care and solemnity, judicially, before commissions innumerable, each consisting of many members, all chosen for integrity and intelligence, and constituting reports more voluminous perhaps than exist upon any other class of cases, is worth anything, it is difficult to deny, or even to doubt the existence of such a phenomenon as the vampire."
>
> J. SHERIDAN LE FANU, "CARMILLA"

IT WAS the general understanding that the world was falling apart in all directions. Bad things had happened and worse were on the way. Everyone understood that – the rich and the poor, old and young (although for the young it might be more dimly sensed, an intuition). But they also understood that there was nothing much anyone could do about it, and so you concentrated on having some fun while there was any left to have. Tawana chewed kwash, which the family grew in the backyard alongside the house, in among the big old rhubarb plants. Once they had tried to eat the rhubarb, but Tawana had to spit it out – and a lucky thing, too, because later on she learned that rhubarb is poison.

The kwash helped if you were hungry (and Tawana was hungry even when her stomach was full) but it could mess up your thinking at the same time. Once in the third grade when she was transferred to a different school closer to downtown and had missed the regular bus, she set off by herself on foot, chewing kwash, and the police picked her up, crying and shoeless, out near the old airport. She had no idea how she'd got there, or lost her shoes. That's the sort of thing the kwash could do, especially if you were just a kid. You got lost without even knowing it.

Anyhow, she was in high school now and the whole system had changed. First when there was the Faith Initiative, she'd gone to a Catholic school, where boys and girls were in the same room all day and things were very strict. You couldn't say a word without raising your hand, or wear your own clothes, only the same old blue uniform every day. But that lasted less than a year. Then the public schools got special teachers for the Somali kids with Intensive English programs, and Tawana and her sisters got vouchers to attend Diversitas, a charter school in what used to be a parking garage in downtown Minneapolis near the old football stadium that they were tearing down. Diversitas is the Latin word for Diversity, and all cultures were respected there. You could have your own prayer rug, or chant, or meditate. It was the complete opposite of Our Lady of Mercy, where everybody had to do everything at the same time, all together. How could you call that freedom of religion? Plus, you could wear pretty much anything you wanted at Diversitas, except for any kind of jewelry that was potentially dangerous. There were even prizes for the best outfits of the week, which Tawana won when she was in the sixth grade. The prize-winning outfit was a Swahili Ceremonial Robe with a matching turban that she'd designed herself with duct tape. Ms. McLeod asked her to wear it to the assembly when the prizes were given out, but that wasn't possible since the towels had had to be returned to their container in the bathroom. She wasn't in fact Swahili, but at that point not many people (including Tawana) knew the difference between Somalia and other parts of Africa. At the assembly, instead of Tawana wearing the actual robe, they had shown a picture from the video on the school's surveillance camera. Up on the screen Tawana's smile must have been six feet from side to side. She was self conscious about her teeth for the next week (kwash tends to darken teeth).

Ms. McLeod had printed out a small picture from the same surveillance tape showing Tawana in her prize-winning outfit, all gleaming white with fuzzy pink flowers. But in the background of that picture there was another figure in white, a man. And no one who looked at the picture had any idea who he might have been. He wasn't one of the teachers, he wasn't in maintenance, and parents rarely visited the school in the daytime. At night there were remedial classes for adult refugees in the basement classrooms, and slams and concerts, sometimes, in the auditorium.

Tawana studied his face a lot, as though it were a puzzle to be solved. Who might he be, that white man, and why was he there at her ceremony? She taped the picture on the inside of the door of her hall locker, underneath the magnetic To Do list with its three immaculately empty categories: Shopping, School, Sports. Then one day it wasn't there. The picture had been removed from her locker. Nothing else had been taken, just that picture of Tawana in her robe and the white man behind her.

That was the last year there were summer vacations. After that you had to go to school all the time. Everybody bitched about it, but Tawana wondered if the complainers weren't secretly glad if only because of the breakfast and lunch programs. With the new year-round schedule there was also a new music and dance teacher, Mr. Forbush, with a beard that had bleached tips. He taught junior high how to do ancient Egyptian dances, a couple of them really exhausting, but he was cute. Some kids said he was having a love affair with Ms. McLeod, but others said no, he was gay.

On a Thursday afternoon late in August of that same summer, when Tawana had already been home from school for an hour or so, the doorbell rang. Then it rang a second time, and third time. Anyone who wanted to visit the family would usually just walk in the house, so the doorbell served mainly as a warning system. But Tawana was at home by herself and she thought what if it was a package and there had to be someone to sign for it?

So she went to the door, but it wasn't a package, it was a man in a white shirt and a blue tie lugging a satchel full of papers. "Are you Miss Makwinja?" he asked Tawana. She should have known better than to admit that's who she was, but she said, yes, that was her name. Then he showed her a badge that said he was an agent for the Census Bureau and he just barged into the house and took a seat in the middle of the twins' futon and started asking her questions. He wanted to know the name of everyone in the family, and how it was spelled and how old they all were and where they were born and their religion and did they have a job. An endless stream of questions, and it was no use saying you didn't know, cause then he would tell her to make a guess. He had a thermos bottle hanging off the side of his knapsack, all beaded with sweat the same as his forehead. The drops would run down the sides of the bottle and down his forehead and his cheeks in zigzags like the mice trying to escape from the laboratory in her brother's video game. "I have to do my homework now," she told him. "That's fine," he said and just sat there. Then after they both sat there a while, not budging, he said, "Oh, I have some other questions here about the house itself. Is there a bathroom?" Tawana nodded. "More than one bathroom?" "I don't know," she said, and suddenly she needed to go to the bathroom herself. But the man wouldn't leave, and wouldn't stop asking his questions. It was like going to the emergency room and having to undress.

And then she realized that she had seen him before this. He was the man behind her in the picture. The picture someone had taken from her locker. The man she had dreamed of again and again.

She got up off the futon and went to stand on the other side of the wooden trunk with the twins' clothes in it. "What did you say your name was?" she asked warily.

"I don't think I did. We're not required to give out our names, you know. My shield number is K-384." He tapped the little plastic badge pinned to his white shirt.

"You know *our* names."

"True. I do. But that's what I'm paid for." And then he smiled this terrible smile, the smile she'd seen in stores and offices and hospitals all her life, without every realizing what it meant. It was the smile of an enemy, of someone sworn to kill her. Not right this moment, but someday maybe years later, someday for sure. He didn't know it yet himself, but Tawana did, because she sometimes had psychic powers. She could look into the future and know what other people were thinking. Not their ideas necessarily, but their feelings. Her mother had had the same gift before she died.

"Well," the white man said, standing up, with a different smile, "thank you for your time." He neatened his papers into a single sheaf and stuffed them back in his satchel.

Someday, somewhere, she would see him again. It was written in the Book of Fate.

*

All that was just before Lionel got in trouble with the INS and disappeared. Lionel had been the family's main source of unvouchered income, and his absence was a source of deep regret, not just for Lucy and the twins, but all of them. No more pizzas, no more Hmong takeout. It was back to beans and rice, canned peas and stewed tomatoes. The cable company took away all the good channels and there was nothing to look at but Tier One, with the law and shopping channels and really dumb cartoons. Tawana got very depressed and even developed suicidal tendencies, which she reported to the school medical officer, who prescribed some purple pills as big as your thumb. But they didn't help much more than a jaw of kwash.

Then Lucy fell in love with a Mexican Kawasaki dealer called Super Hombre and moved to Shakopee, leaving the twins temporarily with the family at the 26th Ave. N.E. house. Except it turned out not to be that temporary. Super Hombre's Kawasaki dealership was all pretend. The bikes in the show window weren't for sale, they were just parked there to make it look like a real business. Super Hombre was charged with sale and possession of a controlled substance, and Lucy was caught in the larger sting and got five to seven. Minnesota had become very strict about even minor felonies.

Without Lucy to look after them, the *niños* became Tawana's responsibility, which was a drag not just in the practical sense that it meant curtailing her various extracurricular activities – the Drama Club, Muslim Sisterhood, Mall Minders – but because it was so embarrassing. She was at an age when she might have had *niños* of her own but instead she'd preserved her chastity. And all for nothing because here she was just the same, wheeling the *niños* back and forth from day care, changing diapers, screaming at them to shut the fuck up. But she never smacked them, which was more than you could say for Lionel or Lucy. Super Hombre had been a pretty good care provider, too, when he had to, except the once when he laid into Kenny with his belt. But Kenny had been asking for it, and Super Hombre was stoned.

The worst thing about being a substitute mom were the trips to the County Health Center. Why couldn't people be counted on to look after their kids without a lot of government bureaucrats sticking their noses into it? All the paperwork, not to mention the shots every time there was some new national amber alert. Or the blood draws! What were they all about? If they did find out you were a carrier, what were they going to do about it anyhow? Empty out all the bad blood and pump you full of a new supply, like bringing a car in for a change of oil?

Basically Tawana just did not like needles and syringes. The sight of her own blood snaking into the little clouded plastic tube and slowly filling one cylinder after another made her sick. She would have nightmares. Sometimes just the sight of a smear of strawberry jam on one of the twins' bibs would register as a bloodstain, and she would feel a chill through her whole body, like diving into a pool. She *hated* needles. She hated the Health Center. She hated every store and streetlight along the way to the Health Center. And most of all she hated the personnel. Nurse Lundgren with his phony smile. Nurse Richardson with her orange hair piled up in an enormous bun. Doctor Shen.

But if someone didn't take the twins in to the Health Center, then there would be Inspectors coming round to the house, perhaps even the INS. And more papers to fill out. And the possibility that the *niños* would be taken off to foster care and the child care stipends suspended or even cancelled. So someone had to get them in to the Health Center and that someone was the person in the family with the least clout. Tawana.

Thanksgiving was the big holiday of the year for the Makwinjas, because of the turkeys. Back in the '90s when the first Somalis had come to Minnesota, their grandfather among them, they'd all been employed by E.G. Harris, the biggest turkey processor in the country. Tawana had seen photographs of the gigantic batteries where the turkeys were grown. They looked like palaces for some Arabian sheik, if you didn't know what they really were. One of the bonuses for E.G. Harris employees to this day was a supersized frozen bird on Thanksgiving and another at Christmas, along with an instruction DVD on making the most of turkey leftovers. There were still two members of the family working for E.G. Harris, so well into February there was plenty of turkey left for turkey pot pie, turkey noodle casserole, and turkey up the ass (which was what Lucy used to call turkey a la king).

The older members of the family, who could still remember what life had been like in Somalia, had a different attitude toward all the food in America than Tawana and her sisters and cousins. Their lives revolved around cooking and grocery shopping and food vouchers. So when the neighborhood Stop 'N' Shop was shut down and CVS took over the building, the older Makwinja women were out on the picket line every day to protest and chant and chain themselves to the awnings. (They were the only exterior elements that anything *could* be chained to: the doors didn't have knobs or handles.) Of course, the protests didn't accomplish anything. In due course CVS moved in, and once people realized there was nowhere else for fourteen blocks to buy basics like Coke and canned soup and toilet paper they started shopping there. One of the last things that Tawana ever heard her grandfather say was after his first visit to the new CVS to fill his prescription for his diabetes medicine. "You know what," he said, "this city is getting to be more like Mogadishu every day." Aunt Bima protested vehemently, saying there was no resemblance at all, that Minneapolis was all clean and modern, while Mogadishu had always been a dump. "You think I'm blind?" Grandpa asked. "You think I'm stupid?" Then he just clamped his jaw shut and refused to argue. A week later he was dead. An embolism.

Half a block from the CVS, what used to be a store selling mattresses and pine furniture had subdivided into an All-Faiths Pentecostal Tabernacle (upstairs) and (downstairs) the Northeast Minneapolis Arts Cooperative. There was a sign over the entrance (which was always padlocked) that said "IRON Y MONGERS" and under that what looked almost like an advertisement from *People* or *GQ* showing four fashion models with big dopey grins under a slogan in mustard-yellow letters: "WELL-DRESSED PEOPLE WEAR CLEAN CLOTHES." In the display windows on either side of the locked door were mannikins dressed entirely in white. The two male mannikins sported white tuxedos and there were a number of female mannikins in stiff sheer white dresses and veils like bridal gowns but sexy. There were bouquets of paper flowers in white vases, and a bookcase full of books all painted white – like the hands and faces of the mannikins. The paint had been applied as carefully as makeup. The mannikins' eyes were realistically blue or green and their lips were bright red, even the two men.

The first time she saw them Tawana thought the mannikins were funny, that the paint on their faces was like the makeup on clowns. But then, walking by the windows a few days later, during a late afternoon snow flurry, she was creeped out. The mannikins seemed half-alive, and threatening. Then, on a later visit, Tawana started feeling angry, as though the display in the windows was somehow a slur directed at herself and her family and all the African Americans in the neighborhood, at everyone who had to walk past the store (which wasn't really a store, since it was always closed) and look at the mannikins with their bright red lips and idiot grins. Why would anyone ever go to the trouble to fix up a window like that? They weren't selling the clothes. You couldn't go inside. If there was a joke, Tawana didn't get it.

She began to dream about the two mannikins in the tuxedos. In her dream they were alive but mannikins at the same time. She was pushing the twins in their stroller along 27th Avenue, and the two men, with their white faces and red lips, were following her, talking to each other in whispers and snickering. When Tawana walked faster, so would they, and when she paused at every curb to lift or lower the wheels of the stroller, the two men would pause too. She realized they were following her in order to learn where she lived, that's why they always kept their distance.

The man in charge of the All-Faiths Pentecostal Tabernacle was a Christian minister by the name of Gospel Blantyre Blount, D.D., and he came from Malawi. "Malawi," the Reverend Blount explained to the seventh grade class visiting the tabernacle on the second Tuesday of Brotherhood Month, "is a narrow strip of land in the middle of Africa, in the middle of four Z's. To the west is Zambia and Zimbabwe, and to the east is Tanzania and Mozambique. I come from the town of Chiradzulu, which you may have read about or even seen on the news. The people there are mostly Zulus, and famous for being tall. Like me. How tall do you think I am?"

No one raised a hand.

"Don't be shy, children," said Ms. McLeod, who was wearing a traditional Zulu headdress and several enormous copper earrings. "Take a guess. Jeffrey."

Jeffrey squirmed. "Six foot," he hazarded.

"Six foot, ten inches," said Reverend Blount, getting up off his stool and demonstrating his full height, and an imposing gut as well. "And I'm the short guy in the family."

This was greeted by respectful, muted laughter.

"Anyone here ever been to Africa?" Reverend Blount asked, in a rumbling, friendly voice, like the voice in the Verizon ads.

"I have!" said Tawana.

"Oh, Tawana, you have not!" Ms. McLeod protested with a rattle of earrings.

"I was born here in Minneapolis, but my family is from Somalia."

Reverend Blount nodded his head gravely. "I've been there. Somalia's a beautiful nation. But they got problems there. Just like Malawi, they got problems."

"Gospel," Ms. McLeod said, "you promised. We can't get into that with the children."

"Okay. But let me ask: how many of you kids has been baptized?"

Six of the children raised their hands. Jeffrey, who hadn't, explained: "We're Muslim, the rest of us."

"The reason I asked, is in the tabernacle here we don't think someone is a 'kid' if they been baptized. So the baptized are free to listen or not, as they choose."

"Gospel, this is not a religious matter."

"But what if it is? What it is, for sure, is a matter of life and death. And it's in the *newspapers*. I can show you! Right here." He took a piece of paper from an inside pocket of his dashiki, unfolded it, and held it up for the visitors to see. "This is from the *New York Times,* Tuesday, January 14, 2003. Not that long ago, huh? And what it tells about is the *vampires* in Malawi. Let me just read you what it says at the end of the article, okay?

> In these impoverished rural communities [they're talking about Malawi], which lack electricity, running water, adequate food, education and medical care, peasant farmers are accustomed to being battered by forces they cannot control or fully understand. The sun burns crops, leaving fields withered and families hungry. Rains drown chickens and wash away huts,

> leaving people homeless. Newborn babies die despite the wails of their mothers and the powerful prayers of their elders.
>
> People here believe in an invisible God, but also in malevolent forces – witches who change into hyenas, people who can destroy their enemies by harnessing floods. So the notion of vampires does not seem farfetched.

Rev. Blount laid the paper down on the pulpit and slammed his hand down over it, as though he were nailing it down. "And I'll just add this. It especially don't seem farfetched if you seen them with your own eyes! If you had neighbors who was vampires. If you seen the syringes they left behind them when they was all full of blood and sleepy. Cause that's what these vampires use nowadays. They don't have sharp teeth like cats or wolves, they got syringes! And they know how to use them as well as any nurse at the hospital. Real fast and neat, they don't leave a drop of blood showing, just slide it in and slip it out." He pantomimed the vampires' expertise.

"Gospel, I'm sorry," Ms. McLeod admonished, "we are going to have to leave. Right now. Children, put your coats on. The Reverend is getting into matters that we had agreed we wouldn't discuss in the context of Brotherhood Month."

"Vampires are real, kids," Reverend Blount boomed out, sounding more like Verizon than ever. "They are real, and they are living here in Minneapolis! If you just look around you will see them in their white suits and their white dresses. And they are laughing at you cause you can't see what's there right under your nose."

Before she got up from her folding chair to follow Ms. McLeod out of the tabernacle, Tawana took one of the bulletins from the stack on the window sill next to her. It was the first time in her life that she had taken up any kind of reading matter without being told to. Maybe she wasn't a kid any more. Maybe the words of Gospel Blantyre Blount, D.D., had been the water of her baptism, just like they'd talked about at the Catholic school. They said if you were baptized and you died your flesh would be raised incorruptible. That's how she felt leaving the All-Faiths Tabernacle, incorruptible.

*

In April the Governor declared the ten counties of the Metro area a Disaster Area and called in the National Guard to help where the roads were washed away and in those areas that had security problems, especially East St. Paul and Duluth, where there had been massive demonstrations and looting. In Shakopee, six African-American teenagers were killed when their Dodge Ram pickup was swept off Route 19 by the reborn Brown Beaver River. An estimated twelve thousand acres of productive farmland were lost in that single inundation, and the President (who had vetoed the Emergency Land Reclamation Act) was widely blamed for the damage sustained throughout the state.

Despite all these tragedies there hadn't been one school day canceled at Diversitas, though the bus service was now optional and rather expensive. Morning after soggy morning Tawana had trudged through the slush and the puddles in her leaky Nikes, which she had thrown such a scene to get when Aunt Bima had wanted to get her a cheaper alternative at the Mall of America. Now Tawana had no one but herself to blame for her misery, which made it a lot more of a misery than it would otherwise have been.

It was only the left Nike that leaked, so if she were careful where she stepped, her foot would stay dry for the whole thirty-four blocks she had to walk. Sometimes, if it wasn't raining too hard, she'd take a slightly longer route that passed by the CVS and other stores that had awnings she could walk under, making an umbrella unnecessary. Tawana hated umbrellas.

That longer route also took her past the All-Faiths Tabernacle and the Northeast Minneapolis Arts Cooperative on the ground floor.

There, on the day after the Governor's declaration, the "Well-Dressed People" display had been taken down and a new display mounted. The sign this time said:

ENTERTAINMENT IS FUN—

FOR THE WHOLE FAMILY!

The same white-faced mannikins, in the same white clothes, were seated in front of an old-fashioned TV set with a dinky screen, and gazing at a tape loop that showed a part of a movie that they had all had to watch at school in the film appreciation class. You could hear the music over an invisible speaker: "I'm singing in the rain, just singing in the rain. I'm singing and dancing in the rain!" The same snippet of the song over and over as the man on the TV whirled with his umbrella about a lamp post and splashed in the puddles on the street. Maybe it was supposed to be fun, like the sign in the window said, but it only made Tawana feel more miserably wet.

The next day it drizzled, and the same actor (Gene Kelly it said at one point in the loop) was still whirling around the same lamp pole to the same music. Then, to Tawana's astonishment, a door opened behind the TV set and a real man (but dressed in a white suit like the mannikins) stepped into the imaginary room behind the window. Tawana knew him. It was Mr. Forbush who had been the music and dance teacher at Diversitas two years earlier. His hair was shorter now and dyed bright gold. When he saw Tawana staring at him, he tipped his head to the side, and smiled, and wiggled his fingers to say hello. Then he turned round to get hold of a gigantic, bright yellow baby chick, which he positioned next to the mannikins so it, too, would be looking at *Singin' in the Rain.*

When Mr. Forbush was satisfied with the baby chick's positioning he began to fluff up its fake feathers with a battery-powered hair dryer. From time to time, when he saw Tawana still standing there under the awning, wavering between amusement and suspicion, he would aim the blow dryer at his own mop of wispy golden curls.

"Well, hello there," said a man's voice that seemed strangely familiar. "I believe we've met before."

Tawana looked to the side, where the Reverend Gospel Blantyre Blount, D.D., was standing in a black dashiki in the shadows of the entrance to the tabernacle.

"You're Tawana, aren't you?"

She nodded.

"Would you like something to eat, Tawana?"

She nodded again and followed the minister up the dark stairway, leaving Gene Kelly singing and spinning around in the endless rain.

Rev. Blount poured some milk powder into a big mug and stirred it up with water from a plastic bottle, added a spoonful of Swiss Miss Diet Cocoa, and put the mug into a microwave to cook. After the bell dinged, he took it out and set it in front of Tawana on what would have been the kitchen table if this were a kitchen. It was more like an office or a library, with piles of paper on the table, and two desks, lots of bookcases. There was also a sink in one corner with a bathroom cabinet over it and a pile of firewood though nowhere to burn any of it. A pair of windows let in some light from the back alley, but not a lot, since they were covered by pink plastic shower curtains, which were drawn almost closed so you could only get a peek at the back alley and the rain coming down.

"Nothing like a hot cup of cocoa on a rainy day," Rev. Blount declared in his booming voice. Tawana concurred with a wary nod, and lifted the brim of the cup to her lips. It was more lukewarm than hot, but even so she did not take a sip.

"I'll bet you're wondering why I called you here."

"You didn't call me here," Tawana said matter-of-factly. "I was looking at the crazy stuff inside that window downstairs."

"Well, I *was* calling, sending out a mental signal, and you *are* here, so figure that out. But you're right about that window. It's crazy, or something worse. Aren't you going to drink that cocoa?"

Tawana took a sip and then an actual swallow. Before she set the mug back down she'd drunk down half the cocoa in it. All the while Rev. Gospel Blantyre Blount kept his eyes fixed on her like a teacher expecting an answer to a question.

Finally he said, "It's the vampires, isn't it? You want to know about the vampires."

"I didn't say that."

"But that's what you was thinking." His large eyes narrowed to a sly knowing slit.

Tawana hooked her finger into the handle of the mug. It *was* the vampires. Ever since she'd read the stuff in the church bulletin that she'd taken home she'd wanted to know more than just what was there in writing, most of it taken out of newspapers. She wanted the whole truth, the truth that didn't get into newspapers.

"You actually saw them yourself, the vampires?"

Rev. Blount nodded. His eyes looked sad, the lids all droopy, with yellowish scuzz in the corners. From time to time he'd wipe the scuzz away with a fingertip, but it would be there again within a few blinks.

"What'd they look like?"

"Just the same as people you see on the street. Tall mostly, but then that's so for most us Malawis. They always wear white. That's how they get their name in Bantu. The White Man is what we call a vampire. It's not the same as calling someone a white man over here, though most vampires do have white skin. Not all, but the overwhelming majority."

Tawana pondered this. In the one movie she had ever seen about her own native country of Somalia she had noticed the same thing. All the American soldiers who went into the city of Mogadishu to kill the people there were white with one exception. That one black soldier didn't have a name that she could remember but she remembered him more clearly than all the white soldiers, because he behaved just the way they did, as though they'd turned him into one of them. If there could be black soldiers like him, why not black vampires?

"I saw the movie," she said, by way of offering her own credentials. And added (thinking he might not know which movie), "The one in black and white."

"Dracula!" said the Reverend Blount. "Yeah, that is one kind of vampire all right. With those teeth. Don't mess with that mother. But the White Man is a different kind of vampire. He don't bite into your neck and suck the blood out, which must be a trickier business than they let on in the old movie. No, the White Man uses modern technology. He's got syringes. You know, like at the doctor's office. Big ones. He jabs them in anywheres, sometimes in the neck, or in the arm, wherever. Then when the thing is filled up with blood he takes off the full test tube-thing and wiggles in an empty one. As many times as he needs to. Sometimes he'll take all the blood they got, if he's hungry. Other times, but not that often, he'll only take a sip. Like you, with that cocoa. That's how new vampires get created. Cause there is some vampire blood inside the syringe and it gets into the victim's bloodstream and turns them into vampires themselves. AIDS works just the same. You know about AIDS?"

Tawana nodded. "We have to study it at school. And you can't share needles."

"True! Especially with the White Man."

Tawana had a feeling she wasn't being told the whole story, just the way grown-ups never tell you the whole story about sex. Usually you had to listen to them when they thought you weren't there. Then you found out.

"The vampire you saw," she said, shifting directions, "was it just one? And was it a man or a woman?"

"Good question!" Rev. Blount said approvingly. "Because there can be lady vampires. Not as many as the men but a lot. And to answer your question, the only ones I ever saw for sure was men. But I have met some ladies I thought might of been vampires – black ladies! – but I cleared out before I could find out for certain. If I hadn't of I might not be here now."

Tawana felt frustrated. Rev. Blount answered her questions honestly enough, but even so he seemed kind of...slippery. He wasn't telling her the *details.*

"You want to know the exact details, don't you?" he asked, reading her mind. "Okay, here's what happened. This was back in 1997 and I was studying theology at the All-Faith Mission and Theological Seminary in Blantyre, which is the city in Malawi that has had the biggest vampire problem but which is also my middle name because I was born there. Well, one day Dr. Hopkins who runs the Mission assembled all the seminarians to the hall and told us we would be welcoming a guest from the United Nations health service, and he would be testing us for AIDS! Dr. Hopkins said how we should be cooperative and let the man from the UN do his job, because it was a humanitarian mission the same as ours, and there had to be someone to set an example. The health service, it seems, was having a problem with cooperation. People in Malawi don't like a stranger coming and sticking needles into them."

"I hate needles," Tawana declared fervently.

"Well, we all hate needles, sister. And why us? we had to wonder. Of course, at that time, no one in Blantyre really believed in AIDS. People got sick, yes, and they died, some of them, but there can be other explanations for that. Most people in Malawi thought AIDS was witchcraft. A witch can put a spell on someone and that someone starts feeling bad and he can't...do whatever he used to. And dies. Only this wasn't any ordinary kind of witchcraft."

"It was the White Man!"

Rev. Blount nodded gravely. "Exactly. Only we didn't know that then. So we agreed to go along with what Dr. Hopkins was asking us to do, and this 'guest' came to the Seminary and we all lined up and let him take our blood. Only *I* refused to let him have any of mine, cause I had a funny feeling about the whole thing. Well, some time went by, and we more or less forgot about the visit we had. But then the guest returned, and talked to Dr. Hopkins, and then he talked with four of the seminarians. But I think there was more than talk that went on. It was like he'd drained the blood right out of them. They were dead before they died. And within a month's time they was genuinely dead, all four of them. It was all hushed up, but I was one of the people Dr. Hopkins asked to clean up their rooms after. And you know what I found? Syringes. I showed them to Dr. Hopkins, but he said just get rid of them, that is nothing to do with the Seminary. Well, what was it then? I wondered. They wasn't taking drugs in the Seminary. I don't think so! It wasn't AIDS, not them boys."

"It was the White Man," Tawana said.

Rev. Blount nodded. "It was the White Man. He tasted the different kinds of blood we sent him, and those boys had the taste the White Man liked best. So he kept coming back for more. And once a vampire has had his first taste, there's nothing you can do to stop him coming back for more. That old movie had it right there. I don't know how the vampires got to them, but those four boys sure as hell didn't commit suicide, which was what some of them at the Seminary was insinuating. Their whole religion is against suicide. No. No. The White Man got them, plain and simple."

"Tawana!" Ms. McLeod exclaimed with her customary excess of gusto. "Come in, come in!" The school's principal placed her wire-framed reading glasses atop a stack of multiple-choice Personnel Evaluation forms that had occupied the same corner of her desk since the start of the spring quarter, an emblem of her supervisory status and a clear sign that her rank as principal set her apart from graders of papers and monitors of lunch rooms.

Tawana entered the Principal's office holding up the yellow slip that had summoned her from Numerical Thinking, her last class before lunch.

"Is this your essay, Tawana?" Ms. McLeod asked, producing three pages of ruled paper. The title – OUR SOMALI BROTHERS AND SISTERS: A Minnesota Perspective – was written with orange magic marker in letters two inches high. Under it, on a more modest scale, was the author's name, Tawana Makwinja.

"Yes, Ms. McLeod."

"And the assignment was to write a letter about your family's cultural heritage. Is that right?"

Tawana dipped her head in agreement.

"Would you," purred Ms. McLeod, handing the paper to Tawana, "read it aloud – so I can hear it in the author's own voice?"

Tawana looked down at the paper, then up at Ms. McLeod, whose thin, plucked eyebrows were lifted high to pantomime attentiveness and curiosity. "Just begin at the beginning."

Tawana began to read from her essay:

> It is difficult to determine exactly the number of Somalis living in the Twin Cities. Minnesota Department of Human Services has estimated as many as 15,000, but the Somalia Council of Minnesota maintains that these figures are greatly inflated. Over 95% of Somali people in Minnesota are refugees. Many Somalis in Minnesota are single women with five or more children, because so many men were killed in the war.
>
> According to Mohammed Essa, director of the Somali Community in Minnesota, the role of women as authority figures in U.S. society is different from Somalia where few women work outside the home and men do not take instruction from women. For instance, the two sexes do not shake hands. Somalis practice corporal punishment, and many complain that the child protection workers are too quick to take away their children.
>
> Somali religious tradition requires female circumcision at the youngest possible age, in order in ensure a woman's virginity, to increase a man's sexual pleasure, and promote marital fidelity. However, this practice is outlawed in Minnesota. Before the

circumcision of an infant daughter there is a 40-day period called the "*afartanbah,*" followed by important celebrations attended by friends and family members that involve the killing of a goat.

Somalis are proud of their heritage and lineage. Children and family are deeply valued by Somalis, who favor large families. Seven or more children are common. Due to resettlement and the inability to keep families together in refugee situations, few Somali children in Minnesota live with both parents. The availability of culturally appropriate childcare is a major issue in Minnesota.

Tawana looked up cautiously, as after a sustained punishment. Ms. McLeod had made her read the whole thing out loud. She would rather have been whipped with a belt.

"Thank you, Tawana," said Ms. McLeod, reaching out to take back the essay. "There were a *few* pronunciation problems along the way, but that often happens when we read words we know only from books. I'm sure you know what all the words *mean*, don't you?"

Tawana nodded, glowering.

"This one, for instance – 'corporal'? What kind of punishment might that be? Hmm? Or 'lineage'? Why exactly is that a source of pride, Tawana?"

Ms. McLeod went on with word after word. It really was not fair. Tawana wasn't stupid, but Ms. McLeod was trying to make her look stupid. Making her read her essay aloud had been a trap.

"Have *you* ever attended an 'afartanbah,' Tawana?"

Tawana raised her eyes in despair. What kind of question was that! "What is a...the word you said?"

"You answered that question in your own essay, Tawana. It is a celebration forty days after the birth of a baby sister. Have you had such a celebration at your home, where there was goat?"

"Who eats goats in Minnesota?" Tawana protested. "You can't get goats with food stamps. I don't even *like* goat!"

With a thin smile Ms. McLeod conceded defeat in that line of interrogation and shifted back to pedagogic mode. "I want you to understand, Tawana, that there is nothing *wrong* with quoting from legitimate sources. All scholars do that. But note that I said 'sources,' plural. To copy out someone else's work word for word is not scholarship, it is plagiarism, and that is simply against all the rules. Students are expelled from university classes for doing what you have done. So you will have to write your essay over, from scratch, and not just copy out... this!" She produced a print-out of the same study from the Center for Cross-Cultural Health, "Somali Culture in Minnesota," that the school librarian had called up on the Internet for Tawana's use.

"That was the bad news," said Ms. McLeod with a sympathetic smile. "The *good* news is that you have really lovely handwriting!"

"I do?"

"Indeed. Firm, well-rounded, but not...childish. I don't know where you developed such a hand – not here at Diversitas, I'm sorry to say. The emphasis here has never been on fine penmanship."

"The nuns taught the Palmer Method at my last school."

"Well, you must have been one of their best students. Now, penmanship is a genuine skill. And anyone with a skill is in a position to earn money! How would you like a *job*, Miss Makwinja?"

Tawana regarded the Principal with ill-concealed dismay. "A job? But I'm just...a kid."

"Oh, I don't mean to send you off to a nine-to-five, full-time place of employment. No, this would be a part-time job, but it would pay more than you would earn by babysitting. And you could work as much or as little as you like, if you do a good job."

"What would I have to do?"

"Just copy out the words of a letter with your clear, bold penmanship. We can have an audition for the job right now. Here is the text of the letter I want you to copy. And here is the stationery to write on. You should be able to fit the whole letter on a single page, if you use both sides of the paper. Don't rush. Make it as neat as your essay."

Tawana regarded the letterhead on the stationery:

Holy Angels School of Nursing and Widwifery
4217 Ralph Bunche Boulevard
Kampala
Uganda, East Africa.

"Here." Ms. McLeod placed a fat fountain pen on top of the Holy Angels stationery. "A real pen always makes a better impression than ballpoint."

Tawana began to copy the letter, neatly and accurately, including all its mistakes.

Dear friend in Christ's Name,

I send you warm greeting hoping you are in a good-sounding health. I am so happy to write to you and I cry for your spiritual kindness to rescue me from this distressed moment.

I am Elesi Kuseliwa, a girl of 18 years old, and a first born in a family of 4 children. We are orphans.

I completed Ordinary level in 2003 and in 2004 I joined the above-mentioned school and took a course in midwifery. Unfortunately in October both our parents perished in a car accident on their way from church. We were left helpless in agony without any one to console or to take care of us. Life is difficult and unbearable.

This is my last and final year to complete my course of study. We study three terms a year and each term I am supposed to pay 450 UK pounds. The total fee for the year is 1350 pounds. I humbly request you to sympathize and become my sponsor so I may complete my course and to take my family responsibities, most importantly, paying school fees for my younger sisters.

Enclosed is a photocopy of my end of third term school report. I pray and await your kind and caring response.

Yours faithfully,
Elisi Kuseliwa

"Very good," said Ms. McLeod, when she had looked over the finished copy. "That took you just a little over fifteen minutes, which means that in an hour you should be able to make four copies just like this. Now I understand that girls your age can earn as much as two-fifty at babysitting. I'll do better than that. I'll pay four dollars an hour. Or one dollar for each letter you copy. Do we have a deal?"

What could Tawana say but yes.

Tawana still had one friend left from when she'd gone to Our Lady of Mercy, Patricia Brown. That was not her Somali name, of course. She'd become Patricia Brown when her mother died and she was adopted into the Brown family. She was a quiet, plodding bully of a girl, already two hundred pounds when Tawana had met her in fourth grade, and now lighting up the screen on the scale at 253. Tawana had won her friendship by patiently listening to Patricia's ceaseless complainings about her foster parents, her siblings, her teachers, and her classmates at Our Lady of Mercy, a skill she had learned from having sat still for Lucy's long whines and Grandpa's rants. In exchange for her nods and murmurs Tawana was able to see shows on the Browns' TV that Tawana couldn't get at home. That is how Tawana (and Patricia as well) came to be a fan of *Buffy the Vampire Slayer*.

At first the later afternoon reruns had been as hard to understand as if you arrived at a stranger's house in the middle of a complicated family quarrel that had been going on for years. You couldn't tell who was right and who was wrong. Or in this case who was the vampire and who wasn't. Buffy herself definitely wasn't, but she had her own superhuman powers. When she wanted to she could zap one of the vampires to the other side of the room with just a tap of her finger. Sometimes she would walk up to a vampire and start talking to him and then without a word of warning whack him through the heart with a wooden stake. But other times, confusingly, she would fall in love with some guy who would turn out to be a vampire, but that didn't stop their being in love.

Patricia said there was a simple explanation. The vampires were able to confuse people by their good looks, and Buffy would eventually realize the mistake she was making with Spike and whack him just like the others. Tawana was not so sure. Spike might be a vampire but he seemed to really love Buffy. Also, he looked a lot like Mr. Forbush, with the same bleached hair and thin face and sarcastic smile. Though, as Patricia had pointed out, what did that have to do with anything! It was all just a story like *Days of Our Lives*, only more so since it was about vampires and vampires are only make-believe. Tawana did not tell Patricia about the real vampires in Malawi. Everything that she had learned about the White Man was between her and Rev. Gospel Blount.

But in the course of watching many episodes of *Buffy* and thinking them over and discussing them with other kids at Diversitas Tawana developed a much broader understanding of the nature of vampires and the powers they possessed than you could get from an out-of-date movie like *Dracula*. Or even from reading books, though Tawana had never actually tried to do that. She was not much interested in books. Even their smell could get her feeling queasy.

The main thing to be learned was that here in America just the same as in Rev. Blount's native land of Malawi there were vampires everywhere. Most people had no idea who the vampires were, but a few special individuals like Buffy, or Tawana, could recognize a vampire from the kind of fire that would flash from their eyes, or by other subtle signs.

The vampires in Minneapolis were usually white, and tended to be on the thin side, and older, especially the men. And they would watch you when they thought you weren't looking. If you caught them at it, they would tilt their head backwards and pretend to be staring at the ceiling.

A lot of what people thought of as the drug problem was actually vampires. That was how they kept themselves out of the news. All the people who died from a so-called drug overdose? It was usually vampires.

Then one day in May toward the end of seventh grade Tawana developed a major insight into vampires that was all her own. She was in the Browns' living room with Patricia and her younger brother Michael watching a rerun of *Buffy* that they all had seen before. Patricia and Michael were sitting side by side in the glider, spaced out on Michael's medication, and Tawana was sitting behind them, keeping the glider rocking real slow with her toe, the same as if they were the twins in their stroller. Instead of looking at the story on the TV Tawana's attention was fixed on the big statue of Jesus on the wall. There were silver spikes through his hands and feet, and his naked body was twisting around and his neck stretched up, trying to escape the crucifix. Tawana realized that Jesus looked exactly like one of the vampires when Buffy had pounded a wooden stake into him. Their skin was the same clouded white, the same expression on their faces, a kind of holy pain. Not only that but with Jesus, the same as with vampires, you might think you had killed him but then a day or two later he wasn't in the coffin where you thought. He was out on the street again, alive.

Jesus had been the first White Man!

Tawana kept rocking the two Brown children, and sneaking sideways glances at the crucifix, and wondering who in the world she could ever tell about her incredible insight, which kept making more and more sense.

The priests, the nuns, the missionaries! Hospitals and health clinics. The crucifixes in everybody's homes, just like the story of Moses when the Jews in Egypt marked their doors with blood to keep out the Angel of Death!

Everything was starting to connect. Here in America and there in Africa, for centuries and centuries, it was all the same ancient never-ending struggle of good against evil, human against vampire, Black against White.

On July 3, in preparation for the holidays, the Northeast Minneapolis Arts Cooperative once again changed its window display in the store that was never open underneath the All-Faiths Tabernacle. The old ENTERTAINMENT IS FUN — FOR THE WHOLE FAMILY! sign wasn't taken down. Instead WAR was pasted over ENTERTAINMENT, and the mannikins who had been sitting around the imaginary living room watching Gene Kelly on TV had been dismembered, their detached limbs and white clothes scattered around a cemetery made of cardboard tombstones and spray-on cobwebs. A big flag rippled in a breeze supplied by a standing fan at the side of the window, while the hidden sound system played the Jimi Hendrix version of the Star-Spangled Banner.

Tawana's first reaction, as for the earlier displays, was a perplexed indignation, a sense of having been personally violated without knowing exactly how. But now that she had become more adept at unriddling such conundrums the basic meaning of the display in the window slowly became clear like a face on TV emerging from the green and grey sprinkles of static. This was the cemetery that the vampires lived in, only they weren't home. The White Man was hunting for more victims. The limbs beside the gravestones were the remnants of some earlier feast.

It actually helped to know what the real situation was. When there is a definite danger it is possible to act. Tawana went round to the back of the building. The Arts Cooperative people always used their back door and kept their front door locked, and Rev. Blount did just the opposite. There was no doorbell, so Tawana knocked.

Mr. Forbush answered the inner door and stood behind the patched and sagging screen, blinking. "Yes?" he asked, stupid with sleep.

"Mr. Forbush, can I come in and talk with you?" When he seemed uncertain, she added, "It's about Rev. Blount, upstairs."

Tawana knew from Rev. Blount there were problems between the Arts Cooperative, who owned the building, and the tabernacle, which was behind in its rent and taking its landlord to court for harassment and other reasons. And sure enough Mr. Forbush forgot his suspicions and invited Tawana inside.

She was in a space almost as jumbled and crazy as the shop window out front, with some of the walls torn down, and drywall partitions painted to look like pictures, and rugs on top of rugs and piles of gigantic pillows and other piles of cardboard and plastic boxes and not much real furniture anywhere. Tawana had never been anywhere vampires lived, and this was nothing like she would have expected. She was fascinated, and a little dazed.

"What are you looking for?" Mr. Forbush asked. "The bathroom?"

"Are we by ourselves?" Tawana asked, running her fingers across the top of the gas stove as though it were a piano.

Before he could answer, the phone rang. All the tension inside of Tawana relaxed away like a puff of smoke. The ring of the phone was the sound of heaven answering her prayers. Mr. Forbush swiveled round in the pile of cushions he'd settled down on, reaching for a cell phone on top of the CD player that sat on the bare floor.

Tawana grabbed hold of the cast iron frying pan on the back burner of the stove, and before there was any answer to Mr. Forbush's "Hello?" she had knocked him over the head. The first blow didn't kill him, or the second. But they were solid enough that he was never able to fight back. He groaned some and waved his arms, but that did nothing to keep Tawana from slaying him.

Outside, along the driveway, there was an old, old wooden fence that hadn't been painted for years. That provided the stake she needed. She didn't even have to sharpen the end of it. She drove it through his heart with the same frying pan she'd used to smash his head in. She was amazed at the amount of blood that spilled out into the pile of pillows. Perhaps he had been feasting through the night.

There was no use trying to mop the floor, no way to hide the body. But she did change out of her bloody clothes, and found a white dress that must have belonged to one of the mannikins. She wore that to go home in, with her own dirty clothes stuffed in a plastic bag from CVS.

Mr. Forbush's death received a good deal of attention on WCCO and the other news programs, and Rev. Blount was often on the TV to answer questions and deny reports. But no charges were every brought against him, or against any other suspect. However, it was not possible, after so much media attention, to deny that Minneapolis had a vampire problem just the same as Malawi. There were many who believed that Mr. Forbush had been a vampire, or at least had been associating with vampires, on the principle that where there is smoke there is fire. It was discovered by a reporter on the *Star* that the Arts Cooperative was a legal fiction designed to help Mr. Forbush evade state and local taxes, that he was, in effect, the sole owner, having inherited the property after the bankruptcy of his father's mattress store and the man's subsequent suicide. It was rumored that the father's death might not have been a suicide, and that he had been the first victim of the vampires – or, alternatively, that he had been the first of the vampires.

None of these stories ever received official media attention, but they were circulated widely enough that the All-Faiths Pentecostal Tabernacle became a big success story in the Twin Cities' Somali-American community. Rev. Blount received a special award for his contributions to Interfaith Dialogue from the Neighborhood Development Association, and even after the protests that followed the "Mall of America Massacre" and the effort by the police to close down the

Tabernacle, he was saluted as a local hero and a possible candidate for the State Senate.

Tawana was never to enjoy the same celebrity status, though as a member of All-Faiths' choir she had her share of the general good fortune, including her own brief moment of glory in the spotlight. It was during the NBC Special Report, *The Vampires of Minnesota.* She was in her red and white choir robes, standing outside the Tabernacle after a Sunday service. The camera had been pressed up to her face, close enough to kiss, and she'd stared right into it, no smile on her lips, completely serious, and said, "They said it could never happen here. They said it might happen somewhere *primitive* and *backwards* like Malawi, but never in Minneapolis."

Then she just lowered her eyes and turned her head sideways, and they started to roll the credits.

The Wall of America

MOST PEOPLE got more space along the Wall than they could ever use, even the oddballs who painted leviathan-sized canvases they couldn't hope to sell to anyone who didn't have his own airplane hangar to hang their enormities. But if you did work on such a scale, you must have had money to burn, so what would it matter if you never sold your stuff? The important thing was having it hung where people could see it.

At least that was the important thing for Lester. He did actually sell something from time to time. He could never tell what it was that tickled them to the tune of five hundred dollars. Admittedly, that was not a lot to ask, even taking into account the collapse of the market, and the dollar. Sometimes a satisfied customer would return a year or two later and shell out *another* five hundred and vanish off into the sunset with his trophy in the back of his mini-van.

North Dakota did have pretty wonderful sunsets, no doubt about that. Sitting there by his stretch of the Wall, Lester would mix its colors on the palette of his imagination, heightening cerulean to a kind of dark lavender, or putting an orangish blush into streaks of old rose. Turner would have loved North Dakota: a plain more perfectly Euclidean than the sea's, with skies of a corresponding serenity. The winds blew more swiftly for lack of friction, and jet trails would dissolve with an exquisite *douceur*, as though they knew they were the only thing happening.

His family, back in Des Moines, thought Lester was crazy, spending two months of each year at the Wall. Even so, his wife or one of his sons would sometimes make the trip north and spend a few days at his side, twiddling their thumbs or getting drunk. (Bobby had a definite problem with liquor at this point, just like his uncle Kevin. Very sad.) It was always a relief when they left, and Lester didn't have to invent things to talk about. He wasn't much of a talker.

Ten years ago he wouldn't have figured himself for a painter either. He sold building material for Boardwalk Products. Mostly the new easy-bonding plywood that had been a precursor to the Wall. It cost almost nothing to mill and had the tensile strength of steel. Now it wasn't just diamonds that were forever. With a dab of bonding it was any post and lintel. Whence, the Wall. At least in terms of opportunity. Motive was another matter, and everyone had a different explanation for why the Wall was a practical requirement and a sound investment. The Canadians liked it because it kept out the Yanks, and the States liked it because it kept out the Leafers, and painters liked it most of all because it represented two hundred million square feet of wall space where they could all exhibit their pictures. You just sent in your application and they sent you back a choice of spreads.

Lester had picked the least densely hung stretch that they'd offered him, not so much because his paintings needed room to sprawl but because he did. It was always a shock to step out of the Winnebago and see the sky absolutely everywhere and the beets shivering. Was there any crop so unglamorous as beets?

There was a good reason you never saw beets in still-lifes, or landscapes of beet fields.

For miles in all directions there was nothing to look at but those beets – and Lester's pictures spaced along the Wall. Wall space on that scale was a luxury that even the King of Spain, if there still was one, couldn't lay claim to: the Escorial was too small. Now it was like flu shots or cheese (in Canada, at least), available for the asking. Having the stuff posted on a Web-site didn't begin to compare. This was real, not virtual. Now China was adapting its own Great Wall to the same purpose, and Berlin was rebuilding a new wall where the old one used to be. But there was no public funding behind those projects, and neither had got off the ground. In America the NEA had been behind the project from the start, along with Homeland Security. It also helped that Boardwalk Products was located in the House Speaker's home state of Montana, the state with the longest single stretch of the Wall.

Lester tried to reciprocate the government's generosity. He didn't give his paintings away, except to someone in the family or a close friend, and then only if they wanted one, which they generally didn't. He sold them at five hundred bucks a pop. Which was the average price of paintings of the size he did. He had no illusion about being discovered by a gallery or a collector and suddenly rolling in clover. Since '69, most painters could expect to earn about as much on an hourly basis as a good plumber, which was about what they got back in the Renaissance if they weren't somebody's cousin. Painting was no longer something a person did for the money. It was more on the order of fishing or falconry, something that got its hook or claws in *you*. You did it just for the beauty of it. That seemed as good an explanation as any.

Anyhow, Lester didn't need explanations himself, and these were not his thoughts, but rather an attempt to explain how, when he was out there by the Wall, he would let his mind go blank for hours at time, sitting on a plastic recliner in the shadow of the Winnebago's rolled-out awning. Or sitting inside at his smaller easel while the CD played some old favorite. Harold in Italy or Hank Williams or Schwarzkopf or Cheb Mami. He wondered if there was some secret correlation that he'd never noticed between what he listened to and what he painted. You'd think there would be, wouldn't you?

One thing Lester had not counted on in signing on for this stretch of the Wall was the Northern Lights. At this time of year, mid-summer, they were sensational. Either that or he was losing his mind. Because so far he'd only ever seen the auroras when he was out alone with no other witness to confirm that the sky had really lighted up like a lava lamp, like searchlights after a prison break, like Christmas Eve in New Jersey. And all in a crickety silence far from all frogponds or drive-ins. No one on the road that ran along parallel to the Wall, no visitors. Just Lester and Apocalypse Now but without the sound track. You want some proof that God exists? There it was. Better than that, it was like having a private conversation with Him but not in words, in a succession of lightning flash slides.

It went beyond beautiful and trespassed on scary, as though, if this really was some coded message from Above, then it might turn out to be that God wanted him to kill his only son Isaac. "Bobby, how would you like to go on a hiking trip with me to Mount Rainier?" Except, of course, God wouldn't recycle the exact same storyline. No, the scary part was exactly the beauty of the thing, the way it erased all other considerations, like beauty can, or sex. As though at that moment when you think it can't get any better you just blew a fuse and got trapped there in your own pure bliss, in the dream come true.

Forever. Which is just where beauty seems to take you. Up to the fresco on the vaulted ceiling where all the angels are playing violins and contemplating the perfections of God. But then, as ever, his fuse *wasn't* blown, and the aurora faded, and soon enough had passed from memory. You couldn't paint the Northern Lights, no one ever had. If you brought up the subject, people who had never seen them would give you a blank look, the same as they do when you try to talk about painting.

Painting was one of those things there's no point talking about because when you try it comes out nonsense.

Most of the time Lester slept outside. The Winnebago could get to be a sauna even with two ceiling fans. He would spread out a sheet of foam rubber over the recliner and an unzipped sleeping bag over that, which he'd zip up into a cocoon some time in the course of the night. After a while the crickets went to sleep, and then he would himself a little later, if God hadn't scheduled a light show.

There was rarely traffic on the Wall's service road, since ten miles south was an Interstate that the truckers and long-haul drivers preferred. Whole nights went by without the drama of headlights approaching and dopplering past. But then there came the night when, far off to the west along the service road, a triad of lights appeared, headlights and above them a brighter beam, like a searchlight. Police? he wondered. The third light swiveled and focused on the first and westernmost of the paintings Lester had hung on the Wall. It paused, and the headlights advanced a little closer along the road. The beam of the searchlight fixed on the next painting. Lester was fascinated, he'd never seen his own paintings like this, at night, shrunk by distance.

As the lights drew nearer he realized, from its clunky silhouette, that it was not a police car but a Hummer. Which, when Lester switched on his own outdoor floodlights, signaled back by lifting and lowering its brights. The Hummer's spotlight had reached only the fourth of the thirty-nine paintings, and the survey of Lester's work continued at an unhurried pace, giving Lester time to go into the Winnebago and get his pistol strapped on under his terry robe, just in case. Artists along the Wall rarely ran into problems with would-be felons, except in the areas around Buffalo, Vancouver, and the Idaho panhandle.

"Nice stuff," said the night visitor in a nasal North Dakotan whine, when the Hummer had drawn abreast of the Winnebago opposite Painting #19. He spoke without getting out of the car, his face masked by the glare of his lights.

"I thank you," said Lester. "We don't get many visitors this time of night."

"I can see that. But I like seeing the pictures at night. If they're not too small. Yours are nice and big."

Lester nodded noncommittally.

"Would you like a beer?" the man asked.

He didn't but it seemed more friendly to say that he did.

When the guy dismounted, six-pack in hand, Lester could see he was no more than twenty, with acne that his meager sideburns could not conceal. He was wearing a black tanktop from Guggenheim/Vegas. Lester pressed the cold can to the back of his neck for a moment of gratitude, then popped the top and wet his lips without taking a sip.

"I've been driving along the Wall three days now," the kid told him.

"East to west or west to east?"

"I started in Calgary and hit the Wall in Glacier Park. It was almost solid art for the first fifty miles, then it tapered off. But this stretch tonight has been the sparest. I think the last guy I saw was back at the turnoff to Bottineau."

Lester nodded. "That'd be Mrs. Lloyd. She does those watercolors. Beautiful stuff. I get her propane for her, and she bakes things for me. Some kind of Italian cookie. You want one?"

"Not with the beer, thanks just the same."

"So." Lester pretended to take another sip. "Are you an artist yourself then?"

The kid shook his head. A matted tress of blond hair flopped down over his forehead. He had the pale skin of someone who works indoors or is up all night. Backlit by the glare of the spot mounted on his Hummer, he reminded Lester of one of Le Nain's card sharps, lit by a single candle. The same stoic sadness. Lester lifted the cold can to his lips and this time let himself enjoy a sip of it.

"I guess you've been at it a long time yourself," the kid ventured.

"A while," said Lester. "Back when I was thirty or so I was in an accident and had to spend some time in rehab. They made us have a hobby. I didn't *have* a hobby, didn't believe in them really, so I told the lady in charge that I liked to paint. Sometimes I used to watch that stuff on Channel 21. Western Civilization. I don't know how else I came up with the idea. But they had the equipment there and no one else was using it. So I started painting."

"And now you've got all that stuff there on the Wall," the kid said respectfully.

"And a lot more besides, back in Des Moines."

"I really like it. But you probably painted all of your pictures in the daylight."

"M-hm. For the most part. There are some painters who prefer to paint at night. They're set up for it. But it changes the color. They kind of fade in the light of day."

"Like vampires," suggested the kid.

"I guess. I never met a vampire myself."

The kid laughed, and seemed to blush, and finished off his can in two quick gulps. He crushed it and, turning quickly, threw it through the open window of the Hummer. Then he opened another.

"My name is Lester," Lester said, offering his hand.

"Gulliver," said the kid.

"No shit. I never met a Gulliver before."

"Neither have I. I may be the only one. Plenty of Keanus and Kevins but no Gullivers any more."

"I have a brother named Kevin," Lester said. "And a son named Robert."

Gulliver nodded. "Oh, I figured you were straight. I guess a lot of guys go cruising here along the Wall, but it's only the pictures I'm interested in."

"So," said Lester, reaching back to tilt the recliner into a sitting position. "Tell me about yourself."

Lester woke up in the first glimmering of dawn to the sound of snoring. Still half-drunk, he thought he was back home in bed beside Carla. But then the false horizon of the Wall reminded him of the true situation. The snores were Gulliver's, wrapped in his own sleeping bag, asleep beside his Hummer, with a litter of beer cans about him. His aim, and Lester's, had deteriorated as they had gone on drinking.

So many cans. So much talk. And most of it Lester's. Gulliver had simply run out of information he thought worth sharing. He'd attended high school in a dutiful way, then shunted tracks to a college in Calgary, where it dawned on him that he had little interest in the future to which all his education was leading. He was not a team player. Books bored him. He'd tried to fall in love and failed. He took out a student loan and used it as the down payment for the Hummer and headed off to see what the world beyond Canada was like, beginning with the Wall of America, which was, he'd confided with drunken reverence, the weirdest thing he'd ever seen.

"Why do people do it?" he asked of Lester. "What's in it for them?"

"It's not the money," Lester said virtuously.

"Yeah, I can see that. People with money find other ways to spend it."

"By and large, yes."

"It just doesn't make sense to me."

"That may be the point, partly. You seem to find it *interesting*. Or you wouldn't be following the Wall."

"I suppose."

"Let me ask you: do you iron your own shirts?"

Gulliver squinted down at the logo on his tanktop. "Why would I iron *this?*"

"Well, do you have any flannel shirts? Plaids?"

Gulliver nodded and then slowly a smile began to form. He was one of those people who are only good-looking when they smile, and he didn't smile that often. "You mean the way it changes color when the iron goes across it?"

"Yes. Is that a pleasure for you?"

"Uh-huh. And painting is like that?"

"Basically, yes."

That had got Lester started. He told Gulliver all the things he'd thought about painting, his own, and the ones he'd seen in museums, and the thousands of them all along the Wall. It must have been something like people experienced when they first go to AA, the spillgates opening. Or the joy of bulimia, except this wasn't just one day's excess he was purging, but a lifetime's feast.

Now, as with a dream, he couldn't remember any of the details. The big insights, the droll anecdotes, the shy confidences of what he hoped he might be able to accomplish.

He could only remember Gulliver saying, with great earnestness, when Lester had finally wound down, "You should do that."

"It doesn't sound crazy to you?"

"In a way, yeah. But the same way my buying this Hummer was crazy. You should do it. Truly."

At which point, without even saying good-night, they both stopped talking and fell asleep.

When the Park Rangers checked out the Winnebago, four days later, there was no sign of any mischief having been done. The doors were unlocked, the contents in good order. The paintings were still hanging along the Wall, except for two of them, #24 and #31. The Rangers fastened a security camera to the top of the Winnebago and returned a week later to find that another painting had been taken off the Wall. But it was a legitimate purchase. A check for $500 had been slipped under the door, with a note from the buyer, who was one of Lester's return customers. The Rangers contacted Lester's wife, and a few days later his son Robert and brother Kevin appeared to sign for the Winnebago. When they drove off they left the paintings hanging where they were.

They were well hung and hugged the Wall like moss all through the autumn winds and winter snow, thanks to the Miracle of Boardwalk's Everfast. They were still there in May, when the artists and tourists began to return, but now they'd become a minor news item. No one had ever left so many paintings on the Wall to weather. One commentator on the UND campus TV station declared that the missing artist was another Leonardo da Vinci, and while that was definitely a minority view, the story got picked up by the Drudge Report, and for a while Lester was the most famous Missing Person in the country.

And the paintings stayed where they were through another winter and another tourist season, by order of the Park Service, who contested the family's right to remove them from the Wall, now that they had become a kind of monument to the honesty of the good citizens of North Dakota and perdurability of acrylic paint. The family realized that their attic full of Lester's other paintings was appreciating in value every day the paintings on the Wall continued where they were, so it was in their interest to achieve a stalemate with the Park Service.

They are still there to be looked at, on the Wall where Lester left them.

Ringtime

ONE DAY (my story begins) I found myself on the shady side of Memory Lane, which is a place, like Wall Street, that can be anywhere the sellers and the sold chance to collide. In this case, in the IRT Antique Arcade between 23rd and 28th, where I had come with $400 in over-the-counter unregistered cash and a need, basic to my nature, to spend it all immediately. I knew where. At the downtown end of the Arcade was a dealer ostensibly dealing in old paperbacks, most of them just powder sealed in cellophane, but in fact a fence for hot rings.

Morton Shure had the pale skin and opossum eyes common to the denizens of the IRT Arcade and a straggly beard that looked like acne that had undergone a sea-change. With browsers who stopped to inspect his baggies of powdered prose he affected the tranked-down speech of a zombie in custodial care. With real customers he revved up to a laconic mumble. Not a candidate for Salesman of the Month, but Morton's merchandise mostly sold itself. I told him what I was after, and we stepped to the back of the booth. Morton drew the curtain closed and brought out his black velvet tray of lost silver souls. Most of the rings on the tray were familiar to me from earlier shopping expeditions. One or two I'd tried on for size and resold to Morton. The selection was as varied, and as tempting, as the index to a sex manual. It is my opinion that anyone who buys a ring as an alternative to getting laid in the phenomenological flesh has his ass screwed on backwards. Orgasm is like the sunrise – another will be along soon. Most collectors of any affluence agree, and so raw sex is a buyer's market on Memory Lane. $400 would have bought up half the rings on Morton's tray and left me change for a doughnut and coffee. On the other hand, I knew

$400 wasn't going to buy me the bluebird of happiness. A felony was as much as I could hope for.

"How about a life of crime?" I hinted.

Morton blinked his opossum eyes. "You, uh, wouldn't want me to, uh, break any laws?"

"Laws? Morton, we're grown-ups. Grown-ups can distinguish between entertainment and real life. If I can put on a ring, I can take it off. Right? At my age, with my blood pressure, do you think I can be corrupted by *The Adventures of Robin Hood*?" I continued babbling in this vein until Morton had been soothed sufficiently for greed to get the better of distrust.

"There's one item. I personally know nothing about it."

"Right, right. Show me."

He unlocked a metal file and took out a cassette. He plugged the cassette into a pair of video-specs and handed them to me. "Personally..." he began again.

"You know nothing about it. I understand."

I turned on the spectacles. They bubbled with blue blips, and then a man in a facemold of the aged Woody Allen told me what to expect from the ring he was pawning. I will not anticipate the ring's own spinning of its tale by repeating the description on the cassette, except to say that the masker (who was not the ring's maker, only its third owner) admitted candidly (and a little nervously) that it recorded the commission of a felony. To be found in possession of such a ring brings a mandatory sentence of a year's imprisonment – longer, if the nature of the crime is particularly nasty. It's odd, but when you know a ring is hot, it starts to look different. Evil has its own glitter.

On the whole I am a law-abiding citizen. I understand the reasonableness of outlawing the merchandising of murder, rape, or any other actionable offense. Surely it will not do for honest citizens to subsidize the criminal elements in crimes they have committed on purpose to market their transcription. Surely to traffic in such wares is irresponsible and deserves nothing but disgust, reprobation, and punishment. Even so, consider how common it was, in the days before micromemory-transfer, for the public to be offered as "entertainment" lurid fantasies of criminal behavior. True, in the movies and novels of the pre-now era, law and order usually wound up winning, but you don't have to be Diogenes to suppose that the prime fascination of all those criminous heroes, otherwise known as villains, was the possibility of the audience sharing vicariously in their wickedness. I'm a guilty wretch, I don't deny it, for buying that ring, but am I any guiltier than the wretches who flocked to see *Little Caesar* or *Death Row Studs* or *How to Dismember a Body?* (Or than the readers of this confession?)

The long and short of it was that I gave in to the temptation I'd come looking for. Morton, with a merchant's mysterious sixth sense for any pocket's exact depth, would not budge from a price of $400. The only concession I could pry out of him was to throw in a couple of blank rings, which came with the proviso that he be allowed first refusal on anything I recorded.

"And if you think you might do anything, um, undignified or – " He twiddled the $400 ring thoughtfully. " – devious, stay away from mirrors, hear. You'd be amazed how many guys get busted cause they get careless about that."

"Just call me Dracula."

Morton smiled a pallid smile. "And don't rob any cradles either. I got principles."

The deal was sealed, and I left Memory Lane fizzing with a sense of personal dignity. It had been quite a while since anyone had suggested that I make a recording. I went up the stairs like they were an escalator, whistling the theme from The Myth of Progress.

Arriving home cured me of those delusions. Home is where the heart breaks. Home is what's left when all the collectibles have gone to the auction block. Home is a plasterboard box 14 feet long, 12 feet wide, and 8 feet high, the largest of ten spaces sliced up from what had once been a dentist's office. I still have Dr. Moss's chair, back sprung and vinyl patched, bolted to the center of the floor. Beside it, where once the drill was mounted, is a rented Ringmaster, my central and sustaining self-indulgence. Twenty years ago, when my recording career began to founder, I had the foresight to sign a long lease for both the office and the Ringmaster. Now the rent from the space I sublet is all that keeps me afloat financially.

The Ringmaster is a metered, not a monthly, charge, and since, alas,

I so rarely use it, my bill is less than I'd pay for a phone, if I had one. I have a small stock of rings, but they are either crude mass-market simulations or my own botched jobs of later years. The day a picnic didn't pan out and I, undaunted, recorded eight hours spaced out in a laundromat. The day I bused upstate to view the autumn leaves and sprained my ankle leaving the bus. Those failures were at least vivid. Most of my unmarketable memories are just dull – so many soft tasteless noodles in the soup of the past.

The fun past, the yummy past, the past one sings of on New Year's Eve – all that is unrecapturable, sold off in weekly and monthly lots. There is one entire year, my twenty-ninth, wiped from the slate of memory. What seas of pleasure I cruised that year, what wine cellars were plundered on my behalf, what dainties ravished my tongue, only the Directors and Patrons of the Albright-Knox Museum are privileged to know, since the public, which includes me, is denied access to the documentation (never mind the use) of those 365 rings. But even unremembered pipers must be paid. One cannot gourmandize through the day and into the night and then, just by turning the lights low, summon Romance or even Raunch. Eventually there is an energy crisis. Instead of resisting that eventuality when it came upon me, I began unwisely to live higher off the hog and, at the same time, to sample my own tapes (with the excuse that I would do my own documentation and thus save gallery fees). Alas, pleasures that are remembered cannot be repeated with equal pleasure. I went through cycles of hunger and satiety, excess and disillusion. Instead of living for my public I began to live for myself, with predictable results. My life fell apart, and my recordings got so bad that even I was bored by them. Bye-bye, career.

All that was Auld Lang Syne. To return to the present – there I was in my humble (168 sq.ft.) home, with my own recent acquisition around my finger, itching to be unveiled. I climbed in the dentist's chair, fastened the seatbelt, and stuck my ring-hand into the Ringmaster's maw. I thumbed the switch and felt the prick of the recall needle as it passed through the center of the ring and pierced my finger. The filament began to revolve, and then, poof, nada, night and fog.

I thought (that much of me that could still think independently), *I've been had!* But no, the ring was functioning, and I – the other "I" of the recording – was walking through a foggy night, heart speeding, muscles tense, ears alert to the traffic noises. Conscious, too, in an amateurish way, of the energy-belt that powered my ring.

A city street, but what city I couldn't tell, for my eyes avoided all telltale specifics – street signs, shop-fronts, the license plates of cars. The mind of the woman behind the ring was as featureless, almost, as the pavement underfoot, a blur of anxiety and fear with some black purpose locked in its back room. As the ring's previous owner had warned, this was a rather unprofessional recording, but in a way the very lack of definition added to the fun, if you count suspense as fun.

My temporary self stepped into the recessed entrance to a narrow brick building and reached into her pocket for the simple tools of her trade. Even numbed with cold, her fingers were quick in solving the riddle of the lock. After taping over the tumblers so the door would not lock behind her, she set off, in deeper darkness, down a corridor, up two flights of stairs, and along a longer corridor until her flashlight's beam picked out, stenciled on a gray steel door, the number 33. Here her task was more delicate, her workmanship more ingenious, but on that first viewing it was the thrills more than the skills of the burglary that I took note of. What clarity there can be in a fear defied. What pleasure (impossible to describe, except that it is intensely, specifically visceral) in the slow winning to the forbidden goal. What triumph when at last the till was open and the money in our hands. And (for it would be dishonest to edit out this final fact) what a blast – of panic, horror, and guilt – when she shot the guard returning with his take-out order of pie and coffee. After the murder (if it amounted to that: she didn't stop to find out) she walked (resisted running) four blocks (I counted them) to a public park, where she sat on a bench and wolfed down the pie and coffee. A cherry pie, and never have I taken greater pleasure in a meal than in that slice of pie. And I am accounted something of a gourmet by those who've collected the rings I've made.

After she'd wiped her fingers on a napkin, she counted her take – $87. She seemed quite satisfied. At that point she stopped recording.

To speak in greater detail of what that ring revealed would be to betray the teacher to whom I was to owe so much. (As it is, I have had to disguise the more incriminating facts: "33" is simply the number I favor at roulette; $87 the going price for a blank ring.) Through her I learned not only (on later viewings) effective methods of picking locks and disabling alarms but, more critically, the *tao* of criminality. Just so, a student learns from the ring of a virtuoso musician not only the feel of his fingerings but whatever of *élan,* judgment, and sublimity his artistry can bring to bear. Let me lay a wreath, therefore, on the grave of that Unknown Felon – and pass on to my own malefactions.

As much, at least, as *I* know of them.

My own criminal career was, from its inception, undertaken less for the sake of immediate gain (that $87 was no great incitement) than for the sake of art. Once I had practiced lockpicking on my own and my tenants' locks (some of surprisingly high quality), I determined to profit from my new skill by recording burglaries that would be, like virtue, their own reward. My objective – not loot but luminescence. I have an abiding faith, which no amount of experience has ever been able to shake, in professionalism and quality. From an esthetic point of view the ring I'd bought from Morton Shure was rankly unprofessional – hasty, unstructured, and fuzzy. While even at their most minimal, on days when I had accomplished little more than tying my shoelaces, my own recordings had been clean, clear, and well-paced. "A born recorder," *Art Scene* called me back in my golden youth, "with a knack for making something miraculous out of the most obvious materials."

Now that the gun of present purpose was loaded, all I lacked was a target. It didn't take long to decide what I wanted for Xmas. What else but rings? I wheedled a back-issue of *Ringtimes* from Morton Shure and compiled a list, from its classified pages, of Manhattan dealers whose offerings were modest enough to suggest that their security systems would not be beyond my still-untested capabilities. List in hand, I began to scout the land and found, like Goldilocks, that most candidates were either too big or too piffling, too posh or too drear.

Until I came to, lucky number, 33 New Soho Square. One look at its degentrified facade of sagging black iron and flaking rose-painted brick, another closer look at the lock on the door in the foyer, and instinct told me with a clear click that here was my target and now was the hour. As Shakespeare says, present mirth hath present laughter. I wired ring to belt and started to record.

*

I woke the next morning in my own room, finger ringless and memory's *tabula* entirely *rasa*. No memory, even, of having come home. Which meant that, as so often in the past, I'd been brought home and put to bed by friendly elves. The elves had left behind, in exchange for yesterday, two rings, a sealed 8-hour blank and a second, fully recorded and set to replay, molded in a lion's head design. Beneath the rings was a note in my own handwriting:

Once more, with feeling. Come at 6.

Meanwhile enjoy your plunder.

After breakfast, for which I lacked my usual appetite, I decided to try out the new ring. Like an informer's hand slipping a secret accusation into the stone jaws of the *Bocca del Leone,* the needle of the Ringmaster entered the lion's head ring, and I found myself at the bottom of a well. The water was up to my knees and rising. Rats squeaked nearby, while far above a witch cackled with glee. Things quickly got worse.

I was lucky to have grown up before the entertainment industry had made cradle-robbing a temptation available to the working class. The equipment needed to make recordings was still too bulky and expensive then, and Memory Lane was a county fair compared to the bustling bazaar it's since become. It's no credit to my parents, therefore, that my lousy childhood belongs to me and not to a collector hungry for wonder and innocence.

There was a case in the news lately of parents who had been re-staging Baby's first Xmas every day of Baby's young life from age 4 through age 7, when the IRS finally caught them. (They got ten years for tax evasion. In Utah there's no law against robbing your own children's cradle.) This recording was more like Baby's first Halloween. The hours I spent trapped in rapport with that child's terror were the supreme bad trip of my life. My own adult knowledge that I was being tormented not by literal witches and ghosts but by everyday human monsters was no proof against panic terror. When the ordeal was over and the needle retracted from the ring, I lay a long time inert, reeling with the aftershock. Slowly my heart's rollercoaster eased to a stop and I got off.

I swore revenge and washed my pants at the sink in the hallway.

*

It was dusk when I returned to Soho Square. The painted brick of Number 33 had dulled from rose to sepia. The metal gates of the shops about the square had been drawn down, giving the neighborhood a battered, embattled look. Pigeons fluttered to their roosts in the junked cars stacked monumentally in the basin of the defunct fountain at the center of the square. It seemed as though nothing had changed for a hundred years. Machu Picchu has got nothing on Manhattan, if you catch it on the right day.

I loitered in the square some minutes, circling the stacked cars in the fountain, establishing mood. Who knew but that this would be my last recording, so it had better be good. My eyes' cameras panned across the concrete stumps of benches towards the doorway of Number 33, and then, feet assisting, zoomed in to the shallow foyer and the laminated plastic nameplate of the Happenings Gallery, M. Ruyk, proprietor. A ringed finger rang the bell. Silence replied.

The door was locked. With the ease of borrowed expertise I entered. The gallery, on the third-floor landing was double-locked. I entered again. The place was an ice palace carved from white light – no walls for miles, no furniture, just a pure, tasteful void. M. Ruyk didn't worry much about the electric bill. Illusions like this cost money. The cinematographer in me was delighted, but the thief was taken aback. Feeling less and less like an avenging angel, I inched forward through the mirage until my hand encountered vertical solidity.

"Mr. Whelan, we're so glad you've decided to return." The voice came from the four corners of the void, a flat, throat-miked contralto like the voice announcing time on the telephone.

In the white glare behind me, where the door should have been, two images formed, his and hers, both dressed in icy shades of blue, both upside-down.

"You're inverted," I told them.

"One moment." The man's hand disappeared to the left, and the image righted itself – and sank through the white glow to just below floor level. "Better?"

"You need some vertical adjustment, but that's okay."

The sofa on which they were seated sank another two feet.

The woman leaned forward – seen right side up, she came across as expensive rather than young – and addressed my midriff with an earnest, placating smile. "Excuse us for keeping at such an unfriendly distance, Mr. Whelan, but the metal indicator downstairs suggested you might be armed."

"Excuse me for breaking and entering. And no need to worry about the gun. It's only a replica. Look." I took it from my pocket and fired off a blank.

"Oh my." She fluttered her hands expressively. They were white and bony and roped with veins and about fifty years older than her face. "How violent! Let me say at once, Mr. Whelan, that I am a great admirer of your work. You have such…'Flair' scarcely does justice. Regrettably I can't claim to possess any of your more notable recordings, but I have been allowed glimpses. *Such* glimpses!" She cocked her head and squinted at my knees. (The image had continued sinking, and now their feet were coming into view in the air above their heads.) "Rudy, can't we get better focus than this?"

Rudy gave a martyred sigh. His hand vanished to fiddle a dial.

"Ah, that's better. No doubt you're impatient, Mr. Whelan. There's so much to explain. And I'm so bad at explanations. The loss of short-term memory is the price one pays for a lifetime of vicarious experience. It does something to the synapses." (Now only their heads were left in the lower image. Slowly they sank from sight and were reunited with their bodies in the image above.) "Consequently *my* memory of yesterday is very little better than yours. Though I do have the advantage over you in having just sampled this." She touched the ring on her left forefinger. "Exquisite! You have not lost your touch, Mr. Whelan. Your palette may be darker, so to speak, but your palate is unchanged. Forgive the pun. I was saying?"

"You were explaining to Mr. Whelan," said Rudy, "why he's here."

"Oh yes. Oh dear. Why *is* he here, Rudy? I remember, from the ring, how he got in yesterday. That was fascinating, all that business with the locks. But then, after the guards had got him and he was handcuffed – which in its own way was most absorbing – after that I'm afraid I rather lose the thread. Mr. Whelan himself became confused, and I stopped paying attention. Until dinner. The dinner was superb. As I believe I've said already. You explain, Rudy. You do it better."

"Maybe you could begin with introductions," I suggested.

"Of course; excuse me. This is my mother, Muriel Ruyk, who founded, and owns, this gallery. I'm Rudolph Ruyk. Fortunately for yourself, you do not need an introduction. Muriel recognized you at once from your recordings. Her short-term memory may be poor, but her recall for the more vivid stretches of her past – any time before the last ten to fifteen years – is often proportionally acute. You, Mr. Whelan, are one of my mother's vividest memories."

"Aruba!" she exclaimed. "And the oysters on Belle Ile! I'll never forget those oysters."

"You were there with me?"

"Goodness, no. *You* were there – isn't that enough? The way the waves pounded on the cliffs. And *you* on those slippery rocks! Oh my. We did meet once, in passing, at Dar-es-Salaam, but nothing came of it. I am proud to say, though, that I was one of your first collectors. So long as I could afford your prices. Once you'd moved up to Knoedler, of course, you zoomed out of my range."

"All that was quite a while back. I'm surprised you recognized me."

"Your hair is thinner now, certainly, and you've put on weight, but the indescribable something is still there. If I *hadn't* recognized you, I'm afraid Rudy would have turned you over to the police directly, and that would have been a shame."

"Mm, yes, it would."

"Such a daring, such a *desperate* thing to do. I've always said, haven't I, Rudy, that there is a deep affinity between artistry and criminality."

"Yes, Mother. But crime is crime, for all that."

"Yes, of course, one must take precautions. But I can't help admiring those like you, Mr. Whelan, who are headlong and act out of impulse. I *do* hope we'll work something out."

"We already have, Mother. We have his agreement on videotape. And as a pledge that he'll honor that agreement we have his own recording of how he broke into the gallery. In fact, with the recording he's making now, we have two such recordings. He can scarcely refuse to cooperate."

"That sounds like blackmail to me."

"It is, Mr. Whelan," said Muriel pleasantly, "but I'd like to think that our arrangement would appeal to you on its own merits. You've been leading a rather *mean* sort of life. We're offering you a new chance at the good life. We're offering you, in fact, a comeback."

Despite myself, the word worked its magic: a comeback! I resisted the bait long enough to ask, "On what terms?"

"On *our* terms," said Rudy. "Five nights a week you'll record for us. The recordings will be the property of the gallery. All recording expenses will be approved in advance and charged to the gallery."

"It all sounds rather...unilateral."

Muriel touched her ingenue smile with a crone's finger. "Isn't that always the way of it with galleries, though? But is self-advantage that important to you as an artist? What does money matter, if you enjoy abundantly the pleasures it can buy?"

"Yeah, but you'll enjoy the re-runs. You and your customers."

"I wouldn't deny that. But what better defense against satiety than to awake each day to a present unshadowed by the past? Candidly, I consider the loss of short-term memory a great blessing. It allows me to live for the moment."

"In any case," said Rudy, "you'll get a quid pro quo. After each recording session you'll be allowed to check out a ring from the gallery's current collection. Excepting some few rare recordings that have only one or two replays left. I assume that's what you were after when you broke in here."

"If the ring you left with me last night is any sample of your collection, I'm not enticed."

"What ring was that, Rudy?" Muriel asked.

"One of my nightmares, from when I was four. I did warn you, Mr. Whelan, that it might be too strong for your taste, but you flipped for the price tag."

"I don't believe that was a nightmare. That was real."

"Oh, Rudy had the most vivid imaginable nightmares as a child. Everyone accepts them quite literally. Of course, as Rudy says, they're not to every taste. One sample was enough for me. But people go to horror movies, don't they? It's the same principle."

"Cradle-robbing is not the same as anything. It's a crime in this state, and that ring is evidence."

"There was nothing illegal in any of Rudy's recordings. They were undertaken with a grant from the National Endowment and conducted under the most stringent psychiatric supervision. Every ring is fully documented. And from a strictly ethical point of view, surely it was a kindness to the dear boy to exorcize the memory of such terrible dreams."

"Except, Mother, that as a result I went on having the nightmares."

"That's only a theory, Rudy," Muriel scolded. "All children have nightmares. It's a stage they go through. You just had a special talent. Why in the world are we discussing this? I thought we'd settled this years ago."

"Because Mr. Whelan didn't enjoy his private viewing."

"Oh yes. Well, Mr. Whelan, you must choose more wisely next time. Try athletics. It picks you up wonderfully, and we've got a fine stock. Rudy takes a group of young men skiing every year, and they all have a lovely time. You can have the same lovely time, and *I* can have my own collection of Whelans! One comes to the gallery business, after all, because one lacks the means to be a collector. I'm *sure* I explained all this yesterday."

"You did, Mother. But you also insisted (if you'll remember) that Mr. Whelan should not stop recording till he was back home and put to sleep. You wanted there to be an element of surprise in today's recording. But (as I pointed out then) we would have to explain this all over."

"And so we are. It's good of you, Rudy, to be so patient with us. You won't have to tomorrow. We'll stop recording in a moment, and then, while you put the finishing touches on dinner – (How long has it been, Mr. Whelan, since you've eaten tournedos Rossini?) – *he* can audit the ring he's making now."

"You're assuming that I've agreed to all this," I pointed out.

"And so you did – yesterday."

"Yesterday I hadn't just gone through purgatory."

"Oh pish, Mr. Whelan, pish. Tomorrow today will be yesterday. We must live for the present. Even the Bible says so, somewhere. Mr. Whelan, I implore you. Try it for one week. You see – " She leaned forward confidentially and went out of focus. " – I have been put on this *merciless* diet. No cholesterol, which means, in effect, no sauces. Virtually no desserts but fresh fruit. No *beef* in any form – think of it! And no salt, Mr. Whelan! What kind of life is that?"

"So basically what you want me to do is...."

"To eat for me, Mr. Whelan. Rudy is a wonderful cook, and when he's not in the mood, the city's full of restaurants. My resources are limited, but I can still afford a table at La Pentola."

"But surely you don't need me for such a...a...."

"A bit part?" Rudy asked sarcastically.

"If you meant to say," said Muriel, "that someone else could make such recordings for me, you don't do justice to your own artistry, Mr. Whelan. Believe me, my dinner table has auditioned hundreds of would-be artists. None of them had your taste, your gusto, your concentration."

"Well?" Rudy demanded.

"Well," I replied, "why not? Like Shakespeare says, the best revenge is living well."

While Rudy went off to the kitchen and Muriel replayed, again, our dinner of the night before, I let the gallery's two guards set up a Ringmaster so that I could audit – and thus be able to recall – the recording I'd just been making. There was a flash of discontinuity as the ring was rewound; subjectively no time had intervened since I'd started recording out in the square. But soon the ring was ready, and I started to relive the last hour of my own life.

By the time the ring had finished playing, dinner was waiting in the upstairs dining room to which the guards had escorted me. At the first whiff of the lobster bisque, my salivary glands snapped to attention. I started to record.

The rest is art history.

The Owl and the Pussycat

> "Hush, hush, whisper who dares!
> Christopher Robin is saying his prayers."
> A. A. MILNE, "VESPERS"

THEY LIKED the mornings best, when Mr. and Mrs. Fairfield were asleep upstairs and the house was quiet and they could snuggle together on the love seat and wait for the train to come rumbling by on the other side of the river. There were other trains at other times of day, but things could get so hectic later on that you might not even realize a train was going by until the windows were rattling.

Those windows should have been fixed years ago, especially the combinations on either side of the TV set. Dampy became anxious whenever there was a storm alert, certain that sooner or later a gusting wind would just suck those old windows out of their aluminum frames. The upstairs windows were more solid, because they were made the old-fashioned way and would probably outlast the roof. Though that wasn't saying much. The roof was in sorry shape, too. One of these days, when he had the cash, Mr. Fairfield was going to fix the roof, but that wouldn't be any day soon, since trying to find a full-time job kept him out of the house so much of the time.

After the train went by, and it started to get brighter, the alarm clock in the upstairs bedroom would go off, and then there'd be noises in the bathroom, and after that from the kitchen the smells of breakfast. Breakfast was their favorite meal of the day, because it was always the same. A little glass of apple juice, and then either puffed rice or corn flakes with milk and sugar and then a crisp piece of toast with butter and jam. They would bow their heads along with Mrs. Fairfield, and

Mr. Fairfield too if he were up that early, and thank the Lord for His blessings.

Some Sundays there were even pancakes. Dampy had lived at Grand Junction Day Care before he moved in with the Fairfields (at the time of the *first* Mrs. Fairfield), and once a month there had been a special Pancake Breakfast Benefit in the lunch room of the day care. The first Mrs. Fairfield had helped make the pancakes on the gas grill, as many as twenty at a time. Wonderful pancakes, sometimes with blueberries in them, sometimes with shredded coconut, and you could have all you could eat for just $2 if you were under the age of six. Later on, the Benefits were not so well attended, and only the children came, as though it were just another school day, except with pancakes, and that's when Dampy had the accident that got him called Dampy. The children had a food fight, using the paper plates as Frisbees, even though there was syrup on the plates and Miss Washington said not to. No one paid any attention, they never did with Miss Washington, and one plate hit Dampy and got syrup all over him, so Mrs. Fairfield took him back to the big sink and gave him a sponging off, and when that didn't get off all the syrup, she gave him a real dousing. And he never got entirely dry again.

He didn't mind being called Dampy. Sticks and stones as they say. But then there was the Terrible Accident (that really was no accident at all), but why talk about that. There is no need to dwell on the dark side of things, and anyhow that was a fine example of a silver lining, since if it hadn't been for the Terrible Accident Dampy would probably never have come to be adopted by the Fairfields on a permanent basis. And the Fairfields' house despite the arguments was a better place to live than Grand Junction Day Care. Quite lonely, of course, until Hooter had come to live there too, but Dampy had always tended to keep to himself. The new Mrs. Fairfield was the same way. She preferred her solitude and the TV over a lot of friends.

But special friends are different, of course, and from the very start Hooter was to be Dampy's *special* friend. He had come to live with Dampy and the Fairfields when Mr. Fairfield had abducted him from his home at the Grand Junction Dutch Reformed Church. There he'd been, sitting in his box, listening to the speaker at the Tuesday night

AA meeting, but not listening all that closely, and then Mr. Fairfield grabbed hold of him. Mr. Fairfield was there because he'd been arrested for Driving While Intoxicated, and the judge had said he had to go to AA meetings twice a week. So there he was at the Dutch Reformed Church in the folding chair just beside Hooter's box.

Mr. Fairfield had nervous hands. If he wasn't fiddling with his cigar, he would be cleaning his fingernails with his Swiss Army pocket knife or tearing a piece of paper into the smallest possible shreds. That night, after he'd turned the two-page list of local AA meetings into confetti he began to play with Hooter, not in a rough way exactly, but certainly with no consideration for Hooter's feelings. After the people at the meeting had shared their experience, strength, and hope (except for those, like Mr. Fairfield, who had nothing that needed sharing) everyone joined hands and said the Our Father.

That was when Mr. Fairfield had picked up the young owl and whispered into his black felt ear, "Hooter, I am going to *adopt* you." "Adopt" was what he said, but "abduct" was how it registered on Hooter, who left the church basement concealed beneath Mr. Fairfield's Carhardt jacket, with a feeling that his Higher Power had betrayed him. After all the time he'd lived in the church basement he'd come to assume that he *belonged* there, that no one was ever going to take him away, even if he spent every Saturday in the box that said *Free*. At first that had been a heart-breaking experience, but the AA meetings had been a consolation in coping with the loneliness and isolation. But Hooter had put his trust in his Higher Power and turned over his will, and he'd learned to *accept* his life as a church owl. And now here he'd been abducted.

Mr. Fairfield pulled open the door of his pickup, and Hooter was astonished to find that someone had been waiting out here in the freezing pickup all through the meeting. Sitting in the dark, wrapped in a blanket, and looking very miffed at having had to spend all this time in the cold.

"Hooter," said Mr. Fairfield. "I want you to meet Dampy. Dampy, this is Hooter. He's going to be your new buddy. So say hello."

Dampy did not respond at once, but at last he breathed out a long, aggrieved sigh. "Hello," he said and moved sideways to make room for Hooter under the blanket. When they were touching, Dampy whispered into Hooter's ear, "Don't say anything in front of *him*." With a meaningful look in the direction of Mr. Fairfield, who had taken out a brown paper bag from the glove compartment of the pickup.

Hooter knew from his first whiff of the opened bottle that Mr. Fairfield was another secret drinker, like Rev. Drury, the pastor of the Dutch Reformed Church. Hooter had often been the companion of the Reverend's secret libations in the church basement, and when he didn't polish off his half-pint of peppermint schnapps at one go he would often leave it in Hooter's keeping, in the Free box of broken toys and stained toddler clothes. Now here Hooter was in the same situation again, an enabler.

"Here's to the two of you!" said Mr. Fairfield, starting up the engine of the pickup and lifting the bottle of alcohol towards Dampy and Hooter. They looked at each other, with a sense of shame and complicity, and then the pickup moved out onto Route 97.

"I seen you before, you know that," Mr. Fairfield said. "At the Saturday garage sale. I noticed you there on the Free table. For weeks. They can't give away that ugly little fucker, I thought. So, when I saw you again tonight I thought – I've got just the place for him. The perfect little dork of a buddy. Right, Dampy?"

Dampy was mum. It was a cruel and provoking thing to have said to the poor little owl, who *was* a homely bedraggled creature, to be sure. Dampy was used to having *his* feelings hurt. He was numb to such abuse. But poor Hooter must have been close to tears.

Mr. Fairfield seemed to pick up on that thought. "Hey, I guess I'm no looker myself. You got that beak, I got this gut, and Dampy there is a god-damn basket case. Dampy has got more problems than Dear Abby. But Dampy don't talk about his problems. Not to his family anyhow. But maybe he will to you. What do you say, little fella?"

Neither Dampy nor Hooter said a word.

Mr. Fairfield took another hit from the bottle and they continued the rest of the way in silence.

When they arrived home, it was Mr. Fairfield who introduced Hooter to the new Mrs. Fairfield. "Look, honey, we got another member of the family." He dropped Hooter into Mrs. Fairfield's lap with a loud but not very owlish *Whoo! Whoo!*

"Isn't he a darling?" said Mrs. Fairfield without much conviction. "Isn't he just the sweetest thing?" She took a puff on her cigarette, and asked, "But what *is* he, anyhow?"

"What bird goes *Whoo! Whoo!* He's an owl. Look at him. He's got a beak like an owl, and those big eyes. Got to be an owl. So we called him Hooter."

"But he's got teddy-bear-type ears," Mrs. Fairfield objected.

"So? No one's perfect. He's a fuckin' owl. Give him a kiss. Go ahead."

Mrs. Fairfield put her cigarette in the ashtray, and sighed, and smiled, and planted a delicate kiss on Hooter's beak. Hooter could tell it was a real kiss, with feelings behind it, and so he knew he was a member of the Fairfield family from that point on. He, who'd thought he'd never belong to *any* family but just spend the rest of his life in a box in the basement of the Dutch Reformed Church.

"Okay?" said Mrs. Fairfield, turning to her husband.

"Now tell him you love him."

"I love you," said Mrs. Fairfield, still looking at Mr. Fairfield in an anxious way.

"Okay then," said Mr. Fairfield, rubbing his hand across the fur on his own head, which was the same color brown as Hooter's but much longer. "We got that settled. Now you all better hit the sack. I'm outta here."

Mrs. Fairfield looked disappointed, but she didn't ask where he was off to or whether she could come along.

Mrs. Fairfield was basically a stay-at-home type, and Dampy and Hooter took after her in that respect. They might spend hours at a time on the loveseat watching TV with Mrs. Fairfield, or playing Parcheesi by themselves under the dining room table with its great mounds of folded clothes waiting to be ironed. Rarely did they go out of the house, for they knew there was good reason not to. The woods were just behind the house, and Mr. Fairfield told fearful tales about the woods. Most animals that did not have human families to live with had no home but the woods, which could be a dangerous place, even for owls. Owls are predators themselves, and hunt for mice and smaller birds, but they are preyed upon in turn by wolves and bears and snakes. As for young pussycats, Mr. Fairfield said, the woods meant certain death. Dampy must never, never go into the woods by himself, not even with Hooter, or they would certainly be eaten alive by the predators out there.

Dampy would listen to these stories with a shiver of dread. Hooter, however, sometimes wondered if Mr. Fairfield was not exaggerating about the woods. Of course, the woods *were* out there. You could see them through the windows, and you could see the woodland creatures too, if you were patient – the deer and the two nice groundhogs and all the different kinds of birds, some of whom Mrs. Fairfield could identify, the crows and robins and chickadees, but most of the rest she had no name for. At sunset, in the summers, there were even bats, with their squeaky, unpleasant songs. But were all these woodland creatures as unfriendly and dangerous as Mr. Fairfield made them out to be? Hooter was not convinced.

And – another question entirely – was Dampy really a cat? Mrs. Fairfield had said once that he looked to her much more like a koala bear. She pointed out that he had ears like the koala bear in the advertisements for Qantas Airlines. Qantas was based in Australia, where most koala bears live. And Hooter thought she had a point. Even without a nose, Dampy looked more like a koala bear than a cat.

But Mr. Fairfield was adamant. Dampy was a cat. To prove it he sang a song. The song went like this:

> "The Owl and the Pussycat went to sea
> In a beautiful pea-green boat.
> They took some honey and plenty of money,
> Wrapped up in a five pound note.
> The Owl looked up to the stars above,
> And sang to a small guitar,
>
> "O lovely Pussy! O Pussy my love,
> What a beautiful Pussy you are,

You are,
You are!
What a beautiful Pussy you are!"

"Dampy is not a girl," Hooter objected. It was the first time he'd ever contradicted anything Mr. Fairfield said, and Mr. Fairfield gave him a sour look and then a swat that knocked him halfway across the room.

"If I say he's a girl, he's a fucking girl. And if I say he's a Pussy, he's a Pussy. You *got* that?"

"Harry, please," said Mrs. Fairfield.

"Harry, please," Mr. Fairfield said in a whining tone meant to mock his wife, though in fact it didn't sound at all like her.

"I guess cats are always females then," said Mrs. Fairfield to Hooter. "Dogs are boys, and cats are girls."

No one went to help Hooter until Mr. Fairfield had left the room, but Dampy exchanged a look of sympathy with him, as sad as could be.

Later, when they could talk without being overheard, Hooter protested (in a whisper, with the sheets over his head): "Is there nothing we can do then? Are we just trapped here, and have to suffer every kind of abuse?"

"He can be very mean," Dampy agreed.

"And just as mean to Mrs. Fairfield as he is to us."

"Meaner, actually. Last year, about a week after New Year's, he sent the *first* Mrs. Fairfield to the hospital emergency room and she had to get seven stitches in her head. You could see them when she took off the bandana she had to wear."

"Why would he do that?" Hooter asked aghast. "And what did he do?"

"Well, they'd been singing this song that he likes. Over and over. And finally she said she was too tired to sing any more, and he just sat there where you're sitting now, staring at her, and then he got up and smashed his guitar right over her head. And do you know what I think?"

"What?"

"I think it was really the guitar he was angry with. Cause he never played it very well. But no one ever complained, not with him. But it was a big relief for him not to have people hear how lousy he played his guitar. And he never got another one to replace the one he smashed."

"He's not a nice person," said Hooter gravely.

"He's not," Dampy agreed. "But we should try and get some sleep. Tomorrow is another day." He put his arms round Hooter, and they snuggled.

In such a small household, in a lonely part of the country with no neighbors close by, it was inevitable that Dampy and Hooter would spend so much time together and become the closest friends. From Hooter Dampy learned all about the Dutch Reformed Church and Rev. Drury and the Twelve Steps of Alcoholics Anonymous. Of Hooter's life before he became a church owl there was not much to be told. He'd been a prize at the ring-toss game at the Grand Junction Centennial Street Fair, but the teenage girl who received Hooter from the winner of the ring toss donated him almost at once to the Dutch Reformed's weekly garage sale. Hooter often felt, he confided to Dampy, like one of those Romanian children you hear about on "All Things Considered" (a program that Rev. Drury listened to every day) who have spent their whole childhood in an orphanage and later have trouble relating to their adoptive parents.

To which Dampy had replied, "I'm not so sure that that would be altogether a bad thing. Some parents you might not want to relate to any more than absolutely necessary."

"You mean...Mr. Fairfield?"

Dampy nodded. "And not just him. *She* was just as bad, the *first* Mrs. Fairfield. Our life here is actually an improvement over what it used to be, with her."

"You've never said that much about her before. Was it she who..." Hooter touched the stub of his wing to the end of his beak to indicate the same area on Dampy's face.

"Who pulled off my nose? No, *that* happened at the Day Care. There was a boy there, Ray McNulty, who kept pulling at my nose, and pulling and pulling. Miss Washington told him not to, but he wouldn't listen. Then one day when everyone was supposed to be napping he just ripped it right off. But that wasn't enough for Ray McNulty! Then he took a pair of scissors and opened the seam at my neck."

"And no one's ever tried to sew it up again?"

Dampy went up to the mirror mounted beside the front door and looked at himself morosely. His neck was slit open from the front to just under his left ear, which gave a sad, sideways tilt to his head and meant that you had to listen very intently when he spoke. "Once, yes. Once, Mrs. Fairfield tried to mend my neck – the new Mrs. Fairfield. She means well, but she's hopeless with a needle and thread. I'm used to it now. I don't mind how it looks."

Hooter went up to him and tried to push the stuffing back inside the wound in his neck. "It's such a shame. You'd look so handsome with just a bit of needlework."

Dampy turned away from the mirror. "That's nice of you to say. Anyhow I was telling you about the first Mrs. Fairfield."

"Was she like him?" Hooter asked. "I mean, did she drink?"

"Yes, and when she drank, she became violent. They quarreled all the time, and she liked to break things. She broke dishes. She threw an electric skillet through the kitchen window. She poured a whole bottle of red wine over him when he was lying drunk on the rug, and when the *ants* got to that, oh boy! And then, if he reacted, she called the police. She had him sent to jail twice."

"So what finally happened? Did they get a divorce?"

Dampy's reply was almost inaudible. Hooter had to ask him to repeat what he said. "She died," he said in a hoarse whisper. This time he added, "And it was no accident either."

He was reluctant to supply any further details, and Hooter knew better than to pester him with lots of questions. In any case there was a more important question pending:

Dampy had asked Hooter if he would marry him!

Hooter had objected that they were the same sex, but Dampy pointed out that same-sex marriages were discussed all the time on the news, and while they weren't allowed among Southern Baptists and Catholics and Orthodox Jews, the two of them were Dutch Reformed if they were anything. Besides which, according to Mr. Fairfield, Dampy was a girl not a boy, so it wouldn't be same sex. The important thing was did they love each other and would they go on loving each other to the end of time or death did them part. At last, Hooter had answered, in the words of the song, "O let us be married! too long we have tarried: but what shall we do for a ring?"

In the poem the owl and the pussycat sail off to a wooded island where a pig sells them, for a shilling, the ring that's in his nose, but in real life finding a ring was a lot easier, for Mrs. Fairfield had a jewel case containing as great a variety of rings as you might find in a jewelry store. There were rings with rubies and emeralds and two with amethysts (the new Mrs. Fairfield was an Aquarius, and the amethyst is the birthstone for February) but the ring they finally selected was a four-carat facsimile zirconium diamond mounted in 14-carat gold from the Home Shopping Club.

They were married in the woods in back of the house on a cloudy June afternoon, while Mr. and Mrs. Fairfield were away to talk to their lawyer in Grand Junction. Dampy wore a red-and-white checkered kitchen towel that Hooter said made him look like a Palestinian terrorist. Hooter himself was all in black. It was the first time they'd been in the woods together so far from the house that you couldn't even see the roof. For all *they* knew they were lost!

Dampy took the stub of Hooter's wing in his paw and said, "I thee wed!"

To which the owl replied, "For better or for worse."

"In sickness and in health."

That was as much of the ceremony as they could remember, except for the kissing. Then there was the problem of what to *do* with the ring now that it was theirs. Dampy wanted to return it to Mrs. Fairfield's jewel case, but Hooter got such a hurt look that Dampy at once came up with an alternate plan. They buried it under a stone out in the woods, marking the very spot where they'd been wed.

When they got back to the house, Mr. and Mrs. Fairfield's lawyer, Mr. Habib, was there with them, as well as two policemen and a lady, Mrs. Yardley, with yellow hair like a movie star's, who wanted to talk to them. At first Mr. Habib said she was being ridiculous, the boy was autistic and delusional. Nothing could be gained by speaking with him, and in any case that would be a hopeless task. The boy could not be made to answer questions. Mr. Habib had tried, and so had the police.

"But I understand, from remarks that Mr. Fairfield has made in his deposition, that he *does* speak to, or through, his teddy bears. And I see he has them with him now. I'd like to speak to the teddy bears. Privately."

"You want to speak to a pair of fucking teddy bears!" jeered Mr. Fairfield. "Maybe give 'em the third degree?"

"For the record," said Mrs. Yardley, "we have reason to believe that the child's welfare may be in danger. There has been a history of abuse."

"All those charges had to do with the deceased," Mr. Habib pointed out. "And this boy is surely not fit for a formal interrogation."

Mrs. Yardley smiled a sweet smile and scrunched down beside Hooter. "But I don't want to talk with the boy. It's *this* little fellow I'd like to meet. And his friend." She gave Hooter's beak a gentle tweak and patted Dampy on the head. "If *someone* would introduce me."

Dampy turned his face away, but Hooter was not quite so shy. "I'm Hooter," he confided in a whisper. "And this is Dampy."

Mr. Habib protested vigorously as to the irregularity of Mrs. Yardley's questioning, but she just ignored him and went on talking with Dampy and Hooter, telling them about other teddy bears she knew and respected, an Evangeline, who lived in Twin Forks and was as well-dressed as any fashion model; Dreyfus, who always wore a little bow tie and was knowledgeable about mutual funds; and Jean-Paul-Luc, who spoke French, which made it difficult for Mrs. Yardley to get to know him very well, since she'd only had one year of French in high school, long ago.

She was a really nice lady, but the nicer she was the ruder Mr. Fairfield became, until finally she had to ask the two policemen to escort Mr. Fairfield out to their car. Mr. Habib accompanied Mr. Fairfield to the police car, and Mrs. Fairfield went upstairs.

When they were with Mrs. Yardley, she shifted their conversation away from the other teddy bears she knew and wanted to know all sort of things about the Fairfields. Hooter tried to be cooperative, but there wasn't much he could tell her about the first Mrs. Fairfield. Dampy was not as trustful at first, and there were lots of things that he claimed he couldn't remember, especially about the night the first Mrs. Fairfield had died.

Gradually Hooter realized that Mrs. Yardley thought that Mr. Fairfield had murdered his first wife and was looking for some way to prove it. When she was done asking Dampy questions, Mrs. Yardley asked Hooter the same questions, even after he'd explained to her that he'd been living at the Dutch Reformed Church when Mrs. Fairfield was killed.

"Ah-ha!" said Mrs. Yardley. "Why do you say 'killed'? Is it because you don't believe it was an accident?"

"I don't *know*," Hooter protested, close to tears.

"I guess she must have killed herself," Dampy said unprompted. "That's what Mr. Fairfield says."

"Oh, really? Who did he say that to? To you?"

"No, to me he always says it was an accident and not to think about it. But I heard him say to the *new* Mrs. Fairfield – "

"To Pamela Harper, that is? The lady who just went upstairs?"

"Mm-hm. He told her that no one can take so many sleeping pills by accident. He said he thinks she must of mashed them up in her Rocky Road ice cream. Sometimes she would eat a whole pint of Rocky Road all by herself. Especially if they had got in a fight. He'd apologize by bringing home the ice cream. No one else ever got a bite."

The more Dampy explained to Mrs. Yardley about the ice cream and the liquor and the different arguments there'd been, the clearer it became to Hooter that Mr. Fairfield had probably killed his first wife by mixing up her sleeping pills with the ice cream. Then putting a bottle of whisky somewhere she'd be sure to find it when he left her by herself. Clearly, Mrs. Yardley suspected the same thing.

Then there was a great ruckus when the new Mrs. Fairfield came storming down the steps and out of the house to accuse her husband of having stolen her 4-karat diamond ring from her jewel-case.

Hooter looked at Dampy with alarm, and Dampy tilted his head back and stared at the ceiling's intricate pattern of overlapping water-stains. Mrs. Yardley could coax nothing more from either of them, so she left them to themselves and went to stand in the front door and watch Mr. and Mrs. Fairfield scream at each other until Mr. Fairfield went from just verbal abuse to a whack across the face, and that was all Mrs. Yardley needed. Dampy and Hooter spent that night in a foster-care residence forty miles away from the Fairfield home, and they remained there all through Mr. Fairfield's trial for the murder of his first wife. They were not qualified, legally, to be witnesses at the trial, and Hooter, for one, was glad to be spared such an unpleasant duty. What could he have said that would be any help to Mr. Fairfield? For all his faults the man had been like a father to him, and Hooter would not have wanted to be there when the jury brought in their verdict of Guilty of Murder in the First Degree.

At the foster-care residence Dampy and Hooter had been discouraged from seeing much of each other. When they could get together it would have to be in the laundry room when no one was washing clothes or up in the attic, where they weren't supposed to go. Even when they were able to spend a few minutes together, away from the other residents, they were both at a loss for words. Dampy was gradually slipping back into the sullenness and depression that had kept him from talking to everyone at the time before he'd met Hooter. And Hooter for his part spent a lot of his time, as he had in the basement of the Dutch Reformed Church, practicing the multiplication tables.

Neither of them would speak to Mr. Fairfield when he tried to phone, and Mrs. Fairfield never did ring up. Maybe she wasn't really Mr. Fairfield's wife, but just a girlfriend. Anyhow she moved somewhere that didn't have an address.

"Do you miss her?" Hooter asked Dampy one cold November afternoon when they were sitting behind the clothes dryer in the laundry room.

"Not really. Watching all those programs on the Home Shopping Channel got to be pretty dull. I didn't like the first Mrs. Fairfield that much either, but she was more fun to be with."

Hooter studied one of the big lint balls on the floor with a look of melancholy. "You know what? I miss *him*."

"Oh, we're better off this way," Dampy assured him.

"I suppose so. Will he have to spend a *lot* of time in jail?"

"The newspaper said 25 years at a minimum."

"Goodness! He'll be, let me see..." Hooter did the arithmetic in his head. "...almost 55 when he gets out. Well, I suppose it's what he deserves. If you kill someone, you have to pay the price."

Dampy gave Hooter a funny smile. The matron at the residence had sewn up the wound in his neck and now his head tilted in the other direction in a way that was sometimes unnerving. "True," he agreed. "But you know *he* didn't kill Mrs. Fairfield."

"Yes, yes, it's like Mr. Habib says, there was nothing but circumstantial evidence."

"No, that's not what I meant."

"You mean, she really did kill herself?"

"I mean *I* killed her."

Hooter looked shocked. "But you couldn't! You're just – "

"Just a teddy bear?" Dampy asked with a smile. "And do *you* think teddy bears are just stupid cuddly dumb animals?"

Hooter shook his head

"We may not live in the woods, but we are bears."

"I'm an owl!" Hooter protested.

"And I'm a pussycat. But we're both bears. Don't deny it – look at your ears. Mr. Fairfield is best off right where he is, and as for us I expect we'll be adopted soon by someone nice. Mrs. Yardley says there have been lots of applications."

And that is just what happened. They were adopted by Curtis and Maeve Bennet and moved to a house on the Jersey shore and there, just as in the poem

> ...hand in hand, on the edge of the sand,
> They danced by the light of the moon,
> The moon,
> The moon,
> They danced by the light of the moon.

But their wedding ring is still where they left it, under the rock in the woods, marking the spot where they were wed.

Canned Goods

IN THE DOWNSTAIRS LOBBY Mr. Weyman's handgun was taken from him by one of the four uniformed guards and locked in a mailbox. No such requirement was made of his escort, whose name was Lenny. When Lenny followed him into the dark stairwell, Mr. Weyman went through a short inward crisis of unreasoning paranoia, followed by an inward sigh of resignation to the dictates of fate, followed by a brief but intense rapture of anger at the way he was being made to cooperate in his own fleecing. It was just as well they'd taken his gun away in the lobby, or he might have done something foolish when he finally got to see this Shroder person.

He must not let himself flare up. Survival was all that mattered. He had survived the winter. Now if he could last out the spring, the government would surely have found some way by then to restore the city to a semblance of order. The crisis could not just keep going on and on and on. It had to stop, and then things would return to normal.

On the sixth-floor landing Mr. Weyman was obliged to ask to stop to catch his breath. During the entire long trek downtown his escort had never once offered to help Mr. Weyman with his precious parcel in its swaddlings of old clothes and taped and stapled-together shopping bags. Now Mr. Weyman's arms and back ached, his sinuses were beginning to pulse ominously, and his lungs were heaving. It wouldn't do to arrive at Shroder's door out-of-breath and beet-red.

"Is it much farther up?"

"Fourteen," answered the ever-laconic Lenny.

Mr. Weyman demanded rest stops again on 9 and on 12, and so when Shroder came to the door and asked him in, he was able to respond without major heavings and gaspings. He even had breath to laugh at Shroder's (and all the world's) little joke about having to complain to the landlord to get the elevator fixed.

Shroder led him into a large drawing room made to seem small with overmuch furniture. Not so much furniture that one was put in mind at once of Noah's ark, but a good deal more (Mr. Weyman was certain) than had been here at the start of the crisis. Nor were the walls hung chock-a-block with the choicest of his recent acquisitions, as one might have expected. There was a small flower painting over the mantle (Fantin-Latour?), a vintage Derain between the windows, and, in the place of honor opposite the couch on which Mr. Weyman was seated, a large, expensively framed academic nude, reclining her peaches-and-cream buttocks on masses of maroon velvet, all very correct and not a little lubricious.

From Mr. Weyman's viewpoint this was not entirely reassuring. That nude, in particular, spoke of a taste that caters to the requirements of Arab oil sheiks. The Derain, on the other hand, offered *some* hope. Indeed, despite himself, Mr. Weyman could not resist an altogether incongruous twinge of envy. For all that he delighted in the Fauves, he'd never owned a first-rate work by one of them.

"Shall we," said Shroder, "get right to business?"

"By all means." Mr. Weyman began undoing the swaddlings of his parcel.

"I hope you won't mind if Lenny puts this on videotape. I should like to have evidence that our transaction has been entered into, on both sides, freely and without constraint. Should there ever be any question."

'I quite understand, and I'm scarcely in a position to object. Indeed, I'm grateful to be allowed to come here *and* for the escort your friend provided. No one likes to carry large parcels about on the street these days. Though if I knew I were going to be on camera, I might have dressed with a little more care."

"Oh, we all must wear camouflage on the streets these days. This is the era, necessarily, of *in*conspicuous consumption."

Mr. Weyman placed his first offering on the low table before the couch.

"A-ha!" said Shroder, making no effort to disguise his pleasure. "Fiske Boyd, and a good one. Though, of course, for a woodcut there's an obvious limit to what I can offer."

Mr. Weyman regarded the Boyd woodcut with a regretful love admixed with some vanity. It represented an arrangement of canned goods on a tabletop, very spare, very assured. He had bought it in '88 when Boyd's reputation, and his prices, were already on the rise. His prices since had peaked, but never declined, and Mr. Weyman could congratulate himself (in this instance) on his acumen as an investor.

"It's chiefly for his woodcuts that Boyd's admired," Mr. Weyman pointed out with the confidence that comes of having the judgment of the market behind one.

"Yes, of course. I only meant that there's a limit to what I can afford to offer for even the *finest* woodcut. What is the date, by the way?"

"1930." There was no need to add that it was in miraculously mint condition.

"Yes. Well...." Shroder nodded significantly towards the shopping bag, as much as to say, "Let's move along."

Shyly, with a sense almost of exposing himself, Mr. Weyman took out what he regarded as his trump card – a large, chastely framed Motherwell collage/drawing.

Shroder formed his lips into an O of disappointment.

"I realize, of course, that Motherwell no longer commands the prices he once did."

Shroder emitted a derisive snort, like the erasure of a laugh.

"Indeed! In *that* respect Motherwell remains at the forefront of the avant-garde."

"You're speaking of what happened to the six paintings in the *Elegy* series at the Black Saturday auction? If the gallery had been allowed to put floors on the prices – "

"If pigs could fly! There was no one buying abstract expressionism at that point but museums and investors. Once the museums started unloading, you don't think the *investors* wouldn't follow suit, do you?"

Mr. Weyman looked down at his Motherwell sadly. Only four years ago he'd bought it from a friend in dire circumstances for $200. The friend had paid several thousand dollars for it in the late '60s.

"I was there that day," Mr. Weyman said. "Were you?"

"On Black Saturday? Hardly. I would have been eleven years old."

"It's something I'll never forget. I remember how I lusted after those Motherwells. But by the time they'd come under the hammer I'd already emptied my own bank account, and the Zurich gallery I was acting for wasn't touching anything that went under an artist's established price level by more than 50%. I remember the silences that day. They'd halve a price, and halve it again, and still no one would *bid.* A Pooms for twelve hundred. Well, perhaps that's not unthinkable. Tastes change, and if one paints on such an institutional scale, and institutions decide to stop investing in art, what's to be done? But a Braque for seven hundred? Braque?"

"Mr. Weyman, may I remind you, that it's not Braque's merits at issue here, but Motherwell's."

"Excuse me. I'm in no position to argue. But I must at least be allowed to point out that this drawing was hung at the '65 retrospective at the Modern."

"I don't care if it hung at the Louvre next to the *Mona Lisa.* It is my long-standing opinion that Motherwell was never anything more than the favorite tailor of a very naked emperor. Any third-year art student with savvy coaching from a competent interior decorator could produce such *wallpaper* by the roll. The days are gone when a painter can claim a day's wages for two minutes' work, because he's spent a lifetime refining his taste. I'm sorry, Mr. Whistler, but art is not p.r. Sorry to you too, Mr. Motherwell, but *this* sort of thing – " He tapped the scrap of a Gauloise pack that lent its little note of color to the drawing. " – just won't do. Not in the 21st century."

"Well, if you don't want it," Mr. Weyman said with a resentment he was unable to conceal, "you needn't take it. I have faith that Motherwell's day will return. I am sorry for your sake that you do not."

"As to my *taking* it, Mr. Weyman, I have a fixed policy, as I believe our mutual friend at Sotheby's explained to you: I buy by the lot. My overhead costs don't allow me the luxury of haggling. Now...let's see what else you have."

Mr. Weyman removed the Burchfield canvas from his shopping bag, which, no longer braced by the painting's stretcher, flopped sideways to the carpet (a very choice Sarouk in a floral design).

"Ah. This is more like it!"

Shroder took the Burchfield in his hands and turned it at different angles to the light, as though studying the facets of a gemstone. It was a painting of a Christmas tree, but a Christmas tree seen in its eternal aspect, each light aureoled and the several aureoles overlapping and interweaving in an elaborate seine of interference patterns. The paint seemed to tremble like tinsel on a tree.

"This," said Shroder reverently, "cannot be easy to part with. I'll give you the best price I can. More, I think, than our mutual friend would have led you to expect. Let me think. For the Fiske Boyd I'll give you, let's say, an even ten cans of tuna? No, it's in mint condition; let's make it a round dozen. For the Motherwell – a pound of elbow macaroni. Which is more than it's worth. For the Burchfield – "

He took the small canvas to the window and basked in the glow of its beauty. "For the Burchfield I shall let Lenny take you into the stockroom, and you may fill up one plastic carrier bag with whatever you fancy, excepting only the caviar. There's a limit of three jars per customer on that."

"That's very good of you, Mr. Shroder. Very generous, indeed. Thank you." Mr. Weyman reached for the handles of his shopping bag.

"One moment, Mr. Weyman. I seem to remember that our friend said you would be bringing me *four* pieces to consider."

"Yes...but the fourth is just a...bagatelle. A frippery. Nothing more than a serigraph. If I'd had a better sense, beforehand, of your preferences I'd never have brought it."

"But you have brought it – I see the end of the cardboard tube poking out of your bag. And you've roused my curiosity with what you say. I must remind you I buy only by the lot."

Reluctantly, Mr. Weyman took the cardboard tube from the recumbent shopping bag, undid the knots of the plastic strip that bound the print to the tube, and unrolled the print. He'd bought the print in the first days after the collapse of the market for what he'd then considered a song – considering its sales history. It had been a very famous work of art in its day.

Shroder crowed with pleasure. "Oh, Mr. Weyman! How droll! And of course I have *just* the thing to give you in exchange. The perfect barter."

He went into his stockroom and returned with a can of Campbell's Tomato Soup.

The Abduction of Bunny Steiner, or, A Shameless Lie

WHEN RUDY STEINER'S AGENT, Mal Bitzberg, called up with the idea that Rudy should produce a UFO book after the manner of Whitley Strieber's *Communion, A True Story,* Rudy thought Bitzberg was putting him on. It was April 1, but Rudy's situation was too desperate for April Fools' Day jokes. Bitzberg knew how desperate Rudy was at the present moment, the latest, lowest nadir of a career rich in nadirs. He was: (a) in debt well over his head; (b) apartmentless; (c) obese; (d) an apostate member of A.A.; (e) in his third month of writer's block; and, the crown jewel among Rudy's woes, (f) all the royalties for his best-selling fantasy series, *The Elfin Horde,* et al., were being held in perpetual escrow pending the settlement of a lawsuit that had been brought against him and his subsequently bankrupted publisher, Djinn Books. The lawsuit had been initiated by a Baltimore attorney and professional litigant, Rafe Boone, who specialized in charging best-selling authors with plagiarism and settling with them out of court. Rudy had balked at shelling out $100,000.00 to Boone, a jury had decided in Boone's favor, and then an appeals court had reversed the verdict. While Boone was contesting that appeal, he had been shot dead on the steps of the courthouse by another of his victims. Shortly afterward, the legal remains of Djinn Books had been swallowed up by a German publishing consortium. Boone having died intestate, his estate was now being contested by five separate claimants, and the bulk of that estate consisted of their potential seizure of Rudy's royalties. It was the opinion of Rudy's attorney, Merrill Yates, that Rudy had as much chance of finding the pot of gold at the end of the rainbow as of seeing any further proceeds from

The Elfin Horde and its six sequels. Worse, he'd been enjoined from writing new books in the series and even from using the pseudonym of Priscilla Wisdom. The experience had been embittering.

"A UFO story?" Rudy had marveled. "You've got to be kidding. Besides the Strieber book, Random House is bringing out one just like it by that other jerk."

But Bitzberg was not a kidder. "So? That means it's a trend. All you need is a slightly different angle. Strieber's angle is he's the first name writer who's been inside a UFO. Hopkins has got this whole club of UFO witnesses, which anyone can join: that's his angle, democracy. The whole thing could become a religion. Anyhow that's what Janet Cruse thinks. It was her idea. And she thinks you're the person to write the next book."

"Janet Cruse? You've got to be kidding!"

Bitzberg shook his head and smiled a snaggletoothed smile that had been known to frighten small children. "She's with Knopf now, and she wants *you* to write a UFO book."

"Janet Cruse is with Knopf? I can't believe it."

Years ago, when Janet, a Canadian living in London, had been handling Rudy's English rights, she had sold several of his Priscilla Wisdom titles in foreign markets without telling him. By the time he'd discovered what she'd done, Janet had absconded to Toronto. She'd sold three books in Belgium, two in Portugal, four in Israel, and those were just the sales Rudy had found out about. He'd never seen a cent of the money.

"She realizes you've got reason to be angry with her. But she hoped this might make it up to you."

"If she wants to make it up to me, she could just pay me the money she stole."

"She doesn't have it. Believe me, I've seen where she's living. She's no better off than you."

"And she's at *Knopf*? And Knopf wants a UFO book?"

"Knopf brought her in, because she's considered an expert on occult writers. UFOs are as respectable as astrology these days. Random House, Atlantic Monthly Press – those are not your typical exploitation publishers. Anyhow, do you want to have lunch with her or not?"

"What kind of money are we talking about?"

"Fifty thousand. Half with the portion and outline, half on publication."

"Fifty thousand? Strieber got a *million*."

"So? Maybe he's got a better agent. Or maybe he's got a bigger name. Or maybe it was because he was there first."

Rudy sighed. He had no choice, and Bitzberg knew it. "Set up a lunch."

Bitzberg exposed his terrible teeth. "It's already set up. Tomorrow, one o'clock, Moratuwa Wok."

"And *morituri te salutamus* to you too, old buddy."

Bitzberg lit a cigarette. His fingers trembled, making the flame of the match quaver. His fingers had trembled as long as Rudy had known him. It was some kind of nervous affliction. "I do what I can, Rudy, I do what I can."

"So this is my idea," Janet Cruse explained the next day, sipping lukewarm tea from a dainty cracked teacup. "Strieber's book shows that the audience is there, and Hopkins' book shows that anyone can tell essentially the same story that Strieber did and the similarity only goes to *prove* that something strange has to be happening, or how is it that *everyone* is telling the same story?"

"How indeed," Rudy agreed.

"Now the one thing you *have* to promise, Rudy, is that you never joke about this. Flying saucers are like religion. You've got to be solemn. Have you read Strieber's book?"

He nodded.

"Then you know the basic line to take. You're upset, you're confused, you're skeptical, you can hardly believe what's happened to you. And you're terribly grateful to Strieber and Hopkins for having had the courage to tell their stories, because now at last you can tell the world about you – and Bunny."

"Bunny?"

Janet dabbed at the crisp, crimson corners of her lips with a paper napkin. "Bunny is your daughter." She tilted her head coquettishly and waited for him to express some suitable astonishment.

He maintained a poker face, however, and their waitress chose just that moment to arrive with their bowls of millet, steamed vegetables, and a condiment made of onion and raisins. Moratuwa Wok was a Sri Lankan vegetarian restaurant, and it did not have a liquor license. There were gaudy posters of Hindu gods on the wall, and scented candles burning on each of the six tables. Janet and Rudy were the only people having lunch.

"How old is my daughter Bunny?" he asked, after the waitress had gone away.

"Oh, I'd say five or six. Four would be ideal, it's when kids are cutest, but you've got to consider that a lot of the text will be Bunny's account while she's under hypnosis."

"Mm-hm."

He considered Janet's proposition while she nibbled a stalk of asparagus still so crisp it barely drooped as she lifted it to her lips. Sri Lankans did not overcook their vegetables.

"You see how inevitable it is, don't you?" Janet said, halfway down the stalk. "Strieber *played* with the possibility. His little boy was allowed to hear the reindeer on the roof, so to speak, and who knows but that in his next book he'll go all the way and have the dear boy abducted. And *missing* for a few days. Imagine the anguish a parent must suffer. Especially a *father*. How long was Cosby's *Fatherhood* at the top of the list? And how many copies did it sell? It set a record, I think, and it's still going strong. And what could be a greater torment for a loving father than to have his daughter abducted by aliens, who perform unspeakable acts on her? Which is what mainly goes on, as I understood it, in all those unidentified flying objects. So there you've got another hot issue for a cherry on the sundae: child abuse. Can you imagine any paperback house turning down a package like that?"

"It sounds like a very marketable commodity, Janet, I agree. There's only one problem."

"What's that? Tell me, I'll solve it." She snapped decisively at a carrot stick. "You don't have a daughter, is that it? *That* is why you are the ideal Dad for little Bunny. Because *obviously* we can't rely on a kid that young to go on talk show circuits and be cross-examined. So what *you* say is that Bunny has been so traumatized by her abduction that she can't possibly be exposed to the brutalizing attentions of the press. She has to be protected from all that, which is why there are no photographs in the book. And as for the fact that Bunny doesn't exist, that's what makes it perfect. That way even Woodward and Bernstein themselves couldn't find her."

Rudy shook his head. "No one will buy it."

"Believe me, they'll buy a million copies."

"Anyone who knows me knows I don't have a daughter."

"But who knows you, Rudy? No one, a dozen people. You don't have a job to go to every day. You've been in and out of A.A. You're broke. Obviously you haven't been the best father in the world to Bunny, but that's part of your anguish. She's being raised by her mother, somewhere upstate, and you visit them whenever you can."

"And what's her name, Bunny's mother?"

"Kimberly, Jennifer, Melissa, take your pick. You can spend a couple chapters filling in the background on the guilt you feel for having let her bear all the responsibility for Bunny's upbringing. You've offered to marry her, because she's a beautiful, talented woman, but she's refused to consider it until you've proved you can stay sober one full year. And of course you can't, but you still visit them whenever you can. They live in this *châlet* in the Catskills. Melissa handles real estate. Or does she paint? No, real estate, that's a daydream anyone can handle. So that's Bunny's background. The story proper can begin in June."

"This coming June?"

"Mm-hm, when you've agreed to go and look after Bunny, while Melissa takes a well-deserved vacation. You can guess what happens then."

"She's abducted by the aliens."

"Right. For *five days* she's missing, and you are frantic, but even so an obscure impulse keeps you from notifying the police. You search the woods. You see the clearing where the UFO must have landed. You find Bunny's doll there in the matted-down grass. No, better than that: her dog, her faithful dog who followed her everywhere."

"Wouldn't it be better if the dog were abducted with her?"

"Of course! What am I telling you all this for, anyhow? *You're* the writer."

"Do you really think I've sunk so low that I'd write the book you're talking about?"

"Oh, I think you'd always have *written* it, Rudy. The only difference now is that you'll sign your name to it."

"You think I'm shameless."

She nodded.

She was right.

Five weeks later he'd finished a first draft of 340 pages. *The Visitation* was shorter than either Strieber's book or Hopkins', but it was intense. If Knopf insisted, he could pad out the middle chapters with more paternal anguish and add any number of pages to the transcript of Bunny's testimony under hypnosis. After the nature descriptions – an idyllic walk with Bunny through blossoming mountain laurels and the thunderstorm on the night she disappears – that transcript was the best thing in the book. The Xlom themselves (such was the name he'd given the aliens that both Strieber and Hopkins had left nameless) were no more incredible than darling four-year-old bright-as-a-button Bunny. "Honey Bunny" he called her in moments of supreme paternal doting, or "Funny Bunny" when she was being mischievous, and sometimes (but never in the book, only when he'd finished his day's quota of ten pages), with a fond, bourbon-scented smile, "Money Bunny." Margaret O'Brien had never been more endearing, and Shirley Temple was crass by comparison. Bunny was sugar and spice and everything nice.

And the Xlom were unspeakable. Strieber and Hopkins had both been very equivocal about their aliens. Strieber even allowed as how they might not come from Outer Space but maybe from some Other Dimension or else perhaps they were gods. *Quién sabe?* Half of Strieber's books were devoted to such bootless speculations. Hopkins was less accommodating. His aliens seemed to be conducting genetic experiments on their captive humans, impregnating the women with genetically altered sperm stolen from the men and then, when the unwilling brides were a couple months pregnant, abducting them again and stealing their foetuses. Hopkins supplied no explanation as to why his aliens did this, but it certainly was not an activity that inspired trust.

Rudy himself went easy on the enforced pregnancy fantasy (Bunny, after all, was only four), but he bore down hard on the details of the little darling's physical examinations and on the mysterious scar tissue that came to be discovered all over her body. Hopkins had also done a lot with scars, including some blurry photos of what looked like knees with squeezed pimples. Sometimes Rudy felt a tad uneasy about the transparency of *The Visitation*'s S & M sub-text, but Janet had told him not to worry on that score. The target audience for UFO books could read the entire works of the Marquis de Sade, she insisted, and if the Sadean cruelties were ascribed to aliens, they would remain completely innocent as to what it was they were getting off on. Such had been the wisdom of Priscilla Wisdom in her time, as well, so Rudy didn't have any problem letting it all hang out. He wrote at a pace he hadn't managed for the past five years and enjoyed doing it. It might not be art, but it was definitely a professional job.

Two weeks after he'd turned in the manuscript to Bitzberg and had been duly patted on the back for his speedy performance, Rudy still had not heard from Janet, nor (which was more worrisome) had he got back the executed contracts from Knopf. Feeling antsy, he called the Knopf office and asked to speak to Ms. Cruse.

"Who?" the receptionist asked.

"Janet Cruse," he insisted. "She's my editor there."

The receptionist insisted that there was no editor with Knopf called Janet Cruse, nor any record of there ever having been one.

He realized right away that he'd been conned. The walk back to the Knopf office after the lunch at Moratuwa Wok, the good-bye at the elevators, the freebie copy of the Updike book (*Trust Me*, indeed!), the boilerplate contracts with the Knopf logo (something that any agent would have had many opportunities to acquire, alter, and duplicate), and then the constant barrage of phone calls "just to kibbitz," but really to keep him from ever needing to call her at the Knopf office.

But what about Bitzberg: hadn't *he* ever tried to call her at Knopf? Or talked to someone else there about *The Visitation*? On the other hand, if Bitzberg knew Janet wasn't at Knopf, if he'd been in collusion with her from the start, why would he have advanced Rudy $10,000 from his own pocket to tide him over until the nonexistent Knopf advance came in?

"I didn't," Bitzberg explained, "know that, at first. And when I came to suspect it, I admit that I didn't at once tell you. At that point the book was half done, and I'd received money. Not from Knopf, admittedly, but the check didn't bounce for all that. If you want to bow out now, I expect we could take the money and run. On the other hand, there is a bonafide contract for *sixty* thou, and they're not asking for any revisions. They love the book, as is."

"They?"

"The People."

"Who are the people?"

"A cult, I gather. I asked Janet, and she was not particularly forthcoming. But they have their own imprint, Orange Bangle Press." Bitzberg raised a cigarette in his trembling fingers: "I know what you're going to say. You're going to be sarcastic about the name of the press. *But* they have had a major best-seller, *I Wish I May*."

"I've never heard of it."

"Well, maybe 'major' is an exaggeration. It sold almost forty thousand copies in a trade paperback over the last two years. And they expect to do a lot more with your book."

"You've got a contract?"

Bitzberg smiled, he nodded, he cringed. "I'll show you," he said.

Rudy read the contract.

He signed it.

Only then did he go to the library and find out what there was to be known about the People.

The People had begun, humbly enough, in 1975 as a support group in San Diego for smokers trying to kick the habit by means of meditation and herbal medicine. This original narrow focus gradually came to include other areas of concern, from the therapeutic use of precious stones in the cure of breast cancer and diabetes to the need for a stronger defense posture. One of the group's founding members and the author most often published by Orange Bangle Press was Ms. Lillian Devore, the sole heir of Robert P. Devore of the munitions firm Devore

International, contractors for the Navy's Atreus missile. Most of the information in the library about the People focused on the recent legal proceedings concerning the mental competence of Ms. Devore, and her subsequent demise only two months ago just after a court had found that she was not provably insane, notwithstanding certain passages in her published works and the opinions of psychiatrists hired by her niece and nephew, who had brought the case against her.

Needless to say, that niece and nephew had inherited nothing from Ms. Devore's estate, all of which was bequeathed to the People with the sole proviso that the organization continue to advance the study of herbal medicine and to investigate UFO phenomena. UFOs had become a matter of concern only late in Ms. Devore's life, after she had entertained the hypothesis at her trial that her niece and nephew might conceivably have been the issue of secret genetic experiments being conducted by aliens on the women of Earth (and on her half sister Sue-Beth Smith in particular). This was essentially the same hypothesis being advanced by Budd Hopkins in *Intruders*, and Ms. Devore's defense attorney was able to introduce as evidence both Hopkins' book and an open letter by the head of Random House, Howard Kaminsky, stating that the publisher and his associates were persuaded of the book's veracity, intellectual integrity, and great importance. It followed from this, Ms. Devore's attorney had argued, that his client must be considered at least as sane as Howard Kaminsky, and the jury had agreed. Two weeks later, at the ripe old age of 94, this monument to the efficacy of herbal medicine died in her sleep, and the last to be heard of the People in the news concerned the unsuccessful efforts of one of the People to have Ms. Devore's estate divided equally among the 150 members of the sect. That effort was quickly quashed, and the direction of the organization and the control of its funds was to remain under the direction of Ms. Devore's former financial adviser and dear friend, B. Franklin Grace, the man who had figured so prominently during the competency hearings for his role in protecting Ms. Devore from the attention of the press. It was Grace, as the head of Orange Bangle Press, who had signed the contract for *The Visitation.*

Books In Print listed four titles by Lillian Devore, including her reputed best-seller *I Wish I May*, but none were available either from the library or at any bookstore where Rudy asked for them. So that was the end of his research efforts. Anyhow, it seemed pretty clear what had happened. Janet had contacted B. Franklin Grace and pitched her idea for the *Communion* rip-off to him, got a go-ahead, and then scouted around for someone desperate enough to write it. Why she'd felt she had to diddle Rudy into thinking he was doing the book for Knopf was still a puzzle. Either she thought he needed the extra bait of Knopf's respectability before he took the hook, or else she might have figured he would have been greedier if he'd known he was dipping his royalties from The Fund for The People, Inc. He also wasn't sure whether Janet had come up with the whole scheme by herself or if she and Bitzberg had acted in collusion. But since the final result was a valid contract and money in the bank, Rudy was willing to put his legitimate anger on hold, take the money, and sit tight. On the whole, he felt he'd be happier being published by Orange Bangle instead of by Knopf, since on the basis of Orange Bangle's previous track record, no one might ever find out that *The Visitation* existed. His poor dear imaginary daughter might have endured all her indignities in vain, like the fabled tree that falls, unheard, in the middle of the forest. With luck, he might not even be reviewed in *Publishers Weekly* (Orange Bangle verged on being a vanity press), and his authorship would remain a secret shame, the easiest kind to bear.

He celebrated his windfall by renting a tape of *Close Encounters* and watching it, soused, with the sound off and Mahler's 8th on the stereo. He fell asleep as Richard Dreyfuss was heading for Wyoming to rendezvous with the aliens' mothership. He woke at 4 A.M. feeling just the way he'd felt in *The Visitation* the first time he'd been returned to his summer cabin after having been abducted and experimented on by the Xlom: his head ached, he was ravenously hungry, and he had an obscure sense that something terrible had just happened to him but he didn't know what.

The Visitation appeared in October and disappeared at once into the vast limbo of unreviewed books, at least as far as New York was concerned. Janet assured him that the real market for UFO books was in the sticks and that there the book was selling reasonably well. The lack of reviews was par for the course with crackpot books, since anyone credulous enough to take such revelations seriously was probably too dumb to write coherent prose. What was a source of concern was the lack of media attention due to what Janet diplomatically referred to as Rudy's image problem, meaning his weight. TV talk shows did not like to feature fat people unless they were famously fat. Similar consideration had prompted Orange Bangle not to put Rudy's picture on the book jacket.

Then, early in November, little Bunny Steiner made her TV debut on a late night talk show in St. Paul. The next day Rudy's phone didn't stop ringing. He claimed, quite truthfully, to know nothing about Bunny's appearance and said that until he saw a tape of the show he could not be certain it had actually been *his* Bunny who'd given such a vivid account of her abduction by the Xlom. When he tried to reach Janet, she was unreachable, and B. Franklin Grace (whom Rudy had not, previously, tried to talk to) was likewise not taking calls.

He let it ride.

The phone calls continued: from Milwaukee, from Detroit, from somewhere in West Virginia, from Buffalo, New York. Bunny got around, and everywhere she got to she seemed to make a considerable impression. Some of the phone calls were accusing in tone, with the unspoken suggestion behind them that Rudy had been personally responsible for his daughter's ordeal, a suggestion he indignantly resisted. "What kind of monster do you think I am?" he would demand of his unseen interrogators.

"Maybe a Xlom?" one of them had replied, and then hung up without awaiting his answer.

Finally, by agreeing to go to Philadelphia for his own late-night inquisition (albeit on radio), Rudy was able to obtain, as his quid pro quo, a VHS tape of Bunny's appearance on *The Brotherly Breakfast Hour*. He slipped the tape into his player, and there she was on his own TV, in the living color of her flesh, his imaginary four-year-old daughter, pretty much the way he'd described her: a blonde, curly haired, dimple-cheeked, lisping mini-maniac, who rolled her eyes and wrang her hands and commanded the willing suspension of any conceivable disbelief as she re-told the story of her abduction. While her delivery was not verbatim, Bunny rarely strayed beyond the boundaries of the text that Rudy had written, and she never was betrayed into a significant contradiction. Her few embroideries were all in the area of the ineffable and the unspoken, quavers and semi-quavers and moments of stricken silence when she found herself unable to say just where the funny bald people with their big eyes had touched her or what they'd asked her to do. When asked such intimate questions, she would look away – into the camera – and cry real tears. This child had clearly been through experiences that words could not express. Little wonder that the media was picking up on Bunny's performance. She was a miniature Sarah Bernhardt.

Bunny's star reached its zenith just before Xmas, when *The Nation* (which you'd think would have had more dignity than to interest itself in UFOS) published a long article examining the books of Rudy, Strieber, Hopkins, and the Atlantic Monthly Press's contender, Gary Kinder, whose *Light Years* (released in June) featured color photos of UFOS taken by a one-armed Swiss farmer, Eduard Meier. The Kinder book had been expected to enjoy an even larger success than *Communion,* being buttressed not only with its snapshots but with quotes from bonafide scientists, including Stevie Wonder's sound engineer. However, before *Light Years*' release it was discovered that Wendelle Stevens, one of the investigators who'd acted as matchmaker between Meier and the author (and therefore shared in the book's royalties) was serving time in an Arizona prison on a charge of child molestation. There had been no child involved in the Meier UFO sightings, so Stevens' crime should have had no bearing on the book's credibility, as Kinder was at pains to point out in a last-minute Appendix. Nevertheless, the critic in *The Nation* made every effort to tar all four UFO books with the same brush, concentrating his most sinister innuendoes on the possibility that Bunny may have been subjected to a false abduction in which Rudy had been an accomplice.

"Young children believe in Santa Claus," the man had argued, "because they *see* him, in his red suit and his white beard, filling their stockings with presents. Who could he be *but* Santa? They have no reason to suspect deceit, no suspicion that for many grown-ups bamboozling the young is its own reward. Might Bunny Steiner not have been put in the same position vis-à-vis the Xlom? Perhaps the reason her testimony has such a distressing fascination, even for UFO skeptics like myself, is that she is not lying. Perhaps the terrible events reported in *The Visitation* really did take place. Only Mr. Steiner can say with any certainty whether his daughter is one of the hoaxers – or one of the hoaxed."

Rudy's problem, of course, was that he couldn't say anything with any certainty. Janet, when he finally did get through to her, would only burble on about what a brilliant marketing strategy Bunny's TV appearances represented. She brushed aside all of Rudy's questions about who Bunny was and where she came from and how the book was selling.

"But her *scars,"* he insisted nervously. "They don't look fake. How did she..."

Janet laughed. "Surely you don't think only aliens can perform surgery. Kids are always falling down and getting stitched back together. You shouldn't let yourself be upset by one article in one magazine."

"But what if the *police* become interested? What if they say they want to talk with Bunny?"

"What police, Rudy? Be reasonable. No one knows what state Bunny lives in, for heaven's sake, much less what city. And *you* are not legally responsible for her, are you? Only her mother is, only Melissa, and she's been very careful to keep both herself and Bunny out of the limelight *except* for her carefully scripted minutes before the cameras. The minute they leave that studio, Bunny's little blonde wig comes off, and she's another girl."

"But is it all an act, or...?"

"No, of course not, it's all true, and she really is your daughter, conceived on board a flying saucer with the semen the Xlom stole from you one night when, according to the false memory they've implanted in your brain, you thought you were watching a rerun of the *The Sound of Music.* And *I'm* the reincarnation of Marie Antoinette."

"You know what I mean," Rudy protested, uncajoled.

"I have never met Bunny, or Melissa X. or B. Franklin Grace for that matter. And I don't see what difference it makes, whether Bunny believes what she's saying or not. She's still a consummate little actress, and her performances are earning us all a pot of money. So why look a gift horse in the mouth?"

"For the Trojans those were famous last words."

"You want reassurance? I'll reassure you. I wasn't going to tell you about this till the deal was firmed up, but at this point we're just haggling over sub-rights percentages, so what the hell. Harper & Row is taking over distribution for Orange Bangle, *on condition* that you write a final chapter bringing the story up to date. Which means you've got a real shot at the list."

"And what's in the last chapter – a searing account of my trial for child molestation?"

"No, an account of your disbelief, amazement, horror, and shock when you go to visit Bunny and her mother on Christmas Eve and you find that they've *both* been abducted. This time, since it's winter, you'll be able to take photos of where the UFO landed in the snow. Then after the first thaw you report them missing."

Rudy's jaw dropped. "To the *police?*"

"Do you know how many people are reported missing every week? Thousands. You're not saying abducted, not to the police. You just say that two people are missing who *are* missing. Who knows why? Maybe all the publicity was too much for Melissa and she decided to take Bunny and the money and disappear. Or *maybe* the Xlom decided that Bunny had to be taken somewhere where scientists couldn't examine her. In either case, your fatherly heart is broken, and all you can hope for is that some day, somewhere you'll see your little Bunny again."

"Harper & Row *want* this? You laid this out for them in advance?"

"Well, I couldn't come right out and say what the Xlom may be intending to do. I just promised them that the last chapter would contain sensational new material. I think they got my drift. Of course, you'll have to split your royalties fifty-fifty for the new edition. On the other hand, it's not a sequel, it's just a final chapter that you can write in a weekend."

"Fifty-fifty with whom?"

"With your original publisher, Orange Bangle. I expect a good part of their cut will go to pay off Bunny and her mom. They can't be doing all this for nothing."

"Do you know what the penalty is for reporting a spurious abduction? A $10,000 fine and five years in prison."

"It won't be spurious. Bunny and her mom will have genuinely disappeared. If you *speculate* in your book that the Xlom have taken them from the face of the planet, that's just your theory. And if, later on, they should turn up somewhere else *on* the planet, all that can be inferred from that is that they're trying to avoid public attention, including yours, which they're entitled to do. But I think it highly unlikely they'll be found. The FBI isn't going to make it a top priority, and where are they going to start looking? It's a big country."

"You've discussed this with Grace?"

"Mm-hm. And he's even thrown out hints that Bunny and her mom will be returning to their original happy home, complete with a daddy and sibs. So anyone trying to track down a single woman and her blonde daughter will be following a false scent."

"And when the police ask me for information about them?"

"Grace has created a paper trail that is fairly close to the 'facts' presented in *The Visitation.* Remember all those little changes that appeared in the book after you returned the galleys? That's why they're there. That's why we made Melissa such a mystery woman. Maybe *she* was an alien! Have you ever considered that? Or maybe she's one of the first generation of genetically altered human beings that the aliens have been training to vamp humanity! But that's too good an idea to waste on this book. Keep that one in reserve, and in the ripeness of time we can approach Harper & Row with a sequel: *I Married a Xlom.*"

"But I *didn't* marry her."

"Rudy, you are such a *pedant.* Anyhow, when can I see that last chapter?"

There didn't seem to be any point in further argument. He'd written Bunny into existence. Now he would write her out of existence. "When do you need it?"

"Yesterday."

"You've got it."

The disappearance of Bunny and Melissa, when that event was finally staged, was like a long-postponed visit to the dentist. The worst of it was in the anxiety beforehand, especially in the week from Christmas through New Year's Day that he had to spend alone in the newly vacated chalet. Most of the neighboring vacation houses were standing empty at that time of year, so he was spared having to make a spectacle of himself going about and asking after his missing significant others. Of those people he did approach, only the crippled woman who tended the nearest convenience store claimed to recognize Bunny and Melissa from the photo he showed them, and all she could remember of them was that the little girl had been particularly fond of Pepperidge Farm cookies, which seemed a precocious and expensive taste in such a very young girl. "Mostly at that age their mommies buy them Ding Dongs or Twinkies, but not that little lady. *She* got Brussels cookies, or Milanos, or Lidos. Did they skip out on their bills, is that why you're asking?" Rudy had assured her it was nothing like that.

With the police he had to be more forthcoming. He could not withhold the fact that the missing girl had figured in *The Visitation* for an earlier disappearance, which the book had ascribed to UFOs. To his relief, though the policemen obviously suspected that Bunny's latest disappearance was a repeat performance of her first, they did not seem annoyed to have been called in. Indeed, both men had their own UFO stories to relate to Rudy concerning mysterious lights that had appeared in the area around the Ashokan Reservoir, moving at higher speeds and lower altitudes than could have been the case if they'd been ordinary airplanes. Rudy ended up taking more notes about their UFO sightings than they did concerning the missing girl and her mother. As the friendlier of the two policeman suggested, with a conspiratorial wink, maybe Melissa was just trying to avoid him. Maybe her arranging to spend the holiday with him had been a kind of practical joke. In any case, while it might be mysterious, it was not the sort of mystery the police ought to take an interest in.

When they left the chalet, Rudy called up Janet to jubilate and to ask her to hold up the final production of the new revised edition until he could add something about the testimony of the two policemen.

Saleswise the new edition was something of a letdown. Disappearances are in their nature hard to ballyhoo, since the person who might do the job best isn't around. An effort was made to have Rudy, despite his obesity, appear on the talk shows where Bunny had been such a hit, but most of them declined the opportunity. The few times he did appear, the shows' hosts were openly derisive. Most of their questions had to do with his earnings from *The Visitation* and his relationship with B. Franklin Grace and the People, who were in the news once again for allegedly having tried to poison Ms. Devore's litigious niece and nephew in the period before her competency hearings. Rudy was not enough of a showman to make emotional headway against such currents, and he came off looking sheepish and creepy. He retired from the talk show circuit with a strong conviction that his fifteen minutes on the parking meter of fame had expired, a conviction that was strengthened when Janet Cruse's phone number began to connect with an answering service instead of with Janet. For a little while the answering service went through the motions of taking Rudy's ever-more-urgent messages, and then he was given the address, in Vancouver, where Janet could be contacted. So that, he thought, was the end of the Bunny Steiner story and of his own career as a father.

He was wrong on both counts.

Bunny arrived in New York at the end of May, unannounced except by the driver of the taxi who had taken her from the Port Authority bus terminal to Rudy's new sublet in a brownstone on Barrow Street in the nicest part of the Village. "Your daughter's down here," the man had shouted into the intercom, and then, before Rudy could deny he had a daughter, he added: "And the charge on the meter is $4.70."

"Hello, Daddy," Bunny said, clutching her little knapsack to her chest and smiling at him as sweetly as if he were a camera.

"Bunny!"

"Mommy said I've grown so much you probably wouldn't recognize me."

"This is none of my business, Mister," the taxi driver said, with a sideways commiserating glance in Bunny's direction, "but don't you think she's a little young to be traveling around New York on her own? I mean, this isn't..." He raised his voice and asked of Bunny: "Where'd you say you came here from, sweetheart?"

"Pocatello," she said demurely. "That's in Idaho."

"You came all the way to New York from Idaho *on a bus?*" the taxi driver marveled.

She nodded. "That's how my dress got so wrinkled."

Rudy paid the driver six dollars, took Bunny's knapsack, and held the door open for her.

"Thank you," she said, stepping inside and heading straight for the stairs. Her hand reached up to grasp the banister. Rudy realized he'd never seen a child on the wide wonky staircase in all the time he'd been subletting his apartment. She seemed so small. Of course, children were supposed to be small, but Bunny seemed smaller than small, a miniature child.

"What is the number of your apartment?" she asked from the head of the stairs.

"Twelve. It's two more flights up."

By the time Rudy had reached the fourth floor, huffing and puffing, Bunny had already gone into the apartment and was leaning out the window that accessed to the fire escape. "You really live high up."

"Not by New York standards."

"I hope you're not mad at me," she said in a placatory tone, turning away from the window and wedging herself into the corner of the sofa. "I know I should have phoned first, but I thought if I did, you might call the police before we had a chance to talk together. I didn't know *what* I'd do if you weren't here. Do they have shopping-bag kids in New York? That's what I'd have become, I guess."

"Am I to understand that you're running away from home?"

She nodded.

"From Pocatello?" he asked with a teasing smile.

She laughed. "No, silly. That's where Judy *Garland* was from, in *A Star Is Born*. Which is one of my favorite movies of all time. We made a tape of it, and I must have seen it twenty times."

"Who is 'we'? And for that matter, who are you?"

"It's all right if you call me Bunny. I like it better than my real name, which is – " She wrinkled her nose to indicate disgust: "Margaret."

"Just Margaret? No last name?"

"On my birth certificate it says Margaret Dacey. But the People don't use last names with each other."

"Ah ha! I *wondered* if you weren't one of the People. They never told me anything about you, you know. I thought I was just making it all up, everything in the book. Even you."

"I know. They always used to make jokes about that. How surprised you were going to be when I appeared on TV. Anyhow, I'm not one of the People. My mother is, but that doesn't mean I have to be. Before the People, she was in something like the Hari Krishnas, only they didn't march around in orange clothes. I *really* hated that. Finally the Baba, who was the old man who ran the place and pretended he was an Indian (but he wasn't, he came from Utah), finally he got busted for cocaine. That was two years ago, in Portland."

"It sounds like you've had an exciting life. How old are you?"

"Guess."

"You must be older than you look. Maybe six?"

She shook her head.

"Seven?"

"No – eight and a half. I'm like Gary Coleman, everyone thinks I'm *pre*-school. When the inspectors came round to the commune to see if they were sending their kids to school like they were supposed to, they always made me go with the little kids. I've never been to a real school. But I can read almost anything. I read *your* book a couple times. And I read *The Elfin Horde*, too. And the other ones that came after. When we were living up in the cabin there wasn't much else you could do but read, you couldn't get TV. Mom was going crazy."

"So? What did you think?"

"Of *The Elfin Horde*? Oh, I loved the whole series. Only I hated it when Twa-Loora died. Sometimes at night when I'm going to sleep I'll think about her riding up to the edge of that cliff and looking back and seeing the Black Riders. And then *leaping* to certain death. And I'll start crying all over again. In fact – " She furrowed her forehead and frowned down at her hands, primly folded together in her lap. "In fact, that's why I decided to come here. Because if I went anywhere else, they would just send me right back to the commune. But I thought *you'd* understand. Because you understood Twa-Loora."

"What about your father? Couldn't you go to him?"

"I'm like the Bunny in your book. I don't have a Dad. Unless *you'd* be my Dad."

"Hey, wait a minute!"

But Bunny was not to be checked now. She insisted on sharing her fantasy in its full extent. And it was not (Rudy gradually, grudgingly came to see) so entirely bizarre as to be unfeasible. As Bunny herself pointed out, millions of TV viewers had already come to accept as a fact that she was his daughter, and her mother had been deeply involved in that deception. Admittedly, Bunny's birth certificate (she produced a xerox of it from her knapsack) could not confirm Rudy's paternity, but neither did it contradict it: the space for Father's Name had been left blank. Assuming that her mother and Mr. Grace agreed to let Rudy assume the responsibility for bringing up Bunny, it would probably not be difficult to arrange the legal details. And with the material in the knapsack it was hard to imagine them withholding their cooperation.

"You realize, don't you, that what we're discussing is blackmail?"

"But if I just took all this to the *police,* it wouldn't make things better for anyone. They'd probably put Mr. Grace in jail, and I'd be sent back to my mother, and she'd be furious with me, and we wouldn't have anywhere to live. Anyhow, she doesn't like me any more than I like her. When we're in the commune we hardly ever even talk to each other. I do have *friends* there, or I used to, but Billy's in jail now. We used to play backgammon, and he really didn't mind if I won sometimes. Mother would get furious. I'll bet she'd be tickled pink to let you have custody. She'd have been glad if the Xlom were real and they did take me away in a flying saucer. She said so lots of times, and pretended it was a joke but it wasn't, not really. It's Mr. Grace who's the problem. Every time reporters would come to the commune, he'd always have someone take me down to the basement laundry room, and I wouldn't come out until the reporters went away. It made me feel like a prisoner."

The more Bunny told about her life in the People's commune, the more Rudy realized that the girl was an As-Told-To diamond mine. What's more, she knew it too, for when he suggested that he turn on his tape deck in order to have a permanent record of the rest of the story, she agreed that that would be a good idea and she even was so thoughtful, when they started taping, to return to the point in the story when Mr. Grace first discovered Bunny and her mother busking in downtown San Diego. Bunny, in addition to her other talents, was a proficient tap-dancer, and one of her objects in adopting Rudy as her father was to be able to study dance – tap, jazz, and classic ballet – in New York City, the dance capital of the universe.

"But also," she confided, "I just *like* you. I could tell that from reading *The Visitation*."

"Yes, but that's all made up," Rudy pointed out. "That book is just one lie after another. *You* know that."

"But you tell *nice* lies," Bunny insisted. "If you had a *real* little girl, I'll bet you'd be just the kind of Daddy you say you are in the book. Is it the money you're worried about? Mother was always saying how expensive it is to have a kid."

"I hadn't even considered that side of it."

"Because when I was in Mr. Grace's office and took those other things, the dirty pictures and the rest, I also took this."

Out of her wonderful knapsack Bunny produced a file of papers showing sales figures for *The Visitation* that were, even at a glance, distinctly at variance from the figures Orange Bangle Press had provided to him. Bunny's competence as a fairy godchild was coming to seem uncanny. "How did you know...?"

"They always talked to each other as though I weren't there. Maybe they thought I was that dumb. Or maybe they just forgot about me."

"And where do they think you are now? Did you leave a note, or tell anyone?"

"I left a note saying I was going to visit one of Baba's people and I told them not to go to the police. I don't think they would have anyhow. I didn't steal much more money than I needed for the bus trip. I knew if I took a lot, Mr. Grace *would* go to the police. Do you have something to eat?"

"Sure. What do you want? Is a sandwich okay?"

"Just some cookies and milk would be nice. I didn't have any breakfast when the bus stopped in New Jersey."

Rudy went into the kitchen and poured out a Daffy Duck glass-full of milk. Then he arranged three kinds of cookies on a plate. He took it as an omen that Bunny should have arrived at the moment when his cupboard was so well supplied with her favorite brand of cookie.

"There's clover for bunnies," he called out from the kitchen, quoting from his book.

And Bunny, from the living room, quoted the book back to him, making it theirs: "And here's a Bunny for the clover!"

Jour de Fête

"Accumulated violence...brought on confrontations at every *fête* during this age...as in the *cournée* in Langres in 1386.... This was a game that took place on all feast days, in which people threw stones at one another."

ROBERT MUCHEMBLED, ON THE REVELRIES OF MEDIEVAL FRANCE

THE SKY that morning was as clear as Adam's soul while still he had his home in Paradise. From the city walls you could see as far as Mont Blanc leagues to the south; to the north the Marne formed a silvery scythe that rested against a horizon blue as the Virgin's mantle. One could not have wanted better weather for the day of the *cournée,* nor a worthier wine with which to salute the occasion.

The massive bowl of the *cournée,* with its crude handles, was passed from player to player, and each swore a favorite oath, or called on St. Mammes to favor his team, as he lifted it to his lips and tried to drink from it without bathing in the wine. As easily sip from a barrel.

When each player had been baptized in this way, the pipers struck up their tune, and the two teams rappelled down the inner walls of the city ramparts on either side of the Porte des Moulins. That gate was noted for the many times it had been destroyed and then rebuilt, first by Julius Caesar, then by the Vandals, who burned down the whole town, and by Attila, who burned it down again. Barbarossa had breached the walls but, at the intercession of the bishop, had spared Langres itself, a mercy commemorated by a statue of the Emperor. That statue was subsequently melted down for shot, but its pedestal remained in the square before the Cathedral of St. Mammes, and it was from that pedestal that the first stones of the *cournée* proper were to be flung when the *fête* began.

First, however, that initial advantage had to be gained. Taking possession of the pedestal was always the bloodiest part of the game, for though all weapons forged from metal were proscribed, as well as any hafted weapon, a stone shaped well for both striking and for gripping can do harm enough – as Cain himself will testify.

As each man alighted at the foot of the ramparts he ran to where he had deposited his chosen stone – either hidden in plain sight among the cobbles of the square or secreted in some doorway or on a window ledge, peeking out from behind a pot of herbs. And here is one, a piece of limestone with a wicked edge, that someone has thought to hide beneath his own coiled excrement, and here's the clever fellow who devised that stratagem, the hero of this brief epic, our rustic Ulysses and Ajax of the Marne, Alexandre Meunier, a journeyman cooper fighting this year for the first time with the men of his guild and those affiliated – vintners, brewers, innkeepers. Not a fellow you would have thought destined for victory from the vantage high above the fray shared by most Langresiens, for he did not advertise himself a warrior by stature or bearing. A boyish figure, a beardless face, a mere David facing a whole phalanx of Goliaths; for the opposing Reds were all in the stone-cutting and -milling trades for which Langres has always been noted.

In such broad and callused hands as theirs Alexandre's chunk of limestone would have seemed as little threatening as a child's toy. But in Alexandre's hand it proved effective enough as he zigzigged amongst the Reds, running as point toward the pedestal with his four mates just behind him. As they drew near, the Reds' stones rained down on them like hail, and one of the four was taken from the game by a well-placed two-pounder just above his right ear. The crowd cheered at the sight of first blood, Red and Green indiscriminately, but when, in despite of their loss, Alexandre scrambled to the top of the pedestal on the shoulders of his friends, it was only the Greens who cheered.

All the stones that had fallen like hail were now scooped up and placed at Alexandre's feet, a tribute he spent as fast as it was offered him. In all the annals of the Langres *cournée* there had never been such an arm as Alexandre's, such deadly aim, such carnage among the Reds. Years – decades! – of old debts were settled by the lad's missiles. The quarryman Gilles Choquet lost his left eye, his nephew Jean half of his young teeth. Three members of the Gardinier clan were carried from the square unconscious. Skulls were cracked along with ribcages.

Once the pedestal was mounted it was forbidden, by the rules of the game, to bring new stones into play. The two teams were ranged on either side of the pedestal, the Reds facing Alexandre, who deftly sidestepped any stone thrown at him: the Greens behind him, ready to retrieve those stones that had not hit their mark and relay them back to Alexandre, many marked now by the enemy's blood.

The game would continue until there were no more stones in play – but since this had never been known to happen (there would always be someone hoarding up for some final, all-redeeming Parthian shot), the two teams had to stand their ground until sunset, when the contest would be halted and both teams would process to the cathedral to receive the sacrament.

Like so many other initial triumphs the *cournée* slowly deflated in the course of the long hot summer afternoon, as the Reds sullenly withheld their ammunition and the Greens were reduced to taunts and jeers, to which the townspeople on the ramparts added their own. For they had come to witness blood, and didn't care whose, so long as it was red and flowed freely.

The impasse was brought to an end, at last, by one of these impatient onlookers, who aimed a small stone at Alexandre just as he'd scored a major hit against the Reds. A cheer had gone up; Alexandre lifted his arms in the universal gesture of victory, and the stone struck his forehead almost unnoticed by the mob. Alexandre shook his head, as though to shoo off a fly – and then he simply toppled to the ground.

It has often been remarked that those who live by the sword shall perish by it; that those who rise most high have the farthest to fall, and here was one more proof of such maxims. That very evening, at the service following the game, the bishop of Langres pointed the moral of Alexandre's story to his flock, but, for all his scolding and wisdom he was not such a fool as to declare an end to the revels of Langres. They were an ancient and beloved institution, as integral to the city's identity as the very stones of the Porte des Moulins. How should the people of Langres, especially its youths, celebrate on a major feast day without the excitement of a *cournée?* As well celebrate Christmas without seeing the Infant Jesus asleep in his manger among the adoring animals and shepherds and the Three Magi. There is a ceremonial side to life that is just as important as the manufacture of barrel staves and millstones.

As for young Alexandre, his death, like that of his great namesake, undoubtedly represents a tragic loss, but we may take comfort in knowing that he will always be remembered by the people of Langres and by all who honor the ancient sport of the *cournée* as one of its greatest players and a model citizen ready to lay down his life in the service of his community. The stones he hurled still pave our streets; the blood he spilled is wine upon our tables.

Voices of the Kill

HE LAY AWAKE through much of his first night in the cabin listening to the stream. It was early June. The water was high and made a fair amount of noise. A smooth white noise it had seemed during the day, but now, listening more closely, surprisingly varied. There was a kind of pulse to it. Not like the plain two-beat alternation of tick and tock that the mind projects on the undifferentiated ratcheting of a clock, but a more inflected flow, like a foreign language being spoken far off, risings and fallings such as an infant must hear in its crib as its parents speak in whispers in another room. Soothing, very soothing, but even so he couldn't get to sleep for many hours, and when he did, he slept lightly and did not dream.

The next morning he opened the plastic bag containing the wading boots he'd bought at the hardware store in Otisville. *Tingley,* the bag said. *Tough Boots for Tough Customers.* They came up to just below his knees. The soles were like tire treads, but quite flexible. He tucked his jeans inside the tops of the boots and went wading up the stream.

He had no intention of fishing. He fished only to be sociable and had little luck at it. In any case, he didn't much like to eat fish, and hated cleaning them. He'd got the boots purely for the pleasure of walking up the stream, as his ticket to the natural history museum of Pine Kill. Not exactly the kind of tough customer Tingley usually catered to, but that was one of the pleasures of taking a vacation all by himself. There was no code to conform to, no expectations to meet, no timetables, no one to say, "Mr. Pierce, would you explain the assignment again?"

A hundred feet up the stream and he felt he had penetrated the mystique of trout fishing. It was simply a macho-compatible mode of meditation. Even with the help of rubber boots, you had to step carefully, for many stones were liable to tilt underfoot, and even the stablest could be treacherous in their smoothness. Moving along at this slower pace, the mind had to gear down too. The busy hum of its own purposes died away and nature slowly emerged from the mists. Nature. He'd almost forgotten what that was. No one had *decided* on any of this. The complications, the repetitions, the apparent patterning – all of it had come about willy-nilly. The beauty, for instance, of these lichens hadn't been intended to delight his eye. The placement of those boulders, which looked so much like a monument by Henry Moore, simply one of an infinite number of rolls of dice.

Another hour up the stream and these abstractions, too, had melted away, like the last lingering traces of ice in spring. The city was thawed out of his limbs. A joy in, a warmth for, the ubiquitous hemlocks bubbled up through his genes from some aboriginal arboreal ancestor.

Where the sunlight penetrated the ranks of the high pines, he stood entranced by the play of the jittering interference patterns across the glowing bed of the stream, the wilderness's own video arcade. And there, darting about through the shallows, were the game's protagonists, two nervous minnows who seemed to be trying to escape their own pursuing and inescapable shadows.

He moved to the stream's next subdivision, a brackish pool where water-skates patterned the silt below with spectral wing patterns, six concentric-banded ovals formed by the touch of their rowing limbs on the skin of the water. For as long as the sunlight held steady over the pool he watched the flights of these subaqueous butterflies, continually delighted at how the light and water had conjured up something so ethereal from such unpromising raw material, for in itself the water-skate was not a pretty sort of bug.

And then there were the flowers, high banks of them where the stream swerved near the parallel curves of Pine Kill Road and the slope was too steep for trees to take root; flowers he had never seen before and had no name for. Some grew stemless from the rot of fallen logs, pale green blossoms of orchidlike intricacy, yet thick and succulent at the same time, as though molded from porcelain. There were great masses of pale yellow blooms that drooped from tall hairy stems, and beyond these a stand of clustered purple trumpet-shaped flowers flamboyant as a lipstick ad.

He braved the bees to pick a large bouquet of both the purple and the yellow flowers, but by the time he'd got back to the cabin all of them had wilted and couldn't be revived. He decided, guiltily, to pick no more bouquets.

That night he heard the voices clearly. So perfect was the illusion that at first he supposed there were people walking along the road on the other side of the stream, taking advantage of the full moon for a midnight stroll. But that was unlikely. His was the farthest cabin up Pine Kill Road, his nearest neighbors half a mile away. What women (for they were surely women's voices) would go walking such a distance, after dark, on such a lonely road?

No, it was the stream he heard, beyond a doubt. When he listened intently he could catch its separate voices merging back into its more liquid murmurings, but only to become distinct again, if never entirely articulate. He could pick out their individual timbres, as he might have the voices in a canon. There were three: a brassy soprano, given to emphatic octave-wide swoops, with a wobble in her lower register; an alto, richer-throated and longer-breathed, but somehow wearier even so; a coloratura, who never spoke more than a few short phrases at a time, little limpid outbursts like the exclamations of flutes in a Mahler symphony. Strain as he might, he could not make out a single word in the flow of their talk, only the melodic line, sinuous and continuous as the flowing of the stream, interrupted from time to time by little hoots of surprise and ripples of laughter.

He dreamed that night – some kind of nightmare involving car crashes and fires in suburban backyards – and woke in a sweat. The alarm clock's digital dial read 1:30 A.M. The stream purled soothingly, voicelessly, outside the cabin, and the moonlight made ghosts of the clothing that hung from nails in the wall.

In the morning he felt as though he were already weeks away from the city. Purged by the nightmare, his spirit was clear as the sky. He set a pot of coffee on the stove to perk. Then, faithful to the promise he'd made to himself the day before, he went down the flagstone steps to the stream and waded out to the deepest part, where two boulders and a small log had formed a natural spillway, below which, under the force of the confluent flow, a hollow had been scooped out from the bed of the stream, large as a bathtub. He lay within it, listening, but from this closest vantage there was not the least whisper of the voices he had heard so plainly the night before. The water was cold, and his bath accordingly quick, but as he returned to where he'd left his towel on the grassy bank he felt a shock of pleasure that made him stop for breath, a neural starburst of delight starting in the center of his chest and lighting up every cell of his body in a quick chain reaction, like the lighting of a giant Christmas tree. *Too much!* he thought, but even with the thinking of that thought, the pleasure had faded to the merest afterimage of that first onslaught of well-being.

That day he went up the mountain – a very small mountain but a mountain for all that – that was coextensive with his backyard, a low many-gapped fieldstone wall being the only boundary between his three-quarter acre and the woods' immensity. He bore due west up the steepest slopes, then north along the first, lowest ridge, and not once was there a house or a paved road or a power line to spoil the illusion that this was the primeval, pre-Yankee wilderness. To be sure, he encountered any number of No Trespassing signs, spoor of the local Rod & Gun Club, and once, at the first broadening of the ridge, he came upon a rough triangle of stacked logs intended for a hunting blind, complete with a detritus of bullet-riddled beer cans and shattered bottle glass. But none of that bulked large against the basic glory of the mountain. The grandeur, the profusion, the fundamentality of it.

On a slope of crumbling slate beyond the hunting blind the mountain revealed its crowning splendor to him, a grove, horizon-wide, of laurels in full bloom, each waist-high shrub so densely blossomed that the underbrush was lost to sight beneath the froth of flowers. Laurels: he knew them by the shape of the leaf. But he'd never seen a laurel in blossom, never understood the fitness of Daphne's metamorphosis. For surely if a man, or God, were to be doomed to love a tree, then it would have to be one of these. They were desire incarnate. You couldn't look at them without wanting...

Something.

There was something he wanted, but he could not think what. To faint away, to expire; to become a song or painting or column of stone that could somehow express... What? This inexpressible wonder. But no, that wasn't what he wanted at all. He wanted to feel this place, this mountain, in his own being. To be a bee, moving ineluctably from bloom to bloom; to be the swarm of them converging on their hive.

To be a part of it.

To belong, here, forever.

Sleep came to him that night at once, as automatic as the light that goes off inside a refrigerator when the door is closed. He woke in a wash of moonlight to hear the voice of the kill, one of its voices, whispering to him. Not clearly yet, but as though a message had been left on a tape many times erased, distant and blurred by static. Words. Two words, repeated at long intervals: "Come here...come here..."

"Where shall I come?" he asked aloud.

"Here," said the voice, already fading.

He knew that she meant beside the stream, and he went out of the cabin and down the flagstone steps, obedient as a lamb.

"That's better," she said, pleased. "Lie here, next to me. The night is cool."

He assumed a reclining position on the grass, trying to be unobtrusive as he displaced the small stones that dug into his hip and rib cage. When he lowered his gaze and bent toward her, the stream filled his entire field of vision, a film of blackness flecked with vanishing gleams of purple and pale yellow, neural relics of the flowers he'd seen on the banks upstream.

She did not speak again at once, nor did he feel any eagerness that she should. A strange contentment hovered about him, like a net of finest mesh, an Edenic happiness that did not yet know itself to be happy, a confidence that blessings were everywhere on hand.

"What is your name?" she asked, in the faintest of whispers, as though they spoke in a crowded room where they must not be seen speaking.

He was taken aback. "My name?" It seemed such a prosaic way to begin.

"How can we talk to each other if I don't know your name?"

"William," he said. "William Logan Pierce."

"Then, welcome, William Logan Pierce. Welcome to Pine Kill. To the waters of your new birth, welcome."

Now that was more like it. That was the language one expects from water sprites.

"What is *your* name?" he asked.

She laughed. "Must *I* have a name, too! Oh, very well, my name is Nixie. Will that do?"

He nodded. Then, uncertain whether she could see him in the darkness, he said, "I don't know how to speak to you, Nixie. I've never had a vision before."

"I am no 'vision,' William," she answered with dignity but no perceptible indignation. "I am like you, a spirit embodied in flesh. Only, as I am a Nereid, my flesh is immortal. But you may speak to me as you would to any mortal woman."

"Of what things shall we talk?"

"Why, we may begin with the elements, if you like. Your views on oxygen, your feelings about complex hydrocarbons."

"You're making fun of me."

"And you no less of me, to suppose that I am incapable of ordinary civil conversation. As though I were some nineteenth-century miss only just liberated from the nursery."

"Excuse me."

"It was nothing." Then, in a tone of mocking primness, as though she'd slipped into the role of that hypothetical young miss: "Tell me, Mr. Pierce, what did you think of today's weather?"

"It was beautiful."

"Is that all? I'd imagined you a man of more words."

So, lying with his head back in the grass, looking up at the moon's shattered descent through the swaying hemlocks, he told her of his day on the mountain. She would put in a word from time to time, assurances of her attention.

"You seem to have been quite smitten with those laurels," she commented when he was done. She adopted an attitude of wifely irony, treating the laurels as someone he'd been seen flirting with at a party. "They'll be gone in another two weeks, you know. So, seize the day."

She fell silent, or rather returned to her natural speech, the lilting *fol-de-riddle fol-de-lay* of her infinite liquid collisions.

He rolled onto his stomach, the better to peer down at the silken stirrings of her body. Now that the moon had gone down behind the mountain, the little flashes of phosphorescent color were more vivid and coherent, forming ephemeral draperies of bioluminescence.

"You mustn't touch me," she warned, sensing his intention before he'd lifted his hand. "Not till you've paid."

"Paid! How 'paid'?"

"With money, of course. Do you think we use cowrie shells? I trust you have some ready cash on hand."

"Yes but –"

"Then it is very simple: if you're to touch me, you must pay."

"But I've never..."

"You've never had to pay for it?" she asked archly.

"No, I didn't mean that."

"Visions – to use your term – don't come cheap, William. You must pay now – and pay again each night you come to call. Those are the rules, and I'm afraid *I* have no authority to set them aside."

"Very well. I'll have to go back into the house to get...your pay."

"I'll be right here," she promised.

Dazzled by the glare of the overhead 100-watt bulb, he dug into the sock drawer of the bureau, where there would be quarters set aside for the laundromat. Then he thought better of it. In classic times coins might have served his purpose, but nowadays quarters were worth little more than cowrie shells. He took his billfold from the top dresser drawer. The smallest bill was a twenty. It was probably the smallest she'd accept in any case.

He returned to the stream. "I've twenty dollars. Will that do?"

There was no reply.

"Nixie, are you there?"

"I'm always here, William. Just put it under a stone. A large stone, and not too close to the shore."

He picked his way carefully across the rocky streambed till he came to the middle. The water sweeping around his ankles did not seem different, except in being less chilly, from the water he'd bathed in yesterday morning. Even so, as he knelt to pry up a rock, the shock of immersion was almost enough to dispel the enchantment and send him, shivering and chagrined, back to the cabin. But as he placed the bill beneath the stone, another kind of shock ran up his wet forearms and connected right to the base of his spine, deep-frying his nerves to ecstasy. He cried out, such a cry as must have brought every animal prowling the night woods to pause and ponder.

"Now you have touched me, William. Now let me touch you."

Helpless, enslaved, and craving nothing but a deeper enslavement, he lowered himself into the stream, careless of the stones on which he lay supine.

She ran her hands over his yielding flesh. "O William," she whispered. "O my sweet, sweet William!"

After that second night, he ceased to take count of the time elapsing. Instead of being stippled with the felt-tip *X*'s that filled the earlier pages of his wall calendar, June's page remained blank as a forgotten diary. His days were given to the mountain or the hammock, his nights to the Nereid's ineffable, evanescent caresses, of which he could recall, in the morning, few particulars. But then what bliss is sweeter for being itemized? So long as our delights are endlessly renewed, what harm is there in taking the days as they come and letting them slip away, unchronicled, to join the great drifts of geologic time? As Nixie said, the thing to do was seize the day – and not look either way.

Yet a day did come, toward the end of June, when he lost his grip on this immemorial good advice. It began with a phone call from Ray Feld, the owner of the cabin, who wanted to know if he meant to continue renting for the rest of the summer. He'd paid only to mid-July.

He promised to have his check in the mail that morning – $875, which was almost exactly half of his bank balance. Even eating frugally and borrowing on his credit cards, it was going to be a tight squeeze to Labor Day. And then...

And then it would be back to Newark and Marcus Garvey Junior High School, where, under the pretense of teaching English and social studies, he gave his young detainees a foretaste of their destined incarceration in the prisons, armies, and offices of the grown-up world. On the premises of Marcus Garvey, he was usually able to take a less dismal view of the teaching profession. If there was nothing else to be said for it, there was at least this – the freedom of his summers. While other people had to make do with two or three weeks of vacation, he could spend the entire season by the stream, with the hemlocks perfuming the air. All he need remember – summer's one simple rule – was not to look back or ahead.

And the best way to do that was to take up the cry of the pines: "More light! More light!" For always a climb up the mountain was an antidote to his merely mental gloom. He'd got lazy about giving the mountain its due; that was the only problem. He'd come to rely too much on Nixie's nightly benefactions. Earth and air must have their share of his devotion. So it was up to the laurels, up through the green, hemlock-filtered light to that all-sufficing beauty. The sweatier, the more breathless, the better.

But even sweaty and panting, gloom stuck to his heels as the counterminnows of the streambed kept pace with the living minnows above. A line from some half-remembered poem haunted him: *The woods decay, the woods decay and fall.* It was like a sliver firmly lodged under his thumbnail and not to be got rid of. Every fallen log repeated it, as it lay rotting, devoured by mushrooms or by maggots: *The woods decay, the woods decay and fall.*

As Nixie had foretold, the laurel grove had become a tangle of green shrubs. The blossoms had shriveled and fallen, exposing the russet-red remnants of their sexual apparatus, and the bees had absconded, like sated seducers, to another part of the summer. Somewhere on the periphery of the grove a thrush, pierced by its own sliver of poetry, reiterated a simple two-bar elegy: *Must it be? Must it be? It must! It must!*

He did not linger there, but headed northeast on a course he knew would intersect the higher reaches of Pine Kill. He'd never followed the stream to its source; he would today. He followed paths already familiar, past an abandoned quarry, where great slabs of slate were stacked to form a simple foursquare maze, a tombstone supermarket. Then along a fire trail, where a few stunted laurels, shadowed by the pines, had preserved their maiden bloom. Already, here, he heard her voice ahead of him. Almost intelligible, despite her insistence that her powers of coherent speech were limited to the hours of the night; almost herself, until the kill became visible, twisting down a staircase of tumbled stones, and shifted gender from she to it. Yet even now, as it zigzagged among the boulders and spilled across the ineffectual dam of a fallen log, he thought he recognized, if not her voice, her bearing – headlong, capricious, intolerant of contradiction.

As he made his way upstream, he was obliged to climb, as the kill did, using its larger boulders as stepping stones, since there was no longer level ground on either side, only steep shoulders of crumbly scree. He slipped several times, soaking his sneakers, but only when, mistaking a mulch of leaves for solid ground, he'd nearly sprained his ankle did he yield to what he supposed to be her will. For some reason she did not want him to reach the source of the kill. If he defied her, she might become still more ruthlessly modest.

By the time he'd limped down to Pine Kill Road, his knees were trembling, and his swollen ankle sent a yelp of protest at every step. At home he would fill the tub with hot water and –

But these compassionate plans were blighted the moment he came within view of the cabin and found, parked behind his yellow Datsun, a blue Buick with Pennsylvania plates. *No,* he thought, *it can't be, not all the way from Philadelphia, not without phoning first.* But it was.

It was his cousin Barry, who came out the back door of the cabin, lofting a can of Heineken as his hello.

"Barry." He tried not to sound dismayed. Barry had had a standing invitation to come up any weekend he could get free from the city. This must be Friday. Or Saturday. Damn. "It's good to see you."

"I was beginning to worry. I got here at three, and it's getting on past seven. Where you been?"

"Up there." He waved his hand in the direction of the mountain.

Barry looked doubtfully at the dark wall of hemlocks. The woods did not look welcoming this late in the day. "Communing with nature?"

"That's what I'm here for, isn't it?" He'd meant to sound playful, but his tone was as ill-judged as an intended love-pat that connects as a right to the jaw. He might as well have asked Barry, *And why are you here? Why won't you go away?*

"Well," said Barry, placatingly, "you're looking terrific. You must have dropped some pounds since Bernie Junior's wedding. And you didn't have that many to drop. You got anorexia or something?"

"Have I lost weight? I haven't been trying to."

"Oh, come off it. When I got here I looked in the icebox, and I can tell you everything that was there: a can of coffee, one stick of Parkay margarine, and a bottle of generic catsup. Plus part of a quart of milk that had gone sour. Then I tried the cupboard, and the situation wasn't much better. You can't be living on nothing but oatmeal and sardines."

"As a matter of fact, Barry, sardines and oatmeal are the basis of the Sullivan County Diet. I'll lend you the book. You're guaranteed to take off ten pounds in ten days, at a cost of just ten cents a serving."

Barry smiled. This was the William he'd come to visit. "You're putting me on."

"You laugh – but wait till you've tasted my sour-milk-oatmeal-sardine bread. It's indescribable."

"Well, you'll have to starve yourself on your own time, 'cause while you were off communing, I drove in to Port Jervis and got us some *edible* food. There's spare ribs for dinner tonight, if I can get the damned charcoal started. Bacon and eggs for breakfast, and a big porterhouse for tomorrow night, plus corn to roast with it. And some genuine hundred percent cholesterol to spread on it, none of your mingy margarine. Plus three six-packs – two and a half at this point – and a fifth of Jack Daniel's. Think we'll survive?"

There was no way he could get out of the cabin to be with Nixie that night. Even though he turned in early, using his ankle as an excuse, Barry stayed up drinking and reading a thriller, and finally just drinking. William could hear the stream, but not Nixie's voice.

He didn't dream that night, and woke to the smell of frying bacon. At breakfast Barry announced that they were going to rent a canoe in Port Jervis and paddle down the Delaware to Milford. And that's what they did. The river seemed impersonal in its huge scale. William was aware only of what was unnatural along its shores – the power lines, the clustering bungalows, the clipped lawns of the larger houses, and all the urgent *windows,* jealous of their views. With every stroke of the paddle in his hands, William felt he was betraying the stream he knew. He imagined Nixie lost in this metropolis of a river, murmuring his name, ignored by the hordes of strangers hurrying along on their own business.

Barry, a law-school dropout, tried to get a political argument going, but William refused to take up the challenge. What was the fun of playing straight man to Barry's right-wing one-liners? Barry, balked of that entertainment, proceeded to analyze his relationship with the vice president of another department of his company, a woman whom he'd offended in the elevator. After a while he got to be as ignorable as a radio. William paddled stolidly, seated at the front of the canoe, letting Barry do the steering. Halfway to the goal of Milford, as they came upon a stretch of rapids, William's end of the canoe lodged against a rock and the flow of the river slowly turned them around till they were at right angles to the current. Barry said, "What are we supposed to do in this situation?" just a moment before the canoe overturned.

The dousing was delightful. William came out of the water grinning, as though their capsizing had been one of Nixie's broader jokes and the look on Barry's face, his stupefied indignation, its punch line. They got the waterlogged canoe to the nearer shore without much difficulty, for the water was shallow. Once there, Barry's concern was all for the contents of his billfold and the well-being of his wristwatch, which was Swiss but only water resistant, not waterproof. They didn't even realize that Barry's paddle had been lost till the canoe was bailed out and they were ready to set off again.

That was the end of all *Gemütlichkeit*. The rest of the trip was a slow, wounded slog, with Barry exiled to the prow seat and William maneuvering, carefully and unskillfully, from the bow. At each new stretch of white water they were in danger of capsizing again, but somehow they scraped through without another soaking. The six-pack had been lost with the paddle, and Barry's high spirits declined in proportion as his thirst mounted. By the time they reached Milford, they were no longer on speaking terms. While they waited for the van that would retrieve them and the canoe, Barry headed into town for beer and aspirin, while William spread out on the lawn above the beach, numb with relief. One day with his cousin and he felt as wrought up as if he'd finished a year of teaching.

The beach was full of children. Most of them were younger than the children he taught. There must have been another beach in the area that was reserved for teenagers. There was, however, a single black girl, about fourteen or fifteen years old, in a one-piece pea-green swimsuit, who was intent on digging a large hole in the sand and heaping up an oblong mound (it could not be called a sandcastle) beside it. She had a small, darker-skinned boy in her charge, two years old or even younger. He might have been her sibling or her son. He spent most of his time at the edge of the water, hurling stones at the river with as much satisfaction as if each stone had broken a window. Once he tried to participate in the girl's excavation, but she swatted him with her pink plastic shovel and screamed at him to get away. Some minutes later he toddled out into the water till he was chest-deep, at which point he was retrieved by the lifeguard, who led him back to his mother (William was sure, now, that that was her relationship to the boy), who swatted him a little more soundly, but hissed instead of screaming.

Hers was a type that William was familiar with from his years at Marcus Garvey – severely retarded but able to survive without custodial care, destined for a life as a welfare mother as sure as God makes little green apples. A child abuser, most likely, and the mother of other welfare mothers yet to be. Usually, William regarded such students as a problem that the officials of state agencies should solve in some humane way that researchers had yet to discover. But here on the beach, with the first premonitory breezes of the evening floating in off the water, the pair of them seemed as beautiful in an elementary way as some Italian Madonna and Child. They seemed to have sprung up out of the landscape like the trees and bushes – a presence, and not a problem at all.

Barry returned from town in much-improved spirits, and soon afterward the van arrived and took them back to Barry's Buick and the known world. By the time they were back at the cabin, the sun had sunk behind the pine-crested ridge of the mountain, but there was still an hour of shadowy daylight left. William undertook to cook the steaks, but he didn't adjust the air vents properly and the charcoal went out. Barry insisted that was all right and that the steaks would be better blood rare than too well done. The meat was dutifully chewed and swallowed, all two and half pounds of it, and then William, unable to take any more, asked Barry if he'd mind leaving that night. "The thing is, I've got a girlfriend coming over. And the cabin just doesn't allow any privacy, you know what I mean?" Barry was obviously miffed, but he also seemed relieved to be clearing out.

As soon as the taillights of the Buick had been assimilated by the darkness of Pine Kill Road, William went down to the stream and, kneeling on a flat mossy rock, touched the skin of the water. Quietly, with no intention of waking her, but as one may touch the neck or shoulder of a sleeping spouse, simply for the pleasure of that near presence.

"I'm sorry," he whispered. "It wasn't my fault. I couldn't come to you while he was here. He'd have thought I was crazy."

He hoped she could hear him. He hoped he could be forgiven. But the water rippling through his fingers offered no reassurance.

He went to bed as soon as it was dark, and lay awake, like a child being punished, staring at the raftered ceiling. The day with Barry kept replaying in his mind, keeping him from sleep – and keeping him from Nixie, for it was usually only after his first dreaming sleep that he would rise and go to her. Was it a form of somnambulism then? Could she summon him only when he was in a trance? That would explain why he could remember so little of their conversations now, and nothing at all of the ecstasies he had known in her embrace, nothing but that there had been, at such moments, consummations that a Saint Theresa might have envied.

He slept, but sleep brought no dreams, and he woke just before dawn to the bland, unintelligible purling of the stream. It was like waking to find, instead of one's beloved, her unhollowed pillow beside one in the bed. He felt betrayed, and yet he knew the first betrayal had been his.

What did she want? His tears? His blood? She could name any price, any punishment, as long as she let him be near her again, to hear her again when she called his name, *William, dear William, come to my bed, come rest your head beside mine.*

*

He was made to pay the penalty of her silence for most of July, and grew resigned to the idea that she might never return to him. To have known such joys once was cause for lifelong gratitude – but to suppose himself *entitled* to them? As well ask to be anointed King of England.

The ordinary splendors of the summer remained open to him. Where the laurels had bloomed, blueberries now were ripening. Cardinals and nuthatches offered their daily examples of how good weather could best be enjoyed, as they darted back and forth from his feeder, skimming the stream, living it up, taking no thought for the morrow – or for next year's lesson plans on such suggested topics as Problems of Family Life or the Perils of Drug Abuse. No wristwatch, no calendar, no mealtimes or bedtimes, no tasks to finish, no friends to remember, no books to read. He had three classical music cassettes – one symphony each by Bruckner, Mahler, and Sibelius – that he listened to over and over at night inside the cabin, while a single log burned in the fireplace. He learned to float through his days and nights the way he would have in a dream.

And then, as the blueberries peaked and the huckleberries followed close behind, she spoke to him again. Not in the same voice now, however. It was the alto who, in a tone of maternal reproach, addressed him: "William, you have been too long away. Come here – explain yourself."

"Nixie!" he cried, pushing himself up from the wicker chair in which he had fallen asleep. "Goddess! Forgive me – my cousin was here – I couldn't come to you. Yet I should have, I see that now. I didn't understand, I – "

"Stop babbling, William." She spoke sternly, but with a kind of humor, even indulgence, that set his hopes leaping like gazelles.

"Nixie, you've returned. I always knew you would return. I always – "

"Is your ear so poorly tuned to our speech, William, that you cannot tell my sister's voice from mine? I am Nereis. Nixie has gone elsewhere, and she will *not* return."

"But *you* will let me worship you? And lie beside you? Do you want money, too? I'll give you all I have. Anything."

"I want only you, William. Come, enter me. Let me touch your cheeks, which Nixie has told me are so soft and warm."

He stumbled through the darkened cabin and down the flagstone steps to the stream. There he paused to remove his clothes. Then, his heart in a flutter, his legs trembling, he splashed through the water to where he used to lie with Nixie.

But as he reached that spot, Nereis spoke out loudly: "Not there! Summer has wasted us, it is too shallow there. See where that larger boulder lies, where the moon has broken through: come to me there."

He made his way toward that farther boulder with, it seemed, enchanted ease, placing his feet as firmly as if he'd been wearing his Tingley boots, as confident as a bridegroom marching to the altar.

She received him not as Nixie would have, with a single, singeing blast of joy; it was rather, with Nereis, a sinking inward, a swooning away, a long slow descent into the whirlpool of an ineffable comfort. When she had wholly absorbed him, when her watery warmth was spread across his face like the tears of a lifetime all suddenly released, he knew that she had taken him into her womb and that he had become hers, hers utterly and for all time.

In the morning he awoke atop the boulder she had led him to, his body bruised, his knees and feet still bleeding. A low mist hung over the stream, as though she had veiled herself. He groaned, like a shanghaied sailor, a bag of sexual garbage dumped in the gutter and waiting for collection. *No more,* he told himself. *No more visions.* It was all very well for William Blake to be at home to spirits: his dealings had been with angels, not with water nymphs. Clearly, Nereids had behavioral traits in common with their cousins, the mermaids. Clearly, a man who continued to answer to their solicitations would be lured to his destruction. Clearly, he must pack up his things and leave the cabin before nightfall, before she called him to her again.

Again: the word, the hope of it, was honey and he the fly happily mired in its fatal sweetness.

I will be more careful, he told himself, as he wound gauze about his lower legs. Then, in earnest of this new self-preserving attitude, he made himself a breakfast of oatmeal and sardines. It tasted, to his ravished tongue, like ambrosia.

The sun swung across the sky like the slowest of pendulums, and the shadow of the cabin's roof-tree touched, sundial-like, the nearer shore of the kill. Four o'clock already, and then, as it touched the farther shore, five. As the shadows lengthened, the birds became livelier and more contentious. The nuthatches stropped their beaks on the bark of the trees and made skirmishes against the chickadees, who panicked but kept returning to the feeder, emblems of the victory of appetite.

The colors of the kill shifted from a lighter to a darker green. Where the shadows were deepest he could glimpse the first restless stirrings of her torso, the undulations of gigantic limbs. How long the days are in July. How caressing the sound of rippling water.

Once, in the summer before his junior year at Wesleyan, William had worked in the violent ward of a psychiatric hospital. He'd been pre-med then and planned to become a psychiatrist. Three months of daily contact with the patients had convinced him, first, that he must find some other career, and second, that there was no such thing as insanity, only the decision, which anyone might make, to act insanely – that is, to follow one's whims and impulses wherever they might lead. By the time they'd led to the violent ward, one had become a career patient, as others were career criminals, and for similar reasons, the chief of which was a preference for institutional life. Only by behaving as a lunatic would one be allowed to live in the eternal kindergarten of the hospital, exempt from work, freed of irksome family ties, one's bloodstream the playground for chemicals available only to the certifiably insane. Those who chose to live such a feckless life were not to be pitied when their grimaces of lunacy froze into masks that could not be removed.

And so it was that when she arose and came to him, at dusk, the water running in trickles down her dark legs, shimmering iridescently across the taut curves of the pea-green swimsuit, he did not resist. He did not tell himself, as she unknotted him from the net hammock to which he'd bound himself, like some hick Ulysses, that this was impossible, could not be happening, etcetera. For he had yielded long since to the possibility – and it was happening now.

"Come," she bade him, "follow me." And the smile that she smiled was like a door.

He opened the door and entered the mountain.

His body was never recovered, but the boots were discovered, where he'd left them, beneath a ledge of limestone close by the source of the kill.

Nights in the Gardens of the Kerhonkson Prison for the Aged and Infirm

"CHESTER, how's it going, my man. How's the leg?"

Chester looked down at his legs, as though wondering which of them the question referred to. Before he could come up with an answer, the man in the gray pajamas had settled down beside him on the bench and become an old friend, praising the weather: "We got some sunlight for a change!" blaming the food: "Meatloaf? You call that meatloaf, then I'm Elvis!" and finally, a dealer finally unveiling his best wares: "Did you hear about Cooper?"

"Who?"

"Cooper. He checked out. Last night, in the middle of *Death Dreams.* We'll never know if Christopher Reeve was the murderer or somebody else, 'cause they cleared the TV room like it was a fire drill. Cooper was stretched out on the floor and the new nurse with the big earrings was zapping his chest with that phaser of hers, but he was gone. Down the toilet. After how long, do you think? Take a guess. Fifty-six years. He went into the joint the day before Pearl Harbor. Assault with intent."

"I don't think I knew him," Chester said. Maybe he did, maybe he didn't, but even when they're dead you don't discuss what someone gets sent up for. And they return the compliment.

"You knew him all right. Little bald weasel, with the bifocals. Scabs on his hands, you didn't know what it was, but you would never want to shake him by the hand. And he only talked about baseball. *Ancient* baseball. Had all the stats in his head, until they started leaking away. Alzheimer's."

Chester nodded gravely. He had the same thing. It wasn't as bad as it could get eventually. The worst so far had been when he couldn't play cards, because the part of the brain that does the figuring just wouldn't light up.

"He put away three guys," the volunteer anchorman went on, "*while* he was in the joint. He even went after some old goat here. That would of been a first for Kerhonkson. We've had guys *break* out...and get as far as the train station." He paused, Mr. Stand-up Comedy, waiting for a laugh. When the laugh didn't come, he rolled right along. "But a genuine homicide? Not yet. Think of all this talent going to waste."

Chester said nothing. He was beginning to cop a resentment. He hadn't invited this windbag to share his bench and start a goddamn memorial service. Chester had come here for some peace and quiet, for the sun, and the reservoir. You could not see the reservoir directly, but at certain times of day, in the right weather, the mist rose up off the water and blanked out the hills on the far side. Chester liked watching things disappear. At twilight, when other people on the yard were watching the sunset, and afterwards, he liked to stand at the perimeter fence looking east.

"I read once that any lifer who's killed two and a half other cons while he's in the joint has saved the state the cost of his own incarceration. I couldn't figure out the arithmetic on that. You'd think one would be enough. You got one, you subtract one from it, the result's got to be zero, right? Anyhow, if that's a true statistic, then Cooper had earned his board and room with half a life to spare."

The guy gave him this *hungry* look and out of the blue Chester remembered his name. Decker.

"You want one of my pills, Decker?" Chester said at last, in a tone of peeved surrender. "If that's what you want, just say so."

"Well...if you don't need them for that leg of yours...yeah. See, I get these headaches, but that nurse, she's some kind of sadist, she won't let me have a fucking aspirin. If I knew anywhere else to get them..."

Chester felt around inside the big pocket of his terrycloth robe, trying to decide by touch which was the Kleenex for wiping his nose and which was the one the capsule was wrapped in. "Here," he said, producing the right Kleenex the first time. "But remember. It's time-release. It kicks in about four hours after you take it. Longer, if you've just eaten. So if you take it too late in the day, it'll just be a sleeping pill."

"Thanks, pal. I won't forget this."

"*I* will," said Chester, but not until the guy had left him alone. He smiled at his little joke, and then, with the illegal nailfile that he kept wedged in a crack on the underside of the wooden bench, he made another notch in the neatly spaced series on the topside of the slat.

When he'd finished with the nailfile, he counted his notches. Twelve. The twelfth was for Cooper. He returned the file to its hiding place. Tomorrow would be time enough to make notch 13. Chester did not count his chickens before they were hatched.

"You never have the nights out here, do you?" remarked Mrs. Schultz.

"No ma'am," said Chester. "We're always locked down before it turns dark. They let us out on the yard sometimes, but never into the gardens."

"I think I would miss that most of all."

"It's surprising the things you do miss, and what you can get used to. There's no predicting."

"Did you miss killing people?"

Chester would have resented the question coming from anyone else, but since Mrs. Schultz was in the same deep shit as he was, and since she seemed genuinely curious and not just trying to probe his conscience or find out if he had one, he answered honestly. "That's probably what I missed most of all. Of course, since I did most of the killings at night, and out-of-doors somewhere, it comes out the same as what you were saying. It's nice being out here when it's really dark like this, and mist in the air."

"Did you follow them?"

"No, it was more like I waited for them to come to me. But I like those parts in the movies – the women on the streets, the sound of their high heels, and then the other footsteps. In real life it wasn't like that."

They were both silent for a while. On the other side of the scrim of pines you could hear a semi gearing down to climb the hill. At least that's what Chester imagined the sound to be. Then there was a muffled tap, which he couldn't figure until he realized it must be his own cane. Sure enough, it was gone from where he'd hooked it over the back of the bench.

"When you dream," Mrs. Schultz asked, "do your dreams take place in prison?"

"Sometimes. But not as often as you'd suppose, seeing how much of my life I've been locked up. And yourself?"

"Me?" She segued into a self-deprecating laugh. "Oh, I'm not *here* so often that it's taken root that deeply. Two hours a week with the library cart. Or do you mean: do I dream of what we've been doing? I don't. It's surprised me how little toll our murders have taken, spiritually."

"Yeah, I always figured serial killers probably sleep easier than most people. They can take care of all those nightmare things while they're awake."

"I suppose I *must* account myself a serial killer now."

"Fourteen's a pretty good score, ma'am."

"Fourteen?" she objected. Then it dawned. "Oh – with you."

"You weren't going to count me? Wasn't that why they gave me that so-called sedative before the guard brought us out here? I'm not dumb. Not that dumb anyhow."

"I know that, Chester. I've always respected your intelligence. I think you're quite the brightest of all of the men here."

"That's faint praise, Mrs. Schultz. Faint praise. Anyhow, here we are. If privacy was what you were after, we got privacy. We kiss in the shadows."

"I beg your pardon?"

"That was a popular song, back when. I remember I would sing along with the car radio. 'We kiss in the shadows.' I forget the rest of it."

She filled in the blank. "Our meetings are secret."

"That's right. So it's even the appropriate song for the occasion. Did you ever have sex outside, Mrs. Schultz? Somewhere like this. Or was it always in the bedroom?"

She ignored his question by asking her own: "Did you keep score? Was that part of it?"

"You mean, before I got sent up? Sure. Not written down, that would have been stupid. There was never so many that it was hard to keep track of them all. The fingers on two hands did the job."

"And when you think of...your score, do you include the men here? Or are they somehow separate?"

"Well, the two sexes are very different. But yeah, sometimes I add them all together. The grand total's twenty: thirteen here, and the seven women."

"I thought there were only four."

"Four they prosecuted. The other three they suspected, but they couldn't prove anything."

"And you wouldn't confess?"

"Why make it any easier for them?"

"Didn't the victims have families?"

"Some of them must have, I suppose."

"Weren't they at the trial?"

"Maybe. All that part is a blank now."

"You really feel no remorse?"

"Do you? For the guys here?"

"Actually, I feel a kind of grim satisfaction."

"I know the feeling. So, tell me – do you plan to keep adding to your score? Find another helper?"

"No, that would be too risky now. In any case, the warden has given me my walking papers. There won't be any more library service at Kerhonkson."

"It's not as though there was ever much call for it, Mrs. Schultz. The guys that aren't going blind are zombies or else they couldn't read to begin with. You won't be missed all that much."

"That was always one of the satisfactions of coming here every week. To see just how brutish you all were. Brutish but feeble. A swamp full of geriatric alligators. Just what they deserve, I could tell myself. Crueller than any lethal injection."

Another silence. Mrs. Schultz tapped the bench arrhythmically with the side of his aluminum cane.

"So, tell me, Mrs. Schultz. What got you interested in the sport of shooting alligators?"

"Compassion, actually. Or that's what I thought it was. I'm a Quaker, you know."

"No shit? Now that's a surprise. You don't seem the type. A retired go-go dancer possibly, but not a Quaker."

"My second husband was a Friend, and a crusader against the death penalty. I...joined his crusade. I attended candlelight vigils in other states when there was an execution. I handed out leaflets. I spoke at town meetings. What I would tell people, then, was that the death penalty made us *all* murderers. Each one of us was no better than an executioner. To which a good many of them said fine, they wouldn't mind doing the job.

"When it came their turn, they'd explain why they were in favor of the death penalty. How their husband or wives or children had been killed. Sometimes by criminals who'd been released on parole. Your name was brought up once or twice at those debates, as I recall. That was some twenty years after you'd been put away, but people still remembered you."

"There were a couple books, that's probably why. There's worse than me."

"I know, I've done the research. And quite a few are right here at Kerhonkson. New York did not have the death penalty for all those years. So the prisons are saddled with you in perpetuity. In another ten years Kerhonkson will be the largest facility in the state. And the average annual cost of maintaining each toothless alligator in its own little cage is close to two hundred thousand dollars."

"It's a scandal, I know. I can understand you taxpayers are outraged. But what you gonna do?"

Mrs. Schultz laughed. And then sighed. "If only you hadn't been so impulsive, Chester, we might have accomplished so much more. Why did you have to give that pill to Mr. Decker? It was not intended for him."

"He pissed me off. Anyhow, it killed him, didn't it? So that's another notch in our gun."

"Not at all. He had a minor stroke, after which he dictated a long and circumstantial account of how he had got the pill from you, and his suspicions that you'd 'assisted' Cooper and several others similarly. Fortunately, the legal aide who'd taken down his testimony went directly to the warden."

"And the warden finished the job on Decker himself?"

"A mischance befell. But not before Mr. Decker had communicated his suspicions to others. So you see, Chester, you would be, in any case, a marked man. Not only among your fellow prisoners. There would have been an inquiry. You would be asked where you'd got the pills you'd given to your victims, who had been their Dr. Kevorkian."

"I kind of figured that was the situation. You don't think they might not want to buy your silence, too? The same way they're buying mine? It wouldn't be that hard."

"I have friends, Chester, who share my convictions. They have tapes of my account of all my dealings with you – and with the warden, and the doctors here. I imagine that's as good an insurance policy as I'll need."

"So I'm going to be the one and only scapegoat."

"The wages of sin, Chester, is death. Does that seem unfair?"

"No, I figure I've had a good run. And it's been great working with you. You've put it all in a new light. I used to think the killing was about excitement. But it's not. Not necessarily. With you it's been like…I can't describe it. It's like being out here in the garden, at night. All soft and misty and, like you said, spiritual. I never was afraid of the dark. I've always liked it."

He stretched out his arm to try and touch her, but she'd left the bench.

"How long have I got till the stuff takes hold?"

"Less than an hour, at this point."

"If I could reach you…" he began regretfully.

"You'd try to kill me?"

"If I were younger, probably. Yeah."

"That's why I took away your cane."

"I figured. Well, you can't win 'em all." He smiled in a friendly way.

She couldn't see his smile, but she seemed to sense it, for there was a kind of choked-up tone in her voice when she said, "I'll leave you now, Chester." Like she was burying a pet.

A Family of the Post-Apocalypse

IT WAS CHEAPER living in the danger zone, which was why they'd settled there after everything went haywire. Dad and Mom and the three Big Babies. All this was after the Rapture and the Second Coming (which they never got to see), and the only people left on Earth were the people who hadn't been saved. Things weren't the same as when they'd got their starter house back in Wisconsin, but as Dad would say, When have things ever been the same? Anti-Christ was supposed to be in charge these days, though it wasn't that much different from when the Presidents were being elected. He appeared, as they had, on TV from time to time, to announce the latest disaster and to reassure the survivors that they shouldn't worry.

The major difference, from Mom's point of view, was not having *any* easy listening on the radio. Just heavy metal, which was bad for the kids, especially when they were teething, which was most of the time.

Scorpions could be a problem. Likewise power outages and brownouts. Fortunately Dad had figured out a way to hook up the deepfreeze to the car batteries he'd scavenged after the big pile-up on Route 66. The lawn, for a wonder, was still in good shape, except in one area around the septic tank, which had become a little forest of mushrooms almost overnight.

Since there was no more industry or commerce or employment or such as that, there was plenty of quality time for the family to do those things they'd been neglecting before Armageddon. The trouble with this was that the Big Babies, who'd earlier shown some sort of aptitude for games that didn't involve numeric skills, seemed to have regressed (even as they'd grown so much larger) to a more or less infantile state. Hence their name now. It wasn't just their three, it was all the children left after the Rapture. Their oldest, Buddy, three at the time, was still capable of a game or two of tic-tac-toe, but the twins were dumb as fish. Strong, and cute as the dickens in a strange way, but dumb as fish. Dad had fixed up a kind of harness from the old Buick's safety belts and taught the twins to pull the lawn mower with it, which they seemed to like to do and which was why the lawn looked as good as it did. But intellectually they were not apple-of-the-eye material.

Time had stopped, so clocks didn't work anymore, and the survivors had split up into factions as to what was the exact date and day of the week. But people still tried to get on to church on Sunday on a hit-or-miss basis. In some ways church attendance seemed more important now than it had in pre-Apocalyptic times, even though there wasn't any urgency about whether you'd end up saved or otherwise. Otherwise seemed to be everybody's situation, but even so there could be a kind of comfort in singing the songs together, and now that Reverend Ashburn was no longer in charge of the music program, the menu of songs was larger, albeit rudimentary, out of respect to the survivors' musical capabilities and what they remembered. "Inky-Dinky Spider" was popular; likewise "Chapel of Love." Whatever enough of them could remember the words for. There were a lot of Christmas carols, of course, which are always comforting, whatever the weather, and staples like "Yankee Doodle" and "America the Beautiful." But never "Oh Say Can You See," since everyone agreed that was outside the vocal range of anyone but a professional soprano.

After the service there would be a coffee hour. Usually, instant, or even in a pinch herbal teas – whatever the Refreshment Committee had been able to scavenge. If you had guns, you had to check them with the ushers. The rule wasn't often enforced, since mostly everyone there knew everyone else. Wasn't that what church was about? A sense of solidarity, of belonging, of *communion*. Sundays could be wonderful, if you guessed right and got there when the other survivors did.

They usually avoided discussing the overall situation, partly from a sense of terror but mostly because they simply didn't understand what that situation was. They weren't in hell precisely; in many ways they were still better off than most people had been before Armageddon, people in Bangladesh or Ethiopia, for instance. On the other hand, terrible things did happen pretty regularly to folks in the danger zone, often on quite a large scale. Sometimes, in the middle of the night, you could hear one of the Post-Apocalyptic biker gangs roaring along Route 66, gangs with names like Plague Riders or L.A. Locusts, all of them Satanic drug addicts and ritual child abusers, and the next day down at the Exxon station, where the owner had a working CB radio, you would hear that a whole small town had been turned to rubble. Or you'd see the wrecks alongside the road and the people who'd been chained to their overturned cars and tortured, some still alive. Mom would say, "There must be *something* we can do for them. For the children at least." Dad wouldn't say a thing, just keep driving, eyes on the road, hand on his gun. The bikers hated anyone driving a car. Once, right after the Rapture, a biker drinking outside a 7-Eleven had shot out both of the Buick's back tires, and they'd driven the last three miles home on the rims and shredded radials. Now Dad was driving a Honda Accord, which was embarrassing for someone who'd always believed in buying Made-in-America products. But you had to ask yourself: was this still America?

At night, after the Big Babies had been drugged and put to bed, if there was nothing but re-runs on TV (which was more and more the case), they would reminisce about the America they remembered growing up in. Their favorite sandwiches or brands of soft drinks that no longer existed. But they avoided recollections about old friends and neighbors back in Laurel Heights, since those memories could only rankle now. The months of living under quarantine, the foreclosure on the house, and finally the eviction, and all because of what was happening to the kids, which wasn't *their* fault. Which wasn't anyone's fault, really, unless you believed the theory that it was a result of the fallout that had resulted from Armageddon. The fallout was also supposed to account for what had happened to the wildlife. Whatever the cause, Mom firmly believed that eventually the doctors would find a cure. "Call me an optimist," she'd say, with a forced smile, "but I'm still counting on attending the twins' college graduation. I've got the date marked on the calendar."

*

The war was also blamed for the way the weather had got so scrambled, so that there'd be a string of hot days, and weeds would start shooting up like crazy, and the mushrooms over the septic tank would bloat and turn all mushy, and then overnight it would be like November. The trees got totally confused. Some were trying to sprout new leaves while a block away the same kind of tree would be turning yellow.

But it was more than the seasons that were out of kilter, it was time itself, and the perception of it. The Post-Apocalyptic world seemed to have dipped one foot into the lacy surf of Eternity. Mom could remember one afternoon when she'd been in the kitchen, chopping an onion and listening to Anthrax on the radio, and the chopping and the song had gone on and on and on, the way on old phonographs a record will continue playing if you don't lower the arm that engages with the spindle. The onion became an eternal onion, infinitely choppable. The infernal scream of the song continued shrilling through her mind for days after, like a car alarm that no one will turn off. Meanwhile, in the basement, where Dad had been cutting a dovetail joint with his router, the same thing happened to him. The bit of the router attacked the pine board with an interminable ferocity, yet without any sense of the process happening in slow motion.

Some time later they learned that they had a close brush with one of the great clouds of smoke that passed over the danger zone at intervals like tornados. The clouds seemed to act as a kind of lens focusing the destructive force of the Last Judgment and creating temporal anomalies of the sort Mom and Dad had experienced. These anomalies were even greater, presumably, beneath the center of the cloud, but even the few people who claimed to have survived the clouds' full destructive force were unable to give any account of what had happened to them. They could only liken it to waking from an absolutely terrifying nightmare, which they forgot, all but its impact, at the moment of waking, the moment, an eternity later, that the cloud had passed.

Food was the big worry. Right at the beginning of Armageddon, when China was nuking Israel and vice versa, as had been foretold, Dad had the foresight to lay in supplies of anything he could lay his hands on.

First, shopping at all the malls within driving distance, and then, when the shortages and/or looting had emptied the malls, by foraging in houses that looked to be abandoned. The pickings were generally slim. Most of the people vacating their houses to escape the danger zone had been prudent enough to empty their cupboards of viable foodstuffs, leaving nothing but the contents of their spice racks and the dregs of the vinegar and A-1 Sauce. But a couple times he got lucky and was able to fill the trunk and half the back seat of the Buick with viable foodstuffs, whole cartons of Ronzoni spaghetti, Quaker Oats, dried milk, Ragu Thick 'n' Hearty Spaghetti Sauce, and, for some reason, 48 one-pound bottles of artichoke hearts.

The artichokes did not sort well with the Ragu sauce, and no combination of spices – tarragon, allspice, summer savory, what have you – were able to help. After a while, everything started tasting like artichokes, even the Quaker Oats. Which, unhappily didn't stretch very far, since almost as soon as each canister was opened the dry oatmeal was swarming with multitudes of tiny black weevils. They'd all have preferred oatmeal to be the staple of their diet to one of artichoke hearts, but as Dad declared, trying to sound like a good sport, "Pillagers can't be choosers."

"Pillagers?" Mom repeated, as though she'd never heard the word before. "I don't know what you mean by pillagers."

On some evenings the night sky was lovelier than ever before. The stars didn't just twinkle, they were like flashbulbs popping. Also they changed colors, shifting from a steely blue to a deep dark red that made your eyes feel funny. At the same time there would be a sound almost too low to hear, a kind of rumble as though a Russian all-male choir were humming the bottommost note of the scale. The ground would seem to shake, and then one night, standing behind the house, looking up at the sky, they realized the ground really was shaking, especially in the area around the septic tank.

And then, just as it is written in John's Revelation, Chapter 9, verses 1 to 11, the septic tank erupted like a volcano, spattering everything in sight, themselves, the house, the garage, the moribund maples, and filling the air with a dreadful stench. Yellow smoke billowed from the pit that had opened up, and they realized they were watching the birth of one of the Post-Apocalyptic clouds that were the terror of the danger zone, and the bottomless pit was here in their own backyard, and out of it now, with faces like the faces of men but hair like the hair of women (verses 7 and 8), streamed a legion of locusts.

Big ones, and dressed, according to the prophecies, pretty much like the bikers in *Mad Max*, except that instead of riding Harleys their bikes were incorporated into their exoskeletons. It was the whirring of their huge wings that sounded like the revving of unmuffled engines. The Bible says at this point that in those days men shall seek death and not find it, shall desire to die, and death shall flee from them. But it doesn't go into the details, it only says that the locusts had stings in their tails and the power to torment people five months, if they didn't have a particular mark on their forehead, which Mom and Dad didn't.

Five months is a limited sentence, but when you are being tortured around the clock by giant insects with stings in their tails and sadistic imaginations, it can seem an eternity, and in a sense, because of the temporal dilations produced by the pall of smoke that covered the sun and the moon and even the fluorescent lights in the kitchen, it *was* an eternity.

"How'd ya like a taste of this then!" Abaddon, the leader of the locusts, would sneer, waving his stinger back and forth, brushing their naked flesh with its venomous tip, and then, *Whoop!* he'd give it a flick and connect right to the swollen lymph gland in Dad's armpit, or *Whap! Whap!* across Mom's lacerated breasts. "Oh, I'm a bad one, yes I am," he'd quip, and all his locust cronies would guffaw on cue.

Abaddon also, which is not in the Bible but perfectly in keeping with his character, taught the Big Babies to act as their parents' tormentors, when the locusts in the house were too bored or drunk to torture Dad and Mom themselves.

The human body has a threshold beyond which pain stops registering, so there were times when the locusts would vanish for days at a time, leaving Dad and Mom to recuperate and make lamentations. "I don't understand it," Dad would say, shaking his head and wincing at the pain. "What did we do *wrong?* Why is this happening to us."

"It was our fornications and abominations!" Mom lamented, reaching into the fireplace for a handful of ashes, which she rubbed into her wounds.

"What fornications! We're married, aren't we? Is that fornication?"

Mom groaned. "And what about the time you came home drunk and made me do you know what? Oh, Jesus, I wish I were dead!"

"You always hated sex," Dad complained, for the umpteenth time.

One of their cruelest torments was simply repeating the same conversations over and over, him blaming her, her blaming him, and in the other room, swollen to an outlandish size but screaming to be fed every waking hour, the Big Babies would claw and scrabble at the plywood nailed over the windows.

"You know what I wish?" said Dad. "Sometimes I wish we'd never got married." Immediately after he'd said it he felt guilty.

Mom looked at him with annoyance but not actual hostility. She smiled a sad little smile and patted his hand, but very gently because of the boils. "It isn't your fault, dear. It isn't anyone's fault. It's just the times we live in."

In Praise of Older Women

ONE MORNING, just before breakfast, Oedipus, the King of Thebes, got a letter informing him that quite inadvertently he had married his own mother, Queen Jocasta. At first he suspected this was his brother-in-law Creon's idea of a practical joke, but for one thing, Creon had no sense of humor and for another the letter was signed by Teiresias, a blind seer of well-attested probity and independence of judgment. Moreover, the letter was accompanied by an affidavit from the shepherd who'd taken the infant Oedipus from Thebes and given him to another shepherd who in turn had passed him on to King Polybus and Queen Periboea of Corinth.

It had been an honest mistake, clearly, but Oedipus hated the idea of newspapers getting hold of such a juicy scandal. Incest with his own mother, and him the King of Thebes! He wondered whether the wisest course wouldn't be to shred the letter and forget the whole thing. Jocasta was certain to be upset, and what else could be done to mend matters now.

I won't tell her, he decided. But the moment she came down to breakfast he changed his mind. She looked so beautiful, spreading butter on the flat bottom-side of a croissant, lifting her coffee cup and blowing ripples in the coffee before she took her first little sip. Hard to believe, looking at her, that she was old enough to be his mother!

"There's something you should know, darling," he said, and passed her the letter.

Jocasta read the letter through, then folded it up and put it back in the envelope.

"I'm afraid it's all true," she said. "At least as to my having exposed that child on the mountain."

"That child?" Oedipus gave the words a sarcastic inflection.

Jocasta looked abashed. She began tearing her croissant to bits. Whenever Jocasta wanted to avoid a discussion her hands would become busy – with a cigarette or crewel-work. When the croissant had been thoroughly disassembled, she looked up at her husband and tried to reconsider him as a son. Impossible! "I suppose you blame me," she said tentatively, testing the water.

"Did I say that?"

"It was Laius's fault. He had this idea, from going to some oracle, that if he ever had a son, he'd be murdered by him. There was no arguing with him. So I just —" She wiped her buttery fingers with a napkin. "— took the initiative. When he saw I was pregnant he was furious, but I *refused* to have an abortion. Royalty has to set an example."

"A fine example *we're* setting."

Jocasta sighed.

"We'll have to do something," he said. "We can't just pretend things are the same as before."

She cast up her eyes in the manner of a sacrificial victim and began nervously shredding a second croissant.

"Can we?" he insisted.

"You're the king," she said, almost too softly to be heard.

"And what is *that* supposed to mean?"

"I mean that the old busybody who wrote that letter isn't immortal. You could arrange an accident for her."

"Teiresias is a he, my dear."

"I thought he had a sex change."

"He did, and then he changed back again."

"The nerve," she said angrily. "I mean, you'd think someone like that would be the *last* person to go around casting aspersions on other people. In any case, whether she's a he, or vice versa, *this* —" She tapped the letter. "— is blackmail. Nothing more nor less."

"You're suggesting that I murder him."

"Do you know any other way to deal with blackmail? If you put him in prison, the story will get out sooner or later. Unless you cut out his tongue, and I think that's barbaric."

Oedipus held up the shepherd's affidavit "And what of this?"

"Oh, he's just a shepherd. Sell him to some foreign trader. *He's* not the problem."

"Let us suppose that Teiresias has been eliminated from the picture. The problem remains, my dear, that our marriage is incestuous."

"Why don't you just come right out and say you want a divorce?"

"But we can't go on...um...acting as man and wife."

"Men," she said witheringly, "are all alike."

"Jocasta – be reasonable."

"When was the last time we made love, Oedipus? When? On the Ides of July, that's when. When you came home drunk from that orgy. When a woman is thirty-five and a man is eighteen, we hear a lot of talk about the beauty of 'mature women.' But when she's fifty, it's another story, oh yes!"

"Jocasta, you're twisting everything. I still *love* you. If I haven't been as attentive as usual, well, that's because with the plague, and the war, and inflation, I've been so busy that I just don't have the energy for... um..."

"Hypocrite."

"You're my *mother*, Jocasta."

"Please don't *whine*. I hate whiners. And as to that, I'm also the mother of your four children. What's to become of *them*, if we're divorced?"

"Well, I could take Antigone and Ismene, and you could take the boys to the palace in Corinth. It's been standing empty ever since Polybus died."

"I hate Corinth, as you well know, and that palace is a pig sty. I refuse. I grew up in Thebes. All my friends are in Thebes. I'm the *Queen* of Thebes, for heaven's sake!"

"Very well, then *I'll* go to Corinth. I'll abdicate and leave Thebes to you. We can't go on as though nothing has happened, as though we didn't know who we are and what we're doing."

"We're royalty and we can do what we like. If your conscience forbids you to come to my bed, that's up to you, of course. But as to divorce, or even a trial separation, there could be nothing so certain to provoke scandal, which is what we're trying to avoid. Another thing – what would we tell the children, have you thought of that? That you're their brother as well as their father? Can you imagine what that would *do* to them, at their age? The guilt they'd feel, and the shame?"

"There's certainly no need for *them* to feel shame and guilt."

"But *we* should?" she asked sarcastically.

"That's not what I said."

Jocasta reached across the table and took her husband's hand in hers. "Oedipus, darling, I understand that you've been upset by all this, and I sympathize. But you mustn't do anything you'll regret later. Thebes needs a king. If you leave me here alone, my brother Creon will be conspiring against the throne before you can say Mnemosyne. We have to face facts."

"Oh, I suppose you're right. Practically speaking."

She patted his hand and got up from the table. "You'll take care of the rest?"

He nodded.

But even with that assurance she lingered in the atrium until he'd given his guards the order to kill the blind seer and to sell the old shepherd to traders from Crete. Then, avoiding the courtyard, where a delegation of citizens were continuing their sit-in to protest the plague, she went up to her own chamber to be bathed and scented with myrrh and dressed in her best purple robe.

Painting Eggplants

RICHARD HAD always envied those artists who had been driven mad by their art. Naturally he preferred those who snapped in the direction of erotic frenzy to the suicides, but any madness was to be wished for if the alternative was a lucid equanimity.

He considered himself invincibly level-headed, so any thought of some psychic aurora on his own part was entirely theoretical, like speculations about the shape and age of the universe. But, as the director of the graduate writing program at Indiana State University in Muncie, he had had plenty of opportunity to witness poetic madness at first hand.

In a sense any student who came to Muncie to study to be a writer had to have some kind of mental defect to begin with – either a simplicity of soul bordering on challenged or else a problem with liquor or hard drugs. The latter had become increasingly common during the '80s and '90s to the point where half of each year's new crop of apprentice fiction concerned the joys and sorrows of addiction or spousal abuse or neglect due to alcoholism. The drop-out rate was phenomenal, ditto expulsions for felony crime. At last count Richard knew of five students from the program serving major time in Indiana Correctional facilities. One of them – indeed, the most promising would-be poet to have attended Muncie – was still pursuing her M.A. in Creative Writing by way of Indiana's pioneering prison-to-university electronic link-up.

But now, without warning and in happy conjunction with a sabbatical he had intended to spend, literally, in Burgundy, divine madness had lighted upon Richard Muldoon, and he was transformed. He had become a mad painter like van der Weyden or van Gogh or Goya.

Every day, every hour, was a new rapture of beauty. The on/off switch was broken and he was always on.

It had all begun with the advice of Marc Jaffe, an Israeli painter who taught at the Spring Workshop in Tuscany, a program that Muncie ran in conjunction with Cincinnati's Koch Music Conservatory. 1986: Richard had been there to sail through his usual summer-school special, "Beginning Your Novel," a course guaranteed to earn high grades with little exertion and no risk of failure that couldn't quickly be shrugged off. Every student was guaranteed to be sent home with a portion and outline of a botched novel to be tucked away in a file and thought back on in more mature years with fond regret, the literary equivalent of a semester spent abroad for the purpose of losing one's cherry while learning French or Italian.

Richard had used his free time in Arezzo to sit in on Jaffe's workshop in oil painting. Bliss it was in those summers to smooth a brushload of frothy peach pigment across a ground of palest, creamy yellow. He hadn't painted a thing since his brief mid-life crisis in 1974 when he had a fling with the Art Students' League in New York City, right after getting his Ph.D. In the course of discovering what he finally decided was his irremediable mediocrity as a painter he had filled all his own and his parents' storage space with canvases in the manners, more or less, of Derain, Nolde, Hofmann and a dozen other B-menu painters who seemed within his reach. But weren't. Which, finally, he was ready to admit and so took Indiana's offer. For years the canvases decorated his various rented premises in and around Muncie, never garnering more than a guarded "Interesting" or, at best, "Nice." Gradually "Interesting" and "Nice" were displaced by museum prints and tasteful lithos by faculty members in Muncie and Arezzo.

What Marc Jaffe had told him, passing Richard's muddy still-life of a pot of rosemary, late on a Tuscan afternoon, was "Paint eggplants." Richard had smiled and nodded and went on daubing his muddy olives and viridians, thinking Jaffe's remark had been just a passing sarcasm, as who might say, "Paint it black." Because there was really no saving the mess taking shape on the easel. Not until the farewell dinner, with all the students' opening chapters read and graded (four A's, two A-minuses, two B's and one B-minus) and his own four keeper canvases already boxed and bound for Muncie, did it occur to Richard that Jaffe might have meant it literally. "Paint eggplants" had not been ironic, but straightforward, practical advice, though advice, admittedly, with some flavor of a koan.

But then he re-thought that possibility and decided that, no, Jaffe had been mocking Richard's poor pot of rosemary, only that and nothing more. Too late then to have a look at the thing, since it had not been one of the keepers. For years Richard gave the matter no thought, though every time he was in the produce department at the Stop & Shop he would look at the massed eggplants in their brightly lit bin with a special regard, such as one affords a local celebrity. And he would hear Jaffe's voice in his head, with its wet plosives. Perhaps he even began to buy eggplants more regularly at that time, though surely it was Julia Child who was responsible for that, with her demonstration of how to bake slices of eggplant smeared with tomato paste to be tasty as potato chips and much less fattening than eggplant parmigian. In any case, Richard began to let eggplants alternate with fruit and acorn squash and zucchini as table decorations when he was too cheap to buy cut flowers.

Never did he think of them as aubergines, although "aubergine" was the official name for their color, while "eggplant" was linguistically inexplicable, at least in a visual sense, since neither in form nor in color were eggplants at all egglike. They didn't taste like eggs either, nor were they eggy in consistency when cooked. That was just one more mystery of the eggplant.

The primary mystery, of course, was why Jaffe had told him to paint them. Was it just a way of putting Richard off, like one of the tasks set for the guileless, disinherited prince in a fairy tale to keep him busy and forever uncrowned? Or simply a challenge to his color sense, his ability to splice together the right two or three pigments that would mirror one particular eggplant and no other? The darker hues were the hardest to get, the shaded sides of treetrunks, an asphalt road, mahogony furniture. The skin of eggplants.

For years he had pondered these matters, and then on the day before his birthday in 2001, during his first summer session in years away from the dolce vita of Arezzo, the UPS van pulled into his driveway with a present from his sister Pat. A beautiful ceramic bowl, shallow but not so shallow as to be a platter rather than a bowl. His favorite celadon green, and the perfect place to put the two eggplants already waiting for the Julia Child treatment.

Seeing them side by side in eggplant heaven he knew the time had come to paint eggplants. He brought in the easel from the garage and got down his paintbox from the shelf of the closet in the spare bedroom. The brushes were stiff and the tubes of paint not as yielding as one might wish. All that remained was to decide which of his dinner plates to sacrifice for service as a palette.

And then, opening the second tube of paint, phthalocyanine blue, the spirit descended. As at Pentecost; or when Danae receives Jove's golden showers; or Callas singing "Casta diva." A light shined in the darkness, and this time the darkness comprehended it and grappled it to its eggplant heart. When he was done he could not remember the details, who had kissed what and for how long, but there were the two eggplants in their birthday bowl, round and luscious, a hymn to all harvests, to Eros, to Psyche, and there on the table, looking as smug as two Dutch burghers, were their originals. Well, who isn't pleased with a flattering portrait? But there was no help for it, their fate was fixed. He flayed them alive, paring away their aubergine skin to expose the pale Caucasian flesh beneath. Then egg, bread crumbs, a sprinkle of oregano, and into the olive oil. Not Julia Child, not this time, but a proper eggplant parmigian.

A Médoc would have been nice, but not at the price of a drive to the liquor store. He made do with the Heinekens in the refrigerator. All the wine he really needed was there before him on that oblong of canvasboard, and he gazed his fill.

His subsequent paintings were not concluded with a similar sacramental symmetry. His digestive enthusiasm for eggplant was finite. But he painted eggplants from then on. In groupings of two or three. In mounds. Solitary eggplants. In bowls and in baskets, on tablecloths, and playing on the lawn. In the ocher sink in the bathroom and in the kitchen's squared-off stainless steel sink. A very difficult painting and not entirely successful the first time, but splendid when he got a bigger easel and painted it much larger than life. An eggplant four feet in length – just think! And that was only the first three weeks of June.

Before eggplants became a personal mission he had tended to have a low regard for painters who had one idea that they rode to death, like Noland with his stripes and chevrons. But did God get tired of making pebbles for the beach? Each one a perfect specimen of the universal ideal, each as different from any fellow pebble as the proverbial snowflake from every other snowflake.

All that was theory, a task for Clement Greenberg. In practice Richard painted his eggplants because it afforded him an inexplicable and abiding satisfaction, serene and self-sufficing. He painted as a yogi might do yoga, less and less troubling himself with questions of motive or purpose. His purpose was certainly *not* ambition. He foresaw no career for himself as The Master of the Muncie Eggplant. One might aspire to a Renaissance-fair *reclam* as a painter of rustic scenery or as a flower painter but not doing eggplants. In any case, though the heart undoubtedly has its reasons, Richard just wasn't that curious what his might be. It felt good: wasn't that enough?

He'd been the same with his three novels. He'd never thought to ask himself *why* he'd written *Submissions of a Catholic Boyhood.* Or why *he* had written it. To emulate Mary McCarthy? To revenge himself on the Christian Brothers and Trinity High School (where, in fact, he'd been tolerably happy and surely better educated in most subjects than he would have been at the public schools available to him)? To cash in on the pedophilia scandals already springing up everywhere? But the beatings his hero had received at the hands of Father Bill hadn't been sexual in character. They were part of a simple context of wills, and test of faith. So, all of the above "reasons" had probably been factors, but basically he'd written the book because he could, because the idea had dawned on him, and the prose arose. Just the way, really, these eggplants had come to him.

And still were coming. On through July and into August. Always a good record-keeper, he'd been keeping a systematic inventory right from the get-go, and there were now seventy-eight paintings of eggplants, large and small, not counting the botches and the false starts. The earlier ones were mostly oils, but it was easier to deal with the cleaning up if he used acrylics. And painting on gessoed plywood panels and masonite was so much cheaper. (There were also a couple of lovely large tapestries painted on plastic tablecloths that had been on sale at Wal-Mart's.) They looked as *Italian* as cans of olive oil, as Canalettos! If he continued in spate, using stretched canvas or canvasboard, he could bankrupt himself were the madness to last much beyond his sabbatical. Of course, he didn't envisage the muse continuing her daily visits beyond, at the furthest stretch, September. But who would have supposed it could go on this long? It is in the nature of passion that one doesn't budget one's time. Mad love doesn't make plans.

Just before Labor Day, Sarah, his ex-wife and his agent still, went off to London and other literary cities in Europe, leaving her Greenwich Village apartment in Richard's hands. No entrails could have yielded a more unequivocal omen, for Sarah's apartment was not one hundred feet from that part of Fifth Avenue where every year, at Labor Day, there was a street fair at which vendors sold the wares bohemia was famed for – ceramics, candles, silver jewelry, T-shirts, and fine art. For whatever reason, wares in the latter category had come to take up less and less exhibition space in proportion to more practical items like socks and underwear. But that relative dearth made it easier for Richard – and other throwbacks to the Beaux Arts era – to be licensed to set up a display and sell his paintings. He did have to show a sample of his work to the curatorial committee – a single eggplant, life-size, in that celadon bowl – and he explained to them that his other works were also still-lifes. Their one comment was, "Nice."

So there he was, on the first Saturday morning of the show, in his assigned space on East 12th, halfway between 5th and Waverly, sitting in front of his harvest of eggplants, waiting for the compliments. There were forty-four paintings hanging from three "walls" rigged from P.V.C. piping and canvas-backed chicken wire. He hadn't priced any of them yet, since he'd wanted to check out the competition first. The very cheapest pictures – sad clowns, drab flowers – fetched $50 to $75. Larger sizes and more careful execution doubled those figures, and the asking price for full-size, over-the-sofa oils suitable for a dentist's waiting room was anywhere from $250 to $500. But the higher price tags were always attached to landscapes. The priciest still life – a really nice watercolor of tiers of bouquets outside a deli – was going for $300, but that was from an artist with an impressive track record and lots of ribbons. Richard tagged his largest offering at $250 – an eggplant inflated to fill a 20″ × 24″ panel of masonite in a tasteful gold-leaf frame (optional for $50), and priced the smaller pieces proportionately. He didn't expect to sell a thing, but pricing his wares seemed an essential civility.

The pedestrians going by did sometimes slow down to take a look. Mostly they seemed to do a double-take on the fact that all of the paintings were paintings of eggplants. Some took that in, and gave a smile or nod of recognition and walked on, perhaps after inquiring, "Eggplants – just eggplants, nothing else?" And he would nod and smile. A few times he reaped his familiar reward of "Nice" or "Interesting," usually from someone who seemed not to find his exclusive focus on eggplants remarkable. But only twice did anyone ask the price. "It's on the flip side," he told them, and they turned the picture around, nodded, and walked off.

All that was between ten A.M. and noon, and already he was getting bored. This side of the *vie de bohème* was not the stuff of operas. But it was too late now to back out. He'd bought his ticket and he was on the plane; he would just have to go to the appointed destination. His neighbor vendor, an elfin woman who did cameo-size paintings of TV personalities, agreed to look after his table while he went to get slices of pizza from Stromboli.

And when he came back he'd sold his first painting! To all his questions about the purchaser his neighbor had no more to say than that she seemed like a very nice lady, was well-dressed, and had carried off her painting (a 10″ × 12″ acrylic on canvasboard notable for the single long brushstroke defining the highlight along the eggplant's flank) in a Balducci bag. Balducci's, his neighbor explained, was where the best eggplants came from in New York City. "Though at this time of year," she went on, "you can get great eggplants at the Green Market. Or almost anywhere..."

It pained him to think that he would never know what was to become of his painting, whether it was hanging in the home of the woman who'd bought it or if it were meant to be a gift. And where would it end up being hung? In someone's kitchen? Or in a hallway, among other paintings? And what would those other paintings look like? Once he fantasized a restauranteur who'd embellished every booth in his establishment with one of Richard's paintings. But he'd never imagined not knowing anything about his paintings' destinations, that they might be sent off into the world like messages in bottles. Yet wouldn't it have been just the same for Matisse or Hopper? And what of the models who'd posed for them? Did they ever wonder, in their old age, what had become of the pictures they'd sat for in the Nirvana of a painter's gaze?

But the possibility that nagged him most annoyingly was what if his neighbor had bought his painting herself just to be nice, just to bolster his morale? And if she had: How would that be any less humbling than what he was doing here all day long, hour after hour, sitting with his begging cup, asking for alms? Wasn't that, finally, the secret meaning of the whole undertaking of art?

His neighbor had finished her slice of pizza and returned to her *Times* crossword. The sidewalk traffic became heavier, and more of those going by seemed to have come on purpose to look at the paintings. There were more nods and remarks of bland approval and even a vivid thumbs-down from a fat black teenage girl who thrust out her huge gut and announced, "Eggplants suck!"

Richard declined to argue. He smiled and tilted his head and she went away with a glare of vindication.

A little later another naysayer appeared less easy to shrug off, a dour squinty-eyed fellow who came to a full stop in front of the triple wall of eggplants, dismissing each in turn with an emphatic shake of his head. "You've got a problem," he told Richard. "A big problem." He waited for Richard to take his bait and ask what his big problem was, but Richard would not oblige.

"You know what it means if you *dream* about eggplants, don't you?"

Richard remained mum.

"What they symbolize?"

"Cancer," said Richard.

His critic looked at him dumbfounded. "What?"

He'd only said it as a form of psychic jiu-jitsu, but now that the word had been uttered, he wondered if there might be some truth in it. There *is* something sinister about an eggplant. Was he exhibiting his own dark cloud of forebodings? Was that what had prompted his unknown patron to plunk down $150 for her own slice of death-wish?

"Well, you sure knew how to take care of that one," said the lady at the next table, folding up her *Times* and slipping it into her tote bag once the fellow had gone away.

"Maybe it's true," said Richard.

"I doubt it. Actually, they're kind of cheerful. Everybody likes pictures of things they like to eat. Did you see the Chardin show at the Met?"

"Oh, for Chardin it was the fur and feathers."

"For sure," she agreed. "No one could do fur better than him. But for eggplants? You got no competition."

"Thank you," said Richard. He couldn't think of a nicer compliment.

In the course of the weekend he sold seven more paintings, but he must have done something to offend his muse, because when he went back to Muncie, the impulse was gone. There was not another painting in him. Up in the attic he had a lifetime supply of Christmas and birthday presents – and not a clue as to what had made him start or what had made him stop.

Art is a mystery.

Three Chronicles of Xglotl and Rwang

1: Martian Madness

THIS WAS the first time Pepsi-Cola Levine had attended the Interplanetary Fashion Theory Conference on Mars, and the first time she had worshipped the super-celebrity and monotheistic goddess Rwang at her shrine in the lounge of the Acidalia Hilton. On the second day of the Conference Pepsi (as most of her beaux and ladyfriends called her) had read the paper she had written for the occasion, "The Ties that Blind," a study of color-coding in costumes designed over the course of seven centuries for productions of Molière's *Don Juan*, Mozart's *Don Giovanni*, and Act 4 of Shaw's *Man and Superman*, with especial reference to the "flame-colored ribbons" that Molière's Sganarelle speaks of his master wearing in Act I, scene 2. Were these ribbons not, Pepsi suggested, a full-frontal reference to the ribbons that would represent the flames rising from the pit of Hell into which the Don is dragged as the curtain falls? Might not these red ribbons be a key to later theatrical representation of libertinage down through the ages?

With this key in her hand Pepsi conducted a slide-show tour through the flames and ribbons of hell, with appropriate audio assists from a pirated recording of Cesare Siepi's "*Fin ch'an del vino!*" from a 1958 production at the Metropolitan Opera, with costumes by Eugene Berman. And such costumes! The audience (of mostly, and most appropriately, remote-controlled mannikins) applauded each slide as though it were a living supermodel taking a turn on the runway.

No one was more appreciative than Rwang Herself, who was attending the conference incognito with her inorganic friend and worshipper Xglotl. She loved academic congresses of all kinds – and pajama parties and bingo halls and anything else that might liven the long Martian nights. She was the least particular of goddesses with respect to partying. Any pretext would serve so long as there were suitable and abundant libations.

"That was such a scrumptious presentation," Rwang gushed to the beautifully preserved Ph.D. afterwards beside her shrine in the hotel lounge. "But such a wicked fellow!"

"Wicked?" Xglotl echoed absent-mindedly. He was as usual doing tax audits with more than half his immense consciousness. "Who's that?"

"Why, Don Giovanni, of course. Or Don Juan, if you prefer."

"Because he had sex? But all humans have sex. Unless they've been neutered in some way." It swiveled one sensor toward Pepsi and flickered a roseate beam of light on her enhanced nipples. "*You're* not neutered, are you?" She shook her head. "No, I didn't suppose so." It returned to its spreadsheets, its due courtesy performed.

"Oh, it wasn't the sex," Rwang declared. "It was the man's atheism. I can't abide atheists."

"Me neither," Pepsi concurred. If the goddess had looked into her heart, she would have known Pepsi was lying and was an atheist herself. But she was also a licensed adventuress and would not gratuitously have contradicted anyone so evidently well-heeled as this monstrously obese masquerader, whose necklace alone might have funded the entire academic congress, if the diamonds weren't paste.

"Have another drink, my dear," the goddess offered, and dinged Pepsi's flute with a gilded fingertip. At once it was refilled with the Hilton's choicest Moët-Chandon.

"However did you do that?" Pepsi marveled.

"She's a goddess," said Xglotl. "Didn't you know?"

"I'd no idea," said Pepsi, without in the least seeming to marvel. In fact, she didn't believe it, and supposed that the fat woman had done some kind of bar trick that depended on the peculiar low gravity of Mars. As an atheist she didn't believe in gods or goddesses, even when she met them in the flesh, as she often did on the outer planets. However, she was quite ready to pretend to believe in the divinity of such beings, if it might prove in some way to her advantage.

Which, on this occasion, it did, for Rwang took a fancy to her in the capricious way gods do and suggested that they go shopping together in the Hilton's mall.

"Should I come, too?" Xglotl asked disconsolately.

"No, my dear, this is strictly a girl thing. But do let us use your discount card."

Obligingly Xglotl emitted a plastic card entitling the user to a percent discount on all purchases, with the exception of items from a long list of independent boutiques. In effect the card was only useful for fragrances and souvenir T-shirts from the Verizon-Disney remainder counter in the basement of the mall, but you had to read the small print to know that. "Have fun," it told them.

And off they went in two comic shopping carts provided by the parking attendant. As they putt-putted along, leaving a wake of astonished stares, Rwang told her new friend that today she would be the teacher and Pepsi the student, and that their subject would be shopping.

"You say you are an adventuress. Well, we shall have an adventure – an adventure in Power-Shopping. You shall purchase such a wardrobe of frills and name-brand bangles and XXX-rated erotica as ever a tourist brought home from Bangkok. Hang left at the next aisle and follow me!"

The goddess's cart took a sharp turn into Aisle 7 – Versace Scarves and Bustiers – and Pepsi's came after, listing alarmingly, for Pepsi, a willowy creature, did not offer her cart much in the way of steadying ballast.

The goddess honked and waved at another cart in the crosswalk ahead. "Jimmy!" she caroled. "Jimmy!"

The man driving the cart braked to a stop, and Pepsi recognized him as Jimmy Balboa, the Brazilian Derridean scheduled to appear on Thursday's Postmodern Hair panel with Pepsi. His beard was a veritable banyan tree among beards, but he was otherwise a conservative dresser. Nothing he wore telegraphed the least datum of his income, and so Pepsi did not give much attention to his brief exchange with Rwang.

Rwang began coyly, "Jimmy, if I were not Myself God Almighty...."

"But you are," Jimmy said, interrupting politely, "and I just adore you."

"Thank you, my dear – " accepting the kiss he pressed on her many-diamonded hand, " – that's very devout of you. You almost make me forget what I was going to say. Oh yes: I thought your paper on thirteenth-century West African hair design was brilliant. I realize you haven't *read* it yet, or published, but one of the few advantages of omniscience is that one does keep up to date, and then some. This is my friend, Pepsi Levine, have you met? Well, now you have. We are out Power-Shopping, so we mustn't keep you any longer. Give my love to all those dear children – how many are there now, twenty-three?"

"Thirty," Professor Balboa said, with a modestly assertive twist of his whiskers. "The last one was unboxed just before I caught the shuttle. A girl: Brioche."

Rwang turned to Pepsi and explained, "All Jimmy's little ones are named for French desserts and pastries, isn't that darling? Tartine, Madeleine, Napoleon, Eclaire, Papillote. It gives a new meaning to 'I could just eat you up!' "

With no more adieux, the goddess gave a farewell honk, loud as a tugboat, and headed on to where a semblance of cascading pearls blinked: ARMANI MARS ARMANI.

"Jimmy," the goddess confided, as they pulled into the Armani parking slot, "is ever so clever, and as nearly omniscient as any mortal can be with a degree from Penn State. No one knows more about Benin hair styling. And such a prolific little paterfamilias (if I say so Myself, Who blessed him with his fecundity): twenty children *before* he got tenure and every single one of them a parthenogenic clone."

"He must be quite well-to-do," Pepsi observed.

"He is fabulously wealthy. His kin are *the* Balboas and own half the Amazon. But all that means nothing to him. He lives for art. His whole life revolves around traditional African hair styles. But enough of all that. Let's shop!"

They shopped for hours – with ever increasing pleasure and recklessness. After Armani, they did all the other boutiques and even, as they exited the mall, picked up an ounce of Martian Madness at the

Verizon-Disney counter in the basement, for which Pepsi Levine did receive a percent discount.

Xglotl, for his part, received a kickback of 25 percent on all of Pepsi's other purchases.

And Rwang got half of that.

She smiled as she ingested the wad of bills. "What I liked about her best," she reminisced, as she let Herself sink into the wallow Xglotl had prepared in the Hilton's spa, "was her enthusiasm as we shopped. Enthusiasm is a religious term, you know. It means that one has 'breathed in' the god. As though we gods were some sort of gas! It's devotion raised to the level of madness. Martian Madness, one might say."

"It'll be raised to another level of madness," Xglotl commented, "when she sees the bill."

"As to that, all the gear she got can be reckoned an investment. She's got her eye on Jimmy. They'll be on a panel together Thursday."

"You're thinking wedding bells? With Jimmy! Lots of luck."

"Stranger things have happened," the goddess said, sliding down into the dark ooze of the wallow. Bubbles rose about her immense girth.

"You haven't predestined anything, have you, Divine Rwang?"

"I know what I know," said Rwang, as she submerged. "And I am that I am."

Jimmy and Pepsi were wed on the very Thursday night of their panel in the Hilton's All-Faith Chapel. Napoleon was their ring-bearer, and little Tartine the maid of honor. And they and all the bridegroom's other clones were coifed to perfection.

2: Bingo Night at a Martian Sportsbar

"Big bang, my ass!" grumbled the omnipotent goddess Rwang over her third tall schooner of May wine. "*I* created this entire damn universe and don't you ever forget it."

"Never," Xglotl assured her, "ever." Xglotl, already well lubricated, was running an old-fashioned spreadsheet with half its mind and playing four bingo cards with the other. "This is a lovely universe, I've always thought so, and it's obvious that it had to be created by a god no less lovely. Or goddess. It only stands to reason."

Rwang glowered at the servile mechanism suspiciously. She knew she was being flattered, but was it from piety or same baser motive? With Xglotl she never could tell. "Something like this doesn't just *happen*," she insisted.

"Of course not," said Xglotl, stroking her Medusa hair with one of its extensors. The hair gradually relaxed. "That's quite unthinkable. Any theologian would agree."

The robart slid down the bar towards them. "There's more where that came from," he told Rwang, squirting the May wine unbidden into her willing maw, then refilling the schooner. "How about those Mets then!"

"Oh yes," Rwang concurred with an absent-minded trembling of her chins. "They are something all right. Three in one!"

"Hey!" said the robart. It slid away, job done.

"What in the world was that supposed to mean: three in one?"

"Almost anything you want it to, my little tin can. It could be a vitamin supplement. Or the Holy Trinity, if you're into theology, which I'm not. Or sportstalk."

"Oh, I hate sportstalk. It's so pointless."

"And spreadsheets?" the goddess asked. "*They* have a point?"

"If you want your books to balance at tax time, they certainly do. Anyhow, spreadsheets are fun. Oh, look at that: N-36! If it had been N-35, I'd have had a bingo."

"Don't change the subject," Rwang ordained. "Sportstalk is essential to the entire social fabric. It's all that allows lower-class men and upper-class men to live on the same planet. They can ignore their economic and erotic differences and spend two or three minutes ritually bonding."

"Oh, spare me." Xglotl strobed derisively. "It's all just vector quantities at the lowest level of stimulus and response. How could any modern machine possibly take an interest in inserting sphere A in hole A? In slow motion!"

"You enjoy counterpoint," Rwang noted. "And ancient plastics. And sonnets."

"I *collect* ancient plastics. And for their ingenuous charm, *not* their chemical complexity. I would never collect modern plastics."

Another robart whizzed along the bar dispensing free samples of Falstaff, the new virtual hallucinogen from the Verizon-Disney distillery. "Try this why don't you," it said with each whoosh of its atomizer. Then, like an animate box of Wheaties, the robart added a sports datum. "Did you know that Conan Brinks of the Chicago Felons was genetically a mouse? That's right, he looked like a man and pitched like a man but all his DNA was actually derived from an ordinary laboratory mouse! Think about that!"

"I didn't know that, did you?" said Xglotl.

"I know everything," said Rwang. "That's what it means to be omniscient."

"O-66," announced the bingo caller on the screen above the bar. One of Xglotl's cards lit up to indicate a hit, but it was a solitaire with no other score in the same row or column.

"I used to have a whole congregation of worshipers like that," Rwang said in a nostalgic tone. "They were cloned from mouse DNA. Right here on Mars. That kind of bio-engineering wasn't legal on Earth back then. Droll little creatures. All dwarves, all male, and fanatical as Anabaptists. Regrettably, they tended to die in their teens. I told them they'd all go to Valhalla." She puckered with amusement, then sighed. "I wonder what ever became of them."

"I thought you were omniscient, Rwang, my adorable one."

"You doubt it? I'll tell you the number of the next ping-pong ball that Episcopal haploid is going to pick from the hopper. It will be B-5."

The caller reached into the hopper, caught a ball and held it up to the camera. "B-5," she announced.

Someone at one of the tables beyond the aquarium room divider called out "Bingo!" and there was a short, celebratory twinkling of the bingo's system's lights. Then the winning bingo card's winning column was showcased on all the screens in the bar.

"Damn it," said Xglotl, "I really thought I was going to win that time.

Rwang didn't say a word. She knew that Xglotl would never win a game of bingo, not if he played eight cards at a time till the bar went bankrupt in the year 3011, Common Era. Such was her everlasting and unalterable decree, but she would never have revealed that to Xglotl. She was a cruel goddess, but she wasn't stupid. If you want to be worshipped you have to extend some kind of hope.

3: The Flaneurs of Mars

"I love them all quite dearly," Xglotl declared tipsily, "old and young, male and female, the right-handed *and* the lefties equally. But I shall never – " It siphoned up the last of the lubricant. " – *never* understand them."

"Because they eat meat?" Rwang wondered, glancing up from her plate of cherried vermin. "How hypocritical! *You* think nothing of snacking on *their* embryos, even though you credit them with rational thought."

"Well, it all depends on your definition of 'rational,' Rwang, my sweet. They can build complex machines, I'll give you that. Their kilns and ovens and oasts are quite wonderful, and I will be shipping back several to my compeers in Red Sands. They collect objets d'Earth of that sort."

"Really. I've a small trove of nuclear warheads tucked away somewhere near Irkutsk. Do you think they'd be interested in those?"

"No, they prefer homelier artifacts. And movies with Grace Kelly. They adore Grace Kelly, don't ask me why."

"I won't. Go back, please, to the issue you're avoiding – what it is you don't understand about them, if it's not that they are carnivores."

Xglotl decanted more of the lubricant into his oilcan. "Their religious beliefs."

"But, Xglotl, you're a machine. You can't understand anyone's religious beliefs, whatever planet they may come from."

"Oh, I understand *yours* well enough. You think you're God. It's a very simple faith."

"It suffices to my needs, and that's all a religion has to do."

"Let us begin there then, with regard to the Earthlings and their needs. In the Greco-Roman culture, as it evolved over time, religious faith came ever more to resemble poetic license. Zeus and Hera were a sit-com couple, like Homer and Marge Simpson. Their execution might be of a superior order, the work of a Phidias or a Praxiteles, but their psychology was rudimentary. He was the philandering paterfamilias, she the nagging and vengeful stay-at-home mom."

"Just like the people who worshiped them. People *want* to worship beings just like themselves. It is a universal truth."

"I'll grant that, but I can see no evolutionary advantage in delusions of omnipotence. All those stories about parting the Red Sea and bringing down the walls of Jericho – it's wish fulfillment."

"No, it's the power of prayer. When people pray to me (and I choose to hear them), sometimes I answer their prayers. As in those cases you mention."

Xglotl emitted a subdued strobe of skepticism and continued as though it hadn't heard Rwang's nonsense: "To me religious faith is like children believing they can fly if they wear a bath towel for a cape. And those who act on such a misguided faith will suffer for it."

Rwang used her little paper umbrella to spear one of the cherries decorating the wriggling mice. "Well, *one* evolutionary advantage would be the placebo effect. People of faith recover more quickly from disease. There seems to be some link to the immune system. But the basic reason, I'm sure, is that they're happier. Just as *I* am happier from knowing that I'm God."

"But *everyone* can't be God."

"Indeed no," Rwang agreed quickly. "And a good thing, too! Even several gods in one family is a recipe for trouble. Fortunately I'm an orphan, unmarried, and without friends, except for a few servile mechanisms like yourself, whom I created. I'm ideally suited, therefore, to be the deity of a monotheistic religion."

"You know, don't you, that I consider you delusional?"

"You're entitled to. You have free will – as much as any mere machine may be said to have free will." Rwang popped one of the larger mice into her immense maw. "Also, there's this, which... Mmm, so savory! There is the need for love. As much as we need nourishment we need love. Even machines need to feel there is some Thing that loves them."

"Not that I'm aware," Xglotl said with a supercilious swiveling of its antennae.

"To be unaware of one's need for love is almost as common as the need itself. Oh, that's rather good, isn't it? I think I'll jot it down." Rwang disgorged a pocket notepad and typed a quick memorandum to Herself.

"I can understand such a need in mammals," Xglotl conceded. "It would be an extension of their dependency on the maternal flow of blood while in the womb, and their later reliance on the mother as a source of milk."

Rwang's bosom heaved responsively.

"But just because one has an atavistic hunger for milk – " Xglotl's syphon made a slurping sound in its oilcan. " – cannot be a good reason for believing in – "

"In what, Xglotl? Speak up."

Rwang was sitting facing away from the entrance. She had not seen the crouched panthers materialize beneath the hanging ferns, the grape clusters spilling down the colored glass front of the slot machine. She did not catch the sharp scent of olibanum. She did not see the bartender metamorphose into a fish, his dandruff changing, flake by flake to silvery scales, nor did she witness the cocktail waitress shrink into a lynx and leap onto the bar in a single bound to lick the winestains from its mirrored surface.

She did not see the god Bacchus smile and, as briefly as he'd smiled, vanish.

"But perhaps," said Xglotl, not unastonished, "perhaps I am wrong. Perhaps there is something I've left out of my equations."

"Do you mean to say that you are actually letting me *win* an argument!" Rwang exulted.

"Mm," said Xglotl. "If you pick up the tab."

In Xanadu

Part One

XANADU

His awareness was quite limited during the first so-long. A pop-up screen said WELCOME TO XANADU, [Cook, Fran]. YOUR AFTERLIFE BEGINS NOW! BROUGHT TO YOU BY DISNEY-MITSUBISHI PRODUCTIONS OF QUEBEC! A VOTRE SANTE TOUJOURS! Then there was a choice of buttons to click on, OKAY or CANCEL. He didn't have an actual physical mouse, but there was an equivalent in his mind, in much the way that amputees have ghostly limbs, but when he clicked on OKAY with his mental mouse there was a dull *Dong!* and nothing happened. When he clicked on CANCEL there was a trembling and the smallest flicker of darkness and then the pop-up screen greeted him with the original message.

This went on for an unknowable amount of time, there being no means by which elapsed time could be measured. After he'd *Dong!*ed on OKAY enough times, he stopped bothering. The part of him that would have been motivated, back when, to express impatience or to feel resentment or to worry just wasn't connected. He felt an almost supernatural passivity. Maybe this is what people were after when they took up meditation. Or maybe it *was* supernatural, though it seemed more likely, from the few clues he'd been given, that it was cybernetic in some way.

He had become lodged (he theorized) in a faulty software program, like a monad in a game of JezzBall banging around inside its little square cage, ricocheting off the same four points on the same four walls forever. Or as they say in Quebec, *toujours.*

And oddly enough that was okay. If he were just a molecule bouncing about, a lifer rattling his bars, there was a kind of comfort in doing so, each bounce a proof of the mass and motion of the molecule, each rattle an SOS despatched to someone who might think, Ah-ha, there's someone there!

STATE PLEASURE DOME 1

And then – or, as it might be, once upon a time – CANCEL produced a different result than it had on countless earlier trials, and he found himself back in some kind of real world. There was theme music ("Wichita Lineman") and scudding clouds high overhead and the smell of leaf-mold, as though he'd been doing push-ups out behind the garage, with his nose grazing the dirt. He had his old body back, and it seemed reasonably trim. Better than he'd left it, certainly.

"Welcome," said his new neighbor, a blonde woman in a blouse of blue polka dots on a silvery rayon-like ground. "My name is Debora. You must be Fran Cook. We've been expecting you."

He suspected that Debora was a construct of some sort, and it occurred to him that he might be another. But whatever she was, she seemed to expect a response from him beyond his stare of mild surmise.

"You'll have to fill me in a little more, Debora. I don't really know where we are."

"This is Xanadu," she said with a smile that literally flashed, like the light on top of a police car, with distinct, pointed sparkles.

"But does Xanadu exist anywhere except in the poem?"

This yielded a blank look but then another dazzling smile. "You could ask the same of us."

"Okay. To be blunt: am I dead? Are you?"

Her smile diminished, as though connected to a rheostat. "I think that might be the case, but I don't know for sure. There's a sign at the entrance to the pleasure dome that says Welcome to Eternity. But there's no one to ask, there or anywhere else. No one who knows anything. Different people have different ideas. I don't have any recollection of dying, myself. Do you?"

"I have no recollections, period," he admitted. "Or none that occur to me at this moment. Maybe if I tried to remember something in particular..."

"It's the same with me. I can remember the plots of a few movies. And the odd quotation. 'We have nothing to fear but fear itself.'"

"Eisenhower?" he hazarded.

"I guess. It's all pretty fuzzy. Maybe I just wasn't paying attention back then. Or it gets erased when you come here. I think there's a myth to that effect. Or maybe it's so blurry because it never happened in the first place. Which makes me wonder: are we really people here, or what? And where is here? This isn't anyone's idea of heaven that *I* ever heard of. It's kind of like Disney World, only there's no food, no rides, no movies. Nothing to do, really. You can meet people, talk to them, like with us, but that's about it. Don't think I'm complaining. They don't call it a pleasure dome for nothing. That part's okay, though it's not any big deal. More like those Magic Finger beds in old motels."

He knew just what she meant, though he couldn't remember ever having been to an old motel or lain down on a Magic Fingers bed. When he tried to reach for a memory of his earlier life, any detail he could use as an ID tag, it was like drawing a blank to a clue in a crossword. Some very simple word that just wouldn't come into focus.

Then there was a fade to black and a final, abject *Dong!* which didn't leave time for a single further thought.

ALPH

"I'm sorry," Debora said, with a silvery shimmer of rayon, "that was my fault for having doubted. Doubt's the last thing either of us needs right now. I *love* the little dimple in your chin."

"I'm not aware that I *had* a dimple in my chin."

"Well, you do now, and it's right – " She traced a line up the center of his chin with her finger, digging into the flesh with the enameled tip as it reached, " – here."

"Was I conked out long?"

She flipped her hair as though to rid herself of a fly, and smiled in a forgiving way, and placed her hand atop his. At that touch he felt a strange lassitude steal over him, a deep calm tinged somehow with mirth, as though he'd remembered some sweet, dumb joke from his vanished childhood. Not the joke itself but the laughter that had greeted it, the laughter of children captured on a home video, silvery and chill.

"If we suppose," she said thoughtfully, tracing the line of a vein on the back of his hand with her red fingertip, "that our senses *can* deceive us, then what is there that *can't?*" She raised her eyebrows italic-wise. "I mean," she insisted, "my body might be an illusion, and the world I *think* surrounds me might be another. But what of that 'I think'? The very act of doubting is a proof of existence, right? I think therefore I am."

"Descartes," he footnoted.

She nodded. "And who would ever have supposed that that old doorstop would be relevant to real life, so-called? Except I think it would be just as true with any other verb: I *love* therefore I am."

"Why not?" he agreed.

She squirmed closer to him until she could let the weight of her upper body rest on his, as he lay there sprawled on the lawn, or the illusion of a lawn. The theme music had segued, unnoticed, to a sinuous rill of clarinets and viola that might have served for the orchestration of a Strauss opera, and the landscape was its visual correlative, a perfect Puvis de Chavannes – the same chalky pastels in thick impasto blocks and splotches, but never with too painterly panache. There were no visible brushstrokes. The only tactile element was the light pressure of her fingers across his skin, making each least hair in its follicle an antenna to register pleasure.

A pleasure that need never, could never cloy, a temperate pleasure suited to its pastoral source, a woodwind pleasure, a fruity wine. Lavender, canary yellow. The green of distant mountains. The ripple of the river.

CAVERNS MEASURELESS TO MAN

The water that buoyed the little skiff was luminescent, and so their progress through the cave was not a matter of mere conjecture or kinesthesia. They could see where they were going. Even so, their speed could only be guessed at, for the water's inward light was not enough to illumine either the ice high overhead or either shore of the river. They were borne along into some more unfathomable darkness far ahead as though across an ideal frictionless plane, and it made him think of spaceships doing the same thing, or of his favorite screen-saver, which simulated the white swirl-by of snowflakes when driving through a blizzard. One is reduced at such moments (he was now) to an elemental condition, as near to being a particle in physics as a clumsy, complex mammal will ever come.

"I shall call you Dynamo," she confided in a throaty whisper. "Would you like that as a nickname? The Dynamo of Xanadu."

"You're too kind," he said unthinkingly. He had become careless in their conversations. Not a conjugal carelessness: he had not talked with her so very often that all her riffs and vamps were second nature to him. This was the plain unadorned carelessness of not caring.

"I used to think," she said, "that we were all heading for hell in a handbasket. Is that how the saying goes?"

"Meaning, hastening to extinction?"

"Yes, meaning that. It wasn't my *original* idea. I guess everyone has their own vision of the end. Some people take it straight from the Bible, which is sweet and pastoral, but maybe a little dumb, though one oughtn't to say so, not where they are likely to overhear you. Because is that really so different from worrying about the hole in the ozone layer? That was my apocalypse of choice, how we'd all get terrible sunburns and cancer, and then the sea-level would rise, and everyone in Calcutta would drown."

"You think this is Calcutta?"

"Can't you ever be serious?"

"So, what's your point, Debora?" When he wanted to be nice, he would use her name, but she never used his. She would invent nicknames for him, and then forget them and have to invent others.

It was thanks to such idiosyncrasies that he'd come to believe in her objective existence as something other than his mental mirror. If she were no more than the forest pool in which Narcissus gazed adoringly, their minds would malfunction in similar ways. Were they mere mirror constructs, he would have known by now.

"It's not," she went on, "that I worry that the end is near. I suppose the end is always near. Relative to Eternity. And it's not that I'm terribly curious *how* it will end. I suppose we'll hurtle over the edge of some immense waterfall, like Columbus and his crew."

"Listen!" he said, breaking in. "Do you hear that?"

"Hear what?"

"The music. It's the score for *Koyaanisqatsi.* God, I used to watch the tape of that over and over."

She gave a sigh of polite disapproval. "I can't bear Philip Glass. It's just as you say, the same thing over and over."

"There was this one incredible pan. It must have been taken by a helicopter flying above this endless high-rise apartment complex. But it had been abandoned."

"And?" she insisted. "What is your point?"

"Well, it was no simulation. The movie was made before computers could turn any single image into some endless quilt. We were really seeing this vast deserted housing project, high-rise after high-rise with the windows boarded up. The abandoned ruins of some ultra-modern city. It existed, but until that movie nobody *knew* about it. It makes you think."

"It doesn't make *me* think."

There was no way, at this moment, they were going to have sex. Anyhow, it probably wouldn't have been safe. The boat would capsize and they would drown.

A SUNLESS SEA

It was as though the whole beach received its light from a few candles. A dim, dim light evenly diffused, and a breeze wafting up from the water with an unrelenting coolness, as at some theater where the air conditioning cannot be turned off. They huddled within the cocoon of a single beach towel, thighs pressed together, arms criss-crossed behind their backs in a chaste hug, trying to keep warm. The chill in the air was the first less-than-agreeable physical sensation he'd known in Xanadu, but it did not impart that zip of challenge that comes with October weather. Rather, it suggested his own mortal diminishment. A plug had been pulled somewhere, and all forms of radiant energy were dwindling synchronously, light, warmth, intelligence, desire.

There were tears on Debora's cheek, and little sculptures of sea-foam in the shingle about them. And very faint, the scent of nutmeg, the last lingering trace of some long-ago lotion or deodorant.

The ocean gray as aluminum.

THE WAILING

Here were the high-rises from the movie, but in twilight now, and without musical accompaniment, though no less portentous for that. He glided past empty benches and leaf-strewn flower-beds like a cameraman on roller-skates, until he entered one of the buildings, passing immaterially through its plate-glass door. Then there was, in a slower pan than the helicopter's but rhyming to it, a smooth iambic progression past the doors along the first-floor corridor.

He came to a stop before the tenth door, which stood ajar. Within he could hear a stifled sobbing – a wailing, rather. He knew he was expected to go inside, to discover the source of this sorrow. But he could not summon the will to do so. Wasn't his own sorrow sufficient? Wasn't the loss of a world enough?

A man appeared at the end of the corridor in the brown uniform of United Parcel Service. His footsteps were inaudible as he approached.

"I have a delivery for [Cook, Fran]," the UPS man announced, holding out a white envelope.

At the same time he was offered, once again, the familiar, forlorn choice between OKAY and CANCEL.

He clicked on CANCEL. There was a trembling, and the smallest flicker of darkness, but then the corridor reasserted itself, and the wailing behind the door. The UPS man was gone, but the envelope remained in his hand. It bore the return address in Quebec of Disney-Mitsubishi.

There was no longer a CANCEL to click on. He had to read the letter.

Dear [Name]:

The staff and management of Xanadu International regret to inform you that as of [date] *all services in connection with your contract* [Number] *will be canceled due to new restrictions in the creation and maintenance of posthumous intelligence. We hope that we will be able to resolve all out-*

standing differences with the government of Quebec and restore the services contracted for by the heirs of your estate, but in the absence of other communications you must expect the imminent closure of your account. It has been a pleasure to serve you. We hope you have enjoyed your time in Xanadu.

The law of the sovereign state of Quebec requires us to advise you that in terminating this contract we are not implying any alteration in the spiritual condition of [Name] *or of his immortal soul. The services of Xanadu International are to be considered an esthetic product offered for entertainment purposes only.*

When he had read it, the words of the letter slowly faded from the page, like the smile of the Cheshire cat.

The wailing behind the door had stopped, but he still stood in the empty corridor, scarcely daring to breathe. Any moment, he thought, might be his last. In an eyeblink the world might cease.

But it didn't. If anything the world seemed solider than heretofore. People who have had a brush with death often report the same sensation.

He reversed his path along the corridor, wondering if anyone lived behind any of them, or if they were just a facade, a Potemkin corridor in a high-rise in the realm of faery.

As though to answer his question Debora was waiting for him when he went outside. She was wearing a stylishly tailored suit in a kind of brown tweed, and her hair was swept up in a way that made her look like a French movie star of the 1940s.

As they kissed the orchestra re-introduced their love theme. The music swelled. The world came to an end.

Part Two

XANADU

But then, just the way that the movie will start all over again after The End, if you just stay in your seat, or even if you go out to the lobby for more popcorn, he found himself back at the beginning, with the same pop-up screen welcoming him to Xanadu and then a choice of OKAY or CANCEL. But there was also, this time, a further choice: a blue banner that pulsed at the upper edge of consciousness and asked him if he wanted expanded memory and quicker responses. He most definitely did, so with his mental mouse he accepted the terms being offered without bothering to scroll through them.

He checked off a series of YES-es and CONTINUE-s, and so, without his knowing it, he had become, by the time he was off the greased slide, a citizen of the sovereign state of Quebec, an employee of Disney-Mitsubishi Temps E-Gal, and – cruelest of his new disadvantages – a girl.

A face glimmered before him in the blue gloaming. At first he thought it might be Debora, for it had the same tentative reality that she did, like a character at the beginning of some old French movie about railroads and murderers, who may be the star or only an extra on hand to show that this is a world with people in it. It was still too early in the movie to tell. Only as he turned sideways did he realize (the sound track made a samisen-like *Twang!* of recognition) that he had been looking in a mirror, and that the face that had been coalescing before him – the rouged cheeks, the plump lips, the fake lashes, the mournful gaze – had been his own! Or rather, now, her own.

As so many other women had realized at a similar point in their lives, it was already too late and nothing could be done to correct the mistake that Fate, and Disney-Mitsubishi, had made. Maybe he'd always been a woman. [Cook, Fran] was a sexually ambiguous name. Perhaps his earlier assumption that he was male was simply a function of thinking in English, where *one* may be mistaken about *his* own identity (but not about hers). I think; therefore I am a guy.

He searched through his expanded memory for some convincing evidence of his gender history. Correction: *her* gender history. Herstory, as feminists would have it. Oh dear, would he be one of *them* now, always thinking in italics, a grievance committee of one in perpetual session?

But look on the bright side (she told herself). There might be advantages in such a change of address. Multiple orgasms. Nicer clothes (though she couldn't remember ever wanting to dress like a woman when she was a man). Someone else paying for dinner, assuming that the protocols of hospitality still worked the same way here in Xanadu as they had back in reality. This was supposed to be heaven and already she was feeling nostalgic for a life she couldn't remember, an identity she had shed.

Then the loudspeaker above her head emitted a dull *Dong!* and she woke up in the Women's Dormitory of State Pleasure Dome 2.

"All right, girls!" said the amplified voice of the matron. "Time to rise and shine. *Le temps s'en va, mesdames, le temps s'en va.*"

STATE PLEASURE DOME 2

"*La vie,*" philosophized Chantal, "*est un maladie dont le sommeil nous soulage toutes les seize heures. C'est un palliatif. La Mort est un rémédie.*" She flicked the drooping ash from the end of her cigarette and made a moue of chic despair. Fran could understand what she'd said quite as well as if she'd been speaking English: Life is a disease from which sleep offers relief every sixteen hours. Sleep is a palliative – death a remedy.

They were sitting before big empty cups of *café au lait* in the employee lounge, dressed in their black e-Gal minis, crisp white aprons, and fish-net hose. Fran felt a positive fever of chagrin to be seen in such a costume, but she felt no otherwise, really, about her entire female body, especially the breasts bulging out of their casings, breasts that quivered visibly at her least motion. It was like wearing a T-shirt with some dumb innuendo on it, or a blatant sexual invitation. Did every girl have to go through the same torment of shame at puberty? Was there any way to get over it except to get into it?

"*Mon bonheur,*" declared Chantal earnestly, "*est d'augmenter celui des autres.*" Her happiness lay in increasing that of others. A doubtful proposition in most circumstances, but not perhaps for Chantal, who, as an e-Gal was part geisha, part rock-star, and part a working theorem in moral calculus, an embodiment of Frances Hutcheson's notion that that action is best which procures the greatest happiness for the greatest numbers. There were times – Thursdays, in the early evening – when Chantal's bedside/web-site was frequented by as many as two thousand admirers, their orgasms all blissfully synchronized with the reels and ditties she performed on her dulcimer, sometimes assisted by Fran (an apprentice in the art) but usually all on her own. At such times (she'd confided to Fran) she felt as she imagined a great conductor must feel conducting some choral extravaganza, the *Missa Solemnis* or the Ninth Symphony.

Except that the dulcimer gave the whole thing a tinge and twang of hillbilly, as of Tammy Wynette singing "I'm just a geisha from the bayou." Of course, the actual Tammy Wynette had died ages ago and could only sing that song in simulation, but still it was hard to imagine it engineered with any other voiceprint: habit makes the things we love seem inevitable as arithmetic.

"*Encore?*" Chantal asked, lifting her empty cup, and then, when Fran had nodded yes, signaling to the waiter.

Coffee, cigarettes, a song on the jukebox. Simple pleasures, but doubled and quadrupled and raised to some astronomical power, the stuff that industries and gross national products are made of. Fran imagined a long reverse zoom away from their table at the cafe, away from the swarming hive of the city, to where each soul and automobile was a mere pixel on the vast monitor of eternity.

The coffees came and Chantal began to sing, "*Le bonheur de la femme n'est pas dans la liberté, mais dans l'acceptation d'un devoir.*"

A woman's happiness lies not in liberty, but in the acceptance of a duty.

And what was that duty? Fran wondered. What could it be but love?

IN A VISION ONCE I SAW

There were no mirrors in Xanadu, and yet every vista seemed to be framed as by those tinted looking glasses of the 18th century that turned everything into a Claude Lorrain. Look too long or too closely into someone else's face and it became your own. Chantal would tilt her head back, a flower bending to the breeze, and she would morph into Fran's friend of his earlier afterlife, Debora. Debora, whose hand had caressed his vanished sex, whose wit had entertained him with Cartesian doubts.

They were the captives (it was explained, when Fran summoned HELP) of pirates, and must yield to the desires of their captors in all things. That they were in the thrall of copyright pirates, not authentic old-fashioned buccaneers, was an epistemological quibble. Subjectively their captors could exercise the same cruel authority as any Captain Kidd or Hannibal Lector. Toes and nipples don't know the difference between a knife and an algorithm. Pirates of whatever sort are in charge of pain and its delivery, and that reduces all history, all consciousness, to a simple system of pluses and minuses, do's and don't's. Suck my dick or walk the plank. That (the terrible simplicity) was the downside of living in a pleasure dome.

"Though, if you think about it," said Debora, with her hand resting atop the strings of her dulcimer, as though it might otherwise interrupt what she had to say, "every polity is ultimately based upon some calculus of pleasure, of apportioning rapture and meting out pain. The jukebox and the slot machine, what are they but emblems of the Pavlovian bargain we all must make with that great dealer high in the sky?" She lifted a little silver hammer and bonked her dulcimer a triple bonk of do-sol-do.

"The uncanny thing is how easily we can be programmed to regard mere symbols—" Another do-sol-do. "—as rewards. A bell is rung somewhere, and something within us resonates. And music becomes one of the necessities of life. Even such a life as this, an ersatz afterlife."

"Is there some way to escape?" Fran asked.

Debora gave an almost imperceptible shrug, which her dulcimer responded to as though she were a breeze and it a wind-chime hanging from the kitchen ceiling. "There are rumors of escapees – e-Men, as they're called. But no one *I've* ever known has escaped, or at least they've never spoken of it. Perhaps they do, and get caught, and then the memory of having done so is blotted out. Our memories are not exactly ours to command, are they?"

The dulcimer hyperventilated.

Debora silenced it with a glance, and continued: "Some days I'll flash on some long-ago golden oldie chart, and a whole bygone existence will come flooding back. A whole one-pound box of madeleines and I will be absolutely convinced by it that I *did* have a life once upon a time, where there were coffee breaks with doughnuts bought at actual bakeries and rain that made the pavements speckled and a whole immense sensorium, always in flux, which I can only remember now in involuntary blips of recall. And maybe it really was like that once, how can we know, but whether we could get back to it, that I somehow can't believe."

"I've tried to think what it would be like to be back there, where we got started." Fran gazed into the misty distance, as though her earlier life might be seen there, as in an old home video. "But it's like trying to imagine what it would be like in the Thirteenth Century, when people all believed in miracles and stuff. It's beyond me."

"Don't you believe in miracles, then?" The dulcimer twanged a twang of simple faith. "I do. I just don't suppose they're for us. Miracles are for people who pay full price. For us there's just Basic Tier programming – eternal time and infinite space."

"And those may be no more than special effects."

Debora nodded. "But even so..."

"Even so?" Fran prompted.

"Even so," said Debora, with the saddest of smiles, a virtual flag of surrender, "if I were you, I would try and escape."

THOSE CAVES OF ICE!

eBay was a lonely place, as holy and enchanted as some underwater cathedral in the poem of a French symbolist, or a German forest late at night. If you have worked at night as a security guard for the Mall of America, or if you've seen Simone Simone in *Cat People* as she walks beside the pool (only her footsteps audible, her footsteps and the water's plash), only then can you imagine its darkling beauty, the change that comes over the objects of our desire when they are flensed of their purveyors and consumers and stand in mute array, aisle after aisle. Then you might sweep the beam of your flashlight across the waters of the recirculating fountain as they perpetually spill over the granite brim. No silence is so large as that where Muzak played, but plays no more.

Imagine such a place, and then imagine discovering an exit that announces itself in the darkness by a dim red light and opening the door to discover a Piranesian vista of a further mall, no less immense, its tiers linked by purring escalators, the leaves of its potted trees shimmering several levels beneath where you are, and twinkling in the immensity, the signs of the stores – every franchise an entrepreneur might lease. Armani and Osh-Kosh, Hallmark, Kodak, Disney-Mitsubishi, American Motors, Schwab. A landscape all of names, and yet if you click on any name you may enter its portal to discover its own little infinity of choices. Shirts of all sizes, colors, patterns, prices; shirts that were sold, yesterday, to someone in Iowa; other shirts that may be sold tomorrow, or may never find a taker. Every atom and molecule in the financial continuum of purchases that might be made has here been numbered and catalogued. Here, surely, if anywhere, one might become if not invisible then scarcely noticed, as in some great metropolis swarming with illegal aliens, among whom a single further citizen can matter not a jot.

Fran became a mote in that vastness, a pip, an alga, unaware of his own frenetic motion as the flow of data took him from one possible purchase to the next. Here was a CD of Hugo Wolf lieder sung by Elly Ameling. Here a pair of Lucchese cowboy boots only slightly worn with western heels. Here six interesting Japanese dinner plates and a hand-embroidered black kimono. This charming pig creamer has an adorable French hat and is only slightly chipped. These Viking sweatshirts still have their tags from Wal-Mart, $29.95. Sabatier knives, set of 4. 1948 First Edition of *The Secret of the Old House*. Hawaiian Barbie with hula accessories. "Elly Ameling Singt Schumann!" Assorted rustic napkins from Amish country.

There is nothing that is not a thought away, nothing that cannot be summoned by a wink and a nod to any of a dozen search engines. But there is a price to pay for such accessibility. The price is sleep, and in that sleep we buy again those commodities we bought or failed to buy before. No price is too steep, and no desire too low. Cream will flow through the slightly chipped lips of the charming pig creamer in the adorable hat, and our feet will slip into the boots we had no use for earlier. And when we return from our night journeys, like refugees returning to the shells of their burned homes, we find we are where we were, back at Square One. The matron was bellowing over the P/A, "*Le temps s'en va, mesdames! Le temps s'en va!*" and Fran wanted to die.

GRAIN BENEATH THE THRESHER'S FLAIL

She was growing old in the service of the Khan, but there was no advantage to be reaped from long service, thanks to the contract she'd signed back when. She had become as adept with the hammers of the dulcimer as ever Chantal had been (Chantal was gone now, no one knew whither), but in truth the dulcimer is not an instrument that requires great skill – and its rewards are proportional. She felt as though she'd devoted her life – her afterlife – to the game of Parcheesi, shaking the dice and moving her tokens round the board for ever. Surely this was not what the prospectus promised those who signed on.

She knew, in theory (which she'd heard, in various forms, from other denizens), that the great desideratum here, the magnet that drew all its custom, was beauty, the rapture of beauty that poets find in writing poetry or composers in their music. It might not be the Beatific Vision that saints feel face to face with God, but it was, in theory, the next best thing, a bliss beyond compare. And perhaps it was all one could hope for. How could she be sure that this bliss or that, as it shivered through her, like a wind through Daphne's leaves, wasn't of the same intensity that had zapped the major romantic poets in their day?

In any case, there was no escaping it. She'd tried to find an exit that didn't, each day, become the entrance by which she returned to her contracted afterlife and her service as a damsel with a dulcimer. Twang! twang! *O ciel! O belle nuit!* Not that she had any notion of some higher destiny for herself, or sweeter pleasures – except the one that all the poets agreed on: Lethe, darkness, death, and by death to say we end the humdrum daily continuation of all our yesterdays into all our tomorrows.

The thought of it filled her with a holy dread, and she took up the silver hammers of her dulcimer and began, once again, to play such music as never mortal knew before.

Torah! Torah! Torah!: Three Bible Tales for the Third Millennium

I

The Naming of the Birds

BEFORE the world began there were very few words, and for a good reason. There was nothing to look at, nothing to listen to, nothing to talk about.

Gradually things improved. God created light, so you could see what was there beyond the darkness on the face of the deep.

The light was called Day and the darkness, which was now limited to the hours after six o'clock, was called Night.

Once there was some light it became obvious just how big a mess the universe was in, with no clear distinction between up and down, or left and right. The sky and the sea and the land were all jumbled up in one big smoosh. God, who is basically very neat, didn't like that at all, so he untangled it into separate areas of sky, where there would be room for the sun and the moon and the stars, water, and land. Things started to make sense after that.

Then God filled the oceans and rivers and other bodies of water with all kinds of fish, including whales, although whales aren't fish, strictly speaking, but mammals like us. And he made birds to fly around in the sky.

Then came the animals, lots of them, more than you'll ever see in any zoo. Most of the animals had legs, but there were some without, and all of them – the fish, the birds, the animals – were able to make more creatures just like themselves, which is what God had told them to do: Multiply.

So all the animals paired up. Each pair of two animals multiplied themselves, so then there were four, and those four multiplied themselves, and there were eight, because two times four is eight, and so on, until in a very short time – a short time back then might be millions of years – all the continents and islands and peninsulas were filled with animals, and likewise the oceans and lakes with fish, and the air with birds.

Millions and billions of them all over the place – and none of them had names!

Not just personal names, such as your dog or cat might have – Browny, or Princess, or Catamaran – but the basic name that explains what kind of animal each one is, like dog or cat or rhinoceros. You couldn't point at a cow out in the field and say, "Look at that cow," because the word "cow," which *we* all take for granted, just didn't exist.

For the animals themselves that might not have mattered so much, since animals don't talk to each other, except with snarls and barks and whines, and fish are even less given to conversation, except for whales, who *do* talk to each other and who, unlike everyone else in the ocean, did have their own name. They were whales right from the start, and so an exception to the rule and not really part of this story.

But the birds didn't have names, and birds can be very talkative, so they *wanted* names. Nice names that would set one flock apart from the others. Names they could preen like their feathers. Names that would make someone stop and think and maybe smile and feel friendly toward the bird that bore such a sweet name. And also, thinking ahead (for birds, because they can fly, often see into the future), names that might be used at some later time in a poem or a song. For just the way that flowers love to be in pictures, birds love to be in songs.

Having foreseen the possibility of poetry, the birds were not altogether surprised when God formed Adam out of the dust of the earth and breathed some life into him. He was a person, and it would be people like him who would some day write the poems the birds might appear in.

Because he was the first human being ever, Adam didn't have to go to school. He was born a grown-up, with no one to tell him when to get up or go to bed, or what to eat for breakfast or dinner, except for one kind of fruit that he had to avoid. But that is a story all on its own, which we won't go into here. This story is about how Adam named all the birds in the Garden of Eden, where he lived at that time.

Naming the animals and birds was the first job that God asked Adam to do, and he had to do it entirely on his own, because Eve, who would later be his wife, didn't exist yet. He had no one he could talk with but God himself, and God said the naming would be up to Adam entirely.

"There they are," said God, with a broad gesture toward the field full of beasts that had assembled for their naming. "Name them."

"Anything at all?"

"Whatever you decide. But try to make each name appropriate. The names will stick, and all these animals will have to live with the names you give them for hundreds of years."

"Okay," said Adam. He looked at the animals who had come nearest to where he and God were standing. "That's a dog. And that's a cat. And that little one is a mouse." He noticed that there was a pair of them, and that they were both cute little things, so he made a correction: "Two mice."

God smiled at the embellishment, and Adam, encouraged, turned toward the largest animals close at hand, and said, "That's an ox, and *they* are oxen."

The oxen looked at each other askance and lowered their heads, as though embarrassed. It was too late for Adam to change his mind, but after that he was more sparing in meting out peculiar plurals.

There were even more kinds of animals then than there are now, because many of them would soon drown in the great flood God had planned for the future, as a punishment for all the violence in the world. So Adam had to name all the different kinds of dinosaurs, as well as shaggy mammoths and saber-tooth tigers and other mammals now extinct.

It took a long time to take care of all the animals, and Adam came up with some quite fanciful names once he got going.

There was the pika and the platypus, the zebu and the stoat. The chameleon and the anaconda. The panda and the peccary, and all kinds of great names for the various tribes of apes and monkeys.

The wallaby.

The walrus.

The yak.

The gnu was the very last animal to be named, and when he'd named the gnu, and the field was empty at last of all the assembled beasts – except for the dog, who kept bringing Adam a slobbery old stick, wanting him to toss it – Adam thought, "I could use a day of rest myself."

God could read his thoughts, and said, "The birds are next."

The minute God said that the sky filled with birds of all shapes and colors and sizes, all of them anxious to be named and to begin to have their own unique identities the way the animals now did. From their aerial vantage they could see mountain goats springing from crag to crag, and sloths drooping from treelimbs like clothes on a clothesline, and squirrels scampering across the lawns of Eden. Adam had shown a real talent for naming, because all the animals behaved just the way you'd expect them to if you thought about their names a little while. The names fit them like gloves, and that's what the birds wanted for themselves.

A pretty plump bird with eggshell-colored feathers and bright pink eyes alighted on an olive branch nearby Adam. It tilted its head to the side, gave a little flutter to its feathers, and said, "Coo? Coo?"

"You'd like a name, is that it?" said Adam, for in those days, in the Garden of Eden, a person could understand what the birds meant with all their tweets and cheeps and hooty-hoos. So Adam knew that "Coo? Coo?" was to be understood as "Who? Who will *we* be?" We, meaning me and the Mrs.

"Coombe!" said Adam cheerily. "How would you like to be a coombe?"

The bird glared at Adam and lifted the ruff of feathers about its neck in a manner that left no doubt as to its refusal. It gave no reason. Birds often don't give their reason. They just fly off, and that's that. Which is what this bird did.

All the birds who'd been close by when Adam made his suggestion had fluttered off in different directions, with the exception of a large, mostly black bird with a neck bent over like the handle of a cane and his beak bent the same way. Large as he was, he seemed rather sickly, and the reason for that was that he hadn't had anything to eat since he was created. He belonged to the family of scavengers who live on the flesh of dead animals, and so far death did not exist in Eden, and the scavengers were all quite hungry and dispirited, scraping along on roots and berries, a diet for which they were not well adapted.

"Coombe?" Adam tried again. "Do you think that's a name *you* might like?"

The black bird shook its head sadly, and went "Grawk!" by which it meant to say, No. No, it did not want a name that rhymed with tomb and doom and gloom. For in due course, when people began to write poetry, imagine what it would be like to be the first bird to spring to mind when a poet began to think of death. "O coombe," the poet would write, "thou bird of doom that hast perched here on the tomb of the dead Lenore. Nevermore shall I see her again, O coombe! Nevermore!"

Adam could understand the bird's feeling, and he realized that all the other birds would feel the same way about being called a coombe, so even though it had a nice ring to it, he knew it wouldn't do for any of the birds, and that's how a coombe came to be a deep narrow valley on the side of a hill, and then only in certain lonely parts of Wales.

"Grawk!" said the black bird, with a different emphasis, and this time what it meant was, Can't you think of something with more positive associations? Perhaps to the arts. To painting, or violin concertos, or ballet?

None of those arts had been invented yet, but Adam, like the birds about him, had a certain prophetic streak, and he knew what this bird would like to rhyme with even if he didn't know what Culture was.

"Vulture!" he said. "How would you like to be a vulture?"

The vulture lifted its head, its eyes aglow with a new self-esteem. "Grawk!" it agreed, and its mate, close by, said "Grawk!" as well, and off the two of them flew to a tall yew tree where they settled down to wait for the arrival of death and their first good meal ever.

Not all the birds were so particular. Most of them seemed happy to accept the first name that came to Adam's mind. The booby raised no objection to being a booby, nor the auk to being an auk. And who would *not* like to be a chickadee or a bobolink, a cormorant or a cockatoo?

Oh, there were many birds with plainer names than that, wrens and sparrows and crows and jays, but even they could *rhyme* to something agreeable. A sparrow could speed through the air like an arrow. A wren could say Amen and then say it again, and beyond that it would rhyme to every kind of hen. Crows could form rows on telephone lines and screech and squawk from dawn till dusk, supposing all the while it was music to equal the larks'.

And as for the larks themselves, there was a song in store for them that said it all. It is in a play by William Shakespeare, called *Cymbeline*, and it begins like this: "Hark! hark! the lark at heaven's gate sings."

The birds that Adam named that day would pop up in thousands of songs in the course of time. Not only "Listen to the Mockingbird" but "Mockingbird Hill" as well. There are many good songs about robins, and one about wild geese that is really inspirational. It begins "I must go where the wild goose goes," and it's about how exciting it is always to be traveling to strange places, the way geese do.

There are so many songs about bluebirds the list would fill the page of a newspaper, and you would still have to say et cetera.

But there is one bird who can be found in even more poems than the robin or the bluebird, and that is the bird that first flew off with its mate when Adam suggested it might be known as a coombe. Now, after all the other birds had been named, those two were back with their ruffled feathers and reproachful Coo's, as though to say, Have you forgotten us? Are *we* to have no name?

Adam looked at God, and God looked at Adam, and all at once he knew the perfect name for the two birds with their grey feathers and softly purring song.

"You're doves!" he announced.

At once their breasts swelled with pride, for they could hear, prophetically, their new name echoing down through the centuries in thousands of poems and songs.

Oh, for the wings, for the wings of a dove!
On the wings of a snow-white dove!

And then, where it says in the Psalms in the Bible: "Ye shall be as the wings of a dove that is covered with silver wings, and her feathers like gold."

Or think of what Mercutio says in *Romeo and Juliet*: "Speak but one rhyme and I am satisfied. Cry but 'Ay me!' Couple but 'dove' and 'love.'"

For that, of course, is why the doves were so happy with the name that Adam had found them. For all eternity they'd be the only birds to rhyme with love and with the heavens above.

Their immortality was a sure thing.

II

A Case of Child Abuse

"What can I tell you?" says Sarah mournfully. "He hears voices. And not just voices like you or I might hear: 'Don't do that, dumkopf!' or 'Maybe tomorrow.' No, the voice *he* hears is nothing less than the Lord God Almighty's. 'Abraham,' this voice tells him, 'behold, here I am.' Of course, there's nothing there *to* behold, it's a voice inside his head, but that didn't stop *him*. They get into a discussion, and this Jehovah voice tells him he's got to abduct our only son, Isaac –" She turns to the stenographer. "That's Isaac with two A's."

The stenographer nods.

Sarah continues: "If I told you how old I was when I had that kid, you wouldn't believe me. Anyhow, never mind about that. So, he takes Isaac, who's still no more than a baby – he wets his bed, he cries all night with the teething, he shouldn't even be out of the *tent* – and he takes him off to the land of *Moriah*, which is to hell and gone, but I guess you know that."

"Yes, ma'am," says the police inspector. "That's where he was arrested."

"You know, I still can't believe it," says Sarah, shaking her head. "Why would he *do* such a thing? His own son. His *only* son. I mean, yes, he *says* God told him to, so you could say that's the reason he did it. But you know what I think? I think he was jealous of the little sucker, simple as that. I told you already what he did with the kid the minute he was born. I said, 'Abe, honey, what do you think you're doing with that knife?' And he says, 'The kid's got to be circumcised. I've discussed this already with God.' I swear I thought at first he'd cut his little weenie clean off. I guess I should have got the message then. You've married a lunatic, honey. Take the baby and run. But what could I do? Go to my father? After I'd eloped and stolen the little clay tchotchkes that were *his* gods? Not likely. All men are lunatics, that's my theory, especially when it comes to them and their gods. I was stuck with Abraham. He was 'my man,' as the song says."

"Had he ever threatened you?" asks the police inspector.

"Never," says Sarah. "Usually he's sweet as can be. Ask the neighbors."

"Do you still, um..." The inspector conveys what he means by lowering his eyes.

"Sex, you mean? Not that much, at our age. After you get to be a hundred, the urge diminishes. As for my sister – he's married to her, too, you know – you'll have to ask her yourself, but I don't think he sees that much of Leah anymore, either. Our handmaidens, now that's another matter. He's got a thing for handmaidens. Which I, personally, have always counted a blessing."

The stenographer signals for Sarah to pause until she's caught up with her. Then, when the stenographer has given her a go-ahead, Sarah asks the inspector, "What's going to happen? Is this going to go to court, or what? I'll tell you right now, I couldn't say these things in front of a lot of people."

"No," says the inspector, "I don't think you'll have to worry about that. Your husband has influential friends. I think the whole matter will be settled out of court."

"Temporary insanity?"

The inspector nods.

"There's nothing temporary about it. Who knows what this Jehovah's going to tell him he wants for his next burnt offering? I'll tell you quite honestly, I don't feel safe around the man any more."

"I'm afraid there's nothing we can do about that, ma'am. According to the law, you are your husband's chattel. And so is the kid. That's why we can't press charges. If it had been someone else's kid, we could nail him."

"What's the point of having laws if they can't protect you?" Sarah grumbles.

"Good question," says the police inspector, as he gets up off the rug and smoothes out the wrinkles in his burnoose. "Maybe you should have your husband ask Jehovah." And he winks. He pushes open the flap of the tent and says to one of the patrolmen, "You can send the kid in now."

Little Isaac runs into the tent, and Sarah spreads open her arms. For a while it's all hugs and tears, and then Sarah asks, "So where's your father?"

Isaac looks down at the rug. "I don't know, Mamma. I think he's with the sheep." She waits. He squirms. "Or maybe with Leah."

Sarah raises her eyes to heaven, more for the stenographer's sake than the police inspector's.

"Your husband was released earlier, ma'am," says the inspector. "But he told us to tell you he'd be home for his dinner at the usual time. And he asked us to give you this."

He hands her a string satchel, and then excuses himself, leaving Sarah alone with Isaac and the stenographer.

Sarah looks inside the satchel and announces, "Lamb chops."

Isaac perks up. "Are we having lamb chops for dinner?"

Sarah looks up at the stenographer. "You know what this is, don't you. It's what's left over from the burnt offering. He probably took the haunch over to Leah. Waste not, want not, that's my Abraham."

"So what else is new," says the stenographer. "We get this sort of thing happening every week. If it isn't Jehovah, it's Moloch. If it isn't Moloch, it's Baal. They're all alike: 'Bring me your firstborn son and set him on my altar.' You're lucky your Jehovah changed his mind at the last minute. Not all of those gods do."

Sarah sighs. "You like lamb chops?" she asks the stenographer. "It looks like there's more than enough."

"Thank you, but I can't," says the stenographer. "I'm vegetarian."

III

Jahweh's Wife

Moses did not like women.

Partly this was a result of living with a wife who was certifiably insane, and partly from the trauma of abandonment in infancy. His mother could never leave off with the bulrushes, and of course the way she told the story it was all Pharaoh's fault for telling the midwives, Shiphrah and Puah, who got credit for contravening the Pharaoh's cruel orders. But his mother and those midwives were thick as thieves, and you don't suppose the little basket they had set him afloat in had anything to do with infant sacrifice and luck in the lottery? Oh no, they were saving his life, assisted by yet another female paragon, no less than Pharaoh's daughter. Tell me another!

Women! All of them worshipped idols, and all their idols had great drooping breasts and swollen stomachs by way of reminding anyone who might have forgotten where babies come from and what they drink that keeps them alive. Moses hated idols, any idols at all, male as much as female, animal, mineral, and vegetable, because there was always something the idol wanted you to do, or wouldn't let you do, and always it turned out to be exactly what his mother wanted him to do – or later on, what his wife Zipporah wanted. He could remember watching old Puah cavorting in front of some cow of a goddess and thinking how someday he would smash all the women's idols and start a new religion just for guys, and no one would be allowed to eat snails ever again (his mother loved snails) or even spare ribs. Especially spare ribs! His mother went into ecstasies every year at the Cairo Spare Rib Festival – and afterwards, talk about unclean!

For many years, even after he'd led the Jews out of bondage and started bringing down Jahweh's laws from the mountaintop where he and the Lord his God got together, Moses felt guilty for some of the laws he laid down. Not so much the busywork laws concerning the decoration of the temple with red lambswool and badger skins and shittim wood, and not even the tough laws – eye for an eye, wound for wound, stripe for stripe – since those were a useful deterrent against crime. It was the laws governing leprosy, which were complicated and strict, that he sometimes regretted. Not that there shouldn't be such laws, but perhaps they were harsher than need be, since he'd framed them at a time when he was feeling miffed with his mother, who was getting senile and would go off every weekend whoring after false gods. She would bow down to graven images and commit abomination and eat snails, so something really had to be done. So Aaron, who was a high priest by then, had declared their mother a leper. But he'd also rigged the test, and maybe that had been going too far. Or maybe the fault was with Moses' laws concerning leprosy. It was a chicken-or-the-egg situation.

Years later, when he was writing the story of his life and making a digest of the laws, he left out those details about his mother, and many of the stories about Zipporah, as well. In fact, he wrote almost nothing about Zipporah, except for a brief mention of her "accident" on the way to Egypt, when she'd bloodied his best robe in the process of cutting their younger son's foreskin with a sharp stone. The stains never did come out, and it wasn't as though the boy hadn't been circumcised already. Zipporah just got excited, sometimes, with a sharp stone in her hand. Her father Jethro had been crazy the same way.

Another subject Moses avoided in the Pentateuch was the vexed relationship between Jahweh and his wife Jaweenah. As a result of Moses's reticence, many of Jahweh's actions may strike readers of Genesis as irrational and unmotivated, since the book omits mention of the demands Jaweenah made upon her husband. Like Fricka, the spouse of another Divine Patriarch, Jaweenah could be a jealous and vindictive deity, and her caprices often dictated her husband's actions. Did Fricka insist that Wotan assist in the slaughter of his bastard son and spoiled darling Siegmund? Was she behind the years-long coma of his daughter Brunhilde? Yes, her responsibility in these matters is clear, just as it was Jaweenah who insisted that the child Isaac be executed by his own doting father as punishment for the child's having trespassed into Jaweenah's magic cloud-garden, where he'd picked her invisible violets. Only at the last moment did the henpecked Divinity rebel against his spouse's stern decree and provide Abraham with a ram to serve as a burnt offering in his son's stead. If Jaweenah had had *her* way...

Then there was the little matter of Gomorrah, a city that had been devoted to the worship of Jaweenah in her character as protectress of ovens and kilns. Gomorrah had been filled with temples where Jaweenah's priestesses baked firstborn male offerings in hollow brazen idols representing the goddess with the attributes of a male baker, including a white cap and large potholders. The powdered remains of children baked in this way were thought to secure their parents against sterility and impotence. Jahweh tried to reason with his wife concerning the propriety of her appearing in public dressed in male attire. The firstborns he didn't mind so much. People in those days went through a lot of firstborns: there weren't other forms of contraception. But Jaweenah wouldn't listen to reason, and finally Jahweh realized he was wasting his breath and rained down fire and brimstone on the offending city while his wife was away on a visit to the gods of Olympus.

When Jaweenah returned there was hell to pay. She stormed about the mountaintop, hurling thunderbolts and spewing lava and afflicting half her husband's Chosen People with scabs and sores in those places it is most embarrassing to scratch. Jahweh apologized and promised to have another city built for her particular worship, if only she would put up her baker's hat and the potholders, which it was unbecoming a woman to wear.

She refused.

He insisted.

She said, "Well, then, there are other gods..."

Those were Jaweenah's last words. Jahweh pronounced his spouse's doom. Her breasts withered and fell to the ground like petals from a fruit tree. When she opened her mouth to curse, her teeth broke into splinters and her tongue began to smoke. In less than a minute Jaweenah was a heap of ashes at her husband's feet. Jahweh scattered the ashes with a breath.

After he'd told Moses this story, Jahweh had misgivings. "On the whole, I wonder if it might not be better to leave all this out of the book. People could get the wrong idea as to proper behavior in a domestic crisis. Stoning adulteresses is one thing, but I may have gone too far. It's that darn temper of mine. When I wax wroth..."

"But what will I tell people when they ask about your wife?"

"Say I was never married. Say I'm the only god there ever was, the Alpha and Omega. Period."

"But the other major deities all have wives."

"There *are* no other deities, Moses. How many times do I have to tell you."

"Yes, Lord," said Moses, happy to be his God's submissive instrument.

And that is why to this very day we worship One God, who is male and unmarried.

One Night, Or, Scheherazade's Bare Minimum

"AND THIS," Sara's abductor explained, throwing open the French doors of a room filled with potted plants and hanging ferns, "is the oda."

"An 'oda,' like in crossword puzzles?" Sara marveled.

"I wouldn't know about that." He sounded miffed.

Sara shuffled over to the barred window. With each step the delicate golden chain hobbling her ankles clinked on the marble parquet. In the distance, silhouetted against the lavender twilight, was the dome of the Taj Mahal.

"So this is Agra! That's another word that's always cropping up in crossword puzzles."

"And *this,* my little gazelle – " He unsheathed the long curved sword that dangled from the sash about his waist. "– is a scimitar. The number of wives and concubines who have been beheaded by this blade is many as the stars in the firmament."

"I'll remember that in case you ever propose."

"The Emir of Bassorah does not solicit the favor of his beloved. The arrows of his desire fly directly to their target. The moment I saw you pass through customs at the Rome airport, I said to my vizier: That one! I must possess her for my pleasure tonight. Hijack the plane, abduct her, dress her in costly raiment and bring her to my divan. I spoke, and he obeyed."

"Okay, but before you possess me or have me beheaded, aren't I entitled to tell a story? I've never been a hostage before, and I don't know a lot about Middle Eastern culture, but that's the basic tradition here, right?"

When the Emir of Bassorah heard his abductee speak in this impudent manner he smote hand upon hand and cried, "There is no Majesty and there is no Might save in Allah the Glorious, the Great." And he sat down on the biggest pillow on the oda's floor and folded his legs into a half-lotus position, which was quite an accomplishment for someone of his girth, but people in traditional societies where there is nothing to sit on (not even in the bathroom!) have to learn to be flexible. And he said to Sara, grudgingly: "All right, those are the rules. Tell me a story, like unto the tale of the loves of Al-Hayfa and Yusuf, and if it amuses I may let you live one night longer. Mind you, I'm not promising anything. I'm merciful, but I'm also capricious."

"Well," said Sara, trying to get comfortable on another pillow without ripping the delicate gauze of her harem pants, "I don't know the story you mention, but in the creative writing course I took at NYU our instructor told us that basically there are only a few stories that anyone can tell. It's all a matter of ascending action and descending action, and how they relate to the objectives of the protagonist. He drew some diagrams that made each archetype clear: if I had my notebook here – "

"Listen, my little American pomegranate, I want a story, not a lecture. A tale full of marvels and wonders and sex and violence."

"Okay, okay, I'll tell you a story about...um...Ed Walker and Sally Morton. Ed was a marketing executive for a major manufacturer of... um..." Sara cast about for inspiration. "Ceramic tiles! And Sally was a young woman he'd met at a party in...Babylon (the Babylon on Long Island, not your Babylon in the Middle East)."

"And she was very beautiful?" the Emir inquired.

"Stunning. On the street people often confused her with Vanna White."

"And her breasts?"

"Her breasts were watermelons."

The Emir licked his thick lips. "Ah, very good! Continue."

Sara continued her tale, which was freely adapted from a story she'd written for her creative writing class at NYU. It had a minimal plot, but her instructor had praised it for the way it revealed the hollowness at the center of Ed's and Sally's lives and for its moments of low-key humor and its accurate observation of everyday life in a business-oriented environment.

As Sara's story unfolded with all deliberate speed, the pointy toes of her listener's golden shoes began to beat time to a faster tempo. At last he broke out: "By the beard of the Prophet, enough of this doleful twaddle! This is not fiction, this is accountancy!"

Sara glared at the Emir and, in a tone of ill-concealed resentment, said: "Sire?"

"I want romance! Mystery! Adventure!"

"Your word is my command," said Sara, and she bethought herself. The Emir of Bassorah was, as might be expected of someone in his position, a male chauvinist pig. The story she had been telling, though it had got her an A in the creative writing course and received some highly complimentary rejection slips from major quarterlies, was probably not suited to the emotional needs of a man of his temperament and social position.

So, instead of telling her own story, Sara began to retell, as well as she could remember it, "The Ballad of Jim Beam," a story by Barry McGough that had appeared in a Pushcart Press annual. It was about a famous short story writer in Oregon who had writer's block and whose marriage was on the rocks because of his alcoholism. On the surface of the story nothing appears to happen – the man and his wife go fishing for bass, without success, drink a bottle of bourbon, and argue about their autistic child – but underneath the surface McGough was opening a whole supermarket of cans of worms.

As an indictment of American culture in the '80s, "The Ballad of Jim Beam" was scathing, but the Emir of Bassorah, unlike so many of his Middle Eastern compatriots, seemed indifferent to the framing of such an indictment, for he yawned a mighty yawn, and scratched his crotch, and began to reach for his scimitar, which he'd placed on another pillow beside the one on which he was sitting, for it's hard enough for a fat man to assume the half-lotus position in an unencumbered state, but to do so with a scimitar lodged in his cummerbund is virtually impossible. Just try it some time.

"Wait!" Sara said, sensing the Emir's displeasure, "I've just thought of another story you might like better. About a magician."

"And is he afflicted with arthritis?" the Emir demanded. "And does he cringe like a beaten dog before his wife's rebukes?"

"No, a real magician, who is extremely rich and has strange powers, called Shahbankhan the Munificent. He can shrink down as small as a pea and swell up to the size of a...I don't know, something enormous. And he can fly anywhere in the world on the back of a hummingbird."

"How could he do that?" The Emir's hand drew back from the jeweled pommel of the scimitar.

"The hummingbird had a teeny-tiny saddle."

"Yes. Go on."

Sara continued her tale, throwing in some new wonder or marvel whenever the Emir showed signs of restlessness or inattention. When his eyes drifted to the window's view of the Taj Mahal, she introduced a veiled maiden who ministered with great skill to the pleasures of Shahbankhan and then mysteriously disappeared. When he began to scrape at the dirt under his fingernails with a golden nail-clipper, she had Shahbankhan fall into a pit of vipers.

All the while the klepsydra, or waterclock, on the wall was dribbling away the minutes of the night. One o'clock found Shahbankhan contending against an army of invisible skeletons. At one-fifteen he was in Samarkand in pursuit of the legendary Blue Scarab of Omnipotence. At one-thirty in Zagzig being plied with a love elixir by an Egyptian enchantress. The Emir listened to it all like a drowsy but querulous child, and the night dripped on endlessly.

It was only a few minutes before dawn, but Sara was at her wit's end. Had it been like this for the original Scheherazade? If so, it was small wonder that so many other wives and concubines had chosen the scimitar to such tiresome and demeaning service. Sara would have much preferred just to give the old fart a blow-job and be done with it. But when she hinted at this possibility, in a narrative aside, the Emir's hand edged toward his damned scimitar. He had a rapist's mentality, unable to conceive of sex as other than a metaphor for murder.

A thousand and one nights of Barry McGough would be bad enough, but a thousand and one nights of rehashing superhero cartoons was an intolerable prospect. Enough! Sara thought, for she was a woman of resourcefulness and courage though not really a great storyteller, notwithstanding her A in creative writing. That had been a tribute more to her looks than any gift for narrative.

She knelt down beside the Emir. Her crimson lips brushed the immense pearl popping from the flesh of his earlobe like a nacreous wart. "And then," she whispered, "the fair enchantress removed the veil from her swanlike neck and, ever so gently, covered the eyes of the guileless magician, so that he was blindfolded now by silk as well as by love." Deftly, Sara demonstrated how this was done with the veil that swathed her own swanlike neck. Then, quick as a mongoose, her hand grasped the pommel of the Emir's scimitar. She lifted it from the pillow on which it rested and raised it high above her head – not an easy thing to do, for scimitars weigh more than you might think, but Sara worked out regularly at Jack LaLanne's and was surprisingly strong. And then, with a sense that she was revenging the grievances of every hack writer who'd ever lived, she beheaded the Emir of Bassorah.

After she'd cleaned up the mess and hidden the Emir's body under a pile of pillows in the oda's farthest corner and found a vase big enough to accommodate his severed head, she tested the various keys on his keyring in the locks of the various locked doors of the harem until she found what she was sure must be there, the "Bluebeard" room in which he had stored the personal possessions of his earlier victims. Sara's own clothes were uppermost in the heap. It was a great relief to change from the constricting and *scratchy* harem clothes into something sensible.

Then she looked through the numerous purses arranged on a malachite display case and took those credit cards that hadn't yet expired.

And then, feeling just like a princess in a fairy tale (but also a bit like the nameless wife in Barry McGough's novella "Born to Shop"), she took a taxi to Agra's main bazaar and had the spree of her life.

A Knight at the Opera

THE APPLAUSE at the end of Act One was enthusiastic if not tumultuous. Lillienthal had surpassed himself, as usual, and the Lohengrin, whom Ann heretofore had seen only on a DVD of *Tristan*, boded well, but no Lohengrin really shows to advantage till Act Three. It's the chorus of maidens, serfs, nobles, and pages who is the collective star of Act One, *das Volk*, together with their ringleader and *Oberstleutnant*, the Herald, tonight an East German baritone in his U.S. premiere, Hans Heckert.

After the headliners had taken their solo turns in front of the curtain, and as the aisles were already filling with people anxious to get to the restrooms, Heckert was allotted his own curtain call, and Ann, in a spirit of populist, standing-room abandon, unloosed her best "Bravo!" The most authoritative Bravos usually seem to be the work of professionals, and though Ann was not a singer herself, had never studied voice or even sung in a church choir, her Bravo cut through the already diminishing rumble of handclapping to inspire one last surge of applause just as the houselights came up and Heckert exited.

"I agree," said an imposing older gentleman, who had turned around mid-exit to applaud Heckert, then turned again to face Ann. "Completely." He stood so near she could smell his breath, sweet as a baby's – or was it the small bouquet he carried, of roses and (naturally) baby's breath partly sheathed in cellophane?

He rattled the bouquet. "If I'd been closer to the stage, I should have tried to heave these his way. I don't suppose the Herald ever gets flowers. Or bravos for that matter. But this guy deserved them." The man smiled in an unflirtatious way.

And Ann fell in love.

But then she had no idea what to say, how to keep him from being swept away from the standing-room rail by the lobby-bound crowd, now at high tide. He solved the problem himself. "Would you like to go out to the lobby for coffee?"

Ann never left a choice place at the rail during intermission from a conviction that another standee would take possession by the time she returned. Tonight she simply draped her coat over the rail, answered the man's smile with an assenting nod, and followed him out to the lobby and down a half-flight of the scarlet-carpeted steps to where a line had already formed before the coffee bar. She felt quite as though she were *in* the opera, her submission as quick and unquestioning as Elsa's when the Herald summons her to judgment.

He seemed, if not a figure of chivalry, the perfect gentleman, with a full head of silver-streaked hair, not quite as leonine as the mane on tonight's Lohengrin but wholly admirable. His navy pinstripe suit, no less so, and the tie with its white fleurs-de-lys speckling a field of electric blue. All so correct but also, somehow, shocking and inordinate. Just what one wanted in a Lohengrin.

"I'm Ann," she began, reaching the bottom step. "Ann Greenwald." She didn't want to be the guest of someone who didn't even know her name.

But he wasn't paying attention. Just like Lohengrin, or Santa Claus for that matter (Christmas was only a week away), he said not a word but concerned himself with the business at hand. Fourteen dollars, for two coffees and two mingy blondies, which he paid without flinching, even leaving the change from his twenty in the concessionaire's plastic cup.

They found a ledge where they could set their coffee cups (beneath the glass were photographs of Elsas, Lohengrins, and Ortruds from days of yore). Ann set her coffee atop the beaming countenance of Lauritz Melchior.

Her own Lohengrin smiled another of his diffidently devastating smiles and said, "The moment that completely laid me low was just before the swordfight, when the Herald sets down the terms of the combat and declares what the penalty will be for anyone who steps inside the ring. A freeman will have his hand cut off, but a serf..."

He shook his head in silent reprehensions.

"Yes! *Mit seinem Haupt büss es der Knecht.* That is so savage." Ann tested her coffee: it was still too hot to sip.

"And then," he went on, "the whole chorus *repeats* what he's said, and with such sincere bloodlust. As though the lot of them had only just graduated from cannibalism."

"Well, it was the Dark Ages. And even today people do still cut off each other's heads, in far-off lands."

"And in *Turandot.* Though that's in one of the far-off lands you speak of. We don't do it in America, not in our operas, anyhow."

"But in France? In England?" Poulenc's *Dialogues* was one of Ann's favorite operas, though she'd only heard recordings. She loved the *thunk* after *thunk* of the guillotine at the end, as one by one each woman in the chorus of nuns was exterminated. But, really, they had to find something else to talk about.

"Do you come here often?" she asked (archly enough, she hoped, that he would hear the quotation marks).

"Now and then. But the prices keep going up, and there are more and more terrific DVDs. With *Lohengrin* there must be four or five. The best, to my mind, is Abbado's, in Vienna. Domingo couldn't be bettered."

"Yes, I've seen it, he's wonderful. A knight in shining armor. When Cheryl Studer *insisted* on asking him his name, I could have killed her. The foolish woman!"

"Oh, it's not just Cheryl Studer. It's any soprano. They can't seem to help themselves."

"Well, *I* wouldn't have. I wouldn't have let Ortrud into my castle, for that matter. You can tell at a glance she's not to be trusted."

"Well, the audience does get to see a side of Ortrud that Elsa doesn't. But I don't think she should bear the blame. Elsa *eventually* would have wanted to know who he was and where he came from. It's in a woman's nature."

"Have I asked *you* your name? Or where you come from?"

"No. But I haven't forbidden it."

"Then forbid it! Go ahead – I still won't ask."

"Very well." He paraphrased Lohengrin's injunction, suggesting the *leitmotif* without actually singing it. "Ann Greenwald, understand me well. Never ask me where I've come from, nor yet my name and rank."

(So he had been listening, she thought.) She laid her hand on her heart, and swore, "It's a promise."

"One further taboo. This – " He placed a silvery cell-phone by Ann's coffee cup. " – is a fancy kind of beeper. You just have to press the little red button. If I don't answer, it will take a message. Or...you can ask one of those forbidden questions. What would be the point of forbidding you to ask a question if there's no one to whom it can be addressed?"

"You're serious?"

"Always. And this – " He placed his ticket stub on top of the cell-phone. " – is yours for acts two and three. I really wish I could stay, but duty – " He patted the cell-phone. " – has called, and I obey. I'm already overdue. I was paged just as the duel got under way, but I was too much of a moral coward to leave my seat and make everyone else along the row stand up. Then when I heard you cheer, I knew I must cede you my seat. You seem to be enjoying the performance so thoroughly. But remember, in Lohengrin's words:

"...du musst mich wohl vernommen:
Nie sollst du mich befragen
Woher ich kam der Fahrt,
Noch nie mein Nam' und Art."

And that was the last she'd seen of him. He left his coffee and blondie on top of the display case, untasted, and vanished into the crowd. Ann was not so willfully wasteful. She finished her blondie and wrapped his in its napkin and made a nest for it in her purse, then snugged the cell-phone into one of the inner compartments of her purse, retrieved her coat from the standing room rail, and took possession of seat K-28 in the orchestra just as the lights began to dim. It wasn't the first time she'd seen the end of an opera in a seat inherited from someone leaving early. Standees often benefit from the kindness of strangers.

It wasn't even the first time she'd fallen in love at first sight and been left in the lurch so abruptly. The most plangent occasion had been years ago by the pool at her gym when a young man with a chiseled torso had spread his arms, flexed his knees, and executed a perfect swan dive. That affair went no further than chit-chat at the gym's juice bar, though she did at least learn his name (Larry something) and rank (assistant dean of a small Catholic law school) before *he* disappeared.

When Act Two began Ann was able to brush away all Ann-ish thoughts and return to her parallel existence as Elsa of Brabant. She was more than ever astonished that Elsa could not see through Ortrud's wiles and overt menaces. Was she herself somehow just as guileless? The question still nagged at her hours later as she unwrapped the second blondie from its damp napkin and nibbled it with some chocolate milk in front of her blank television. For instance, should she suspect her own spur-of-the-moment Lohengrin? Of what? At the very worst, of a whimsical joke. What sinister purpose could he think to accomplish by presenting her with his cell-phone? It was probably defunct, or its service had expired. Ann knew nothing of how cell-phones worked, or how they differed from pagers and beepers. For years she'd entertained an unthinking prejudice against everyone who used them. Indeed, her only misgiving about her anonymous knight was that he'd had one of the nasty things. Could he be a surgeon? a journalist? a spy? Those were occupations that might make a cell-phone a practical necessity.

But whoa! Already she was making Elsa's mistake! She was speculating about his *Nam und Art*, the very thing she'd vowed not to do. Not, not, not. She brushed the last crumbs of the blondie off the tablecloth and retrieved the cell-phone from the compartment in her handbag in which it had made such a Cinderella-perfect fit. Then she dragged the chair she was sitting on across the room and used it as a stepladder to get down the big ceramic vase from the top of the bookcase. She put the cell-phone into the vase, and returned the vase to its exact place on the oak shelf, marked by a film of dust. Then, with a Kleenex from the packet in her bathrobe she wiped away the dust. Just so, she thought, I cleanse my heart of suspicion's uncomely stain! Opera had a way of putting her into an italicizing, declamatory frame of mind. She returned the chair to its place by the table, washed her glass at the sink, and called on the angels to stand about her bed.

Two weeks later the first package arrived. It was sitting by itself on the little table under the mailboxes in the lobby, addressed to A. Greenwald, no apartment number and no zip-code – and no return address. She knew at once who'd sent it, and wasn't at all surprised. Somehow she'd been expecting it. How he'd learned her address (her phone number was no longer listed) wasn't something she puzzled over. That's the sort of thing one would suppose any Lohengrin would be able to do. It went with the territory.

And the contents of the package weren't surprising either. A videotape inside the kind of cloudy plastic container some rental shops use, with the title roughly lettered on the plastic, "Flying Dutchman." As soon as she got inside her door she slid the tape into her VCR. There were two or three minutes of zigzags and splotches that led directly to the overture overseen with stern intensity by a heavyset young maestro who conducted without a baton, flailing about his intensely quivering fingers, like the Kirov's Gergiev.

There could not have been a better *Dutchman.* Its very faults were Wagner's and intrinsic with a storyline as silly and blood-curdling as the most opprobrious gothic novel ever written. Ann was entranced from the first Hoi-ho! of the work crew on Daland's ship, which in this production was a kind of spectral engine room, perhaps on a ship, possibly in a mine or factory, but *very* dismal, the quintessence of every rock-bottom sweat-shop job any wage-slave had ever toiled at. Ann identified totally, and when the second act began it was like being sucked down into an even worse job at a factory in Calcutta or Bombay where emaciated women drudged at assembly lines that maintained a perpetual motion, singing all the while of the nice dinners they will cook for their husbands when they're home from their jobs on the sea. Wagner's Senta was the most wretched of these wraiths and seemed to have been driven mad by years of overtime. Ann *was* Senta, even to the weird correspondence of the little mole on the left side of her too-wide chin, and the Dutchman, when he could finally be seen in close-up (he'd been veiled by stage-smoke all through Act One), was her Lohengrin in the same business suit he'd worn at the opera but a century older now, shabby and rumpled and desolate with loss. Forlorn! That was his condition exactly, and Senta's, and that of the whole miserable world looming about them.

At the end of Act Two, Ann pressed Eject. She knew that Senta would commit suicide next, and couldn't bear to watch the rest of the opera. Not all at one go, this very night.

Where had he found the tape? In what suburb of hell had it been staged and filmed? Ann could recognize none of the singers. They weren't really that good – Daland croaked, Senta hooted, and the Dutchman seemed at times to gasp more than to sing – but they compelled one's belief as better singers might not have. If Auschwitz had had its own opera house, these singers would have been its stars.

It was almost as though (Ann thought) he'd done this just for her – hired the opera house, cast the roles, designed the sets and costumes – and all just to tempt her to betray her vow, to make her press the little button on the cell-phone, and summon him, and ask his name.

She loved him more than ever. She loved him the way that Heloise loved Abelard, the way Theresa of Avila loved the crucified Christ. It gave her migraines she loved him so much.

But then, worse than any migraine, a toothache took hold of her, worse than the toothache that had led to her root canal, missing her finals in her sophomore year at Mount Holyoke, and, ultimately, dropping out without a degree. She knew her teeth were once again in dreadful shape and did not want a dentist to look inside her mouth, but after a single futile day of self-medication with oil of clove, she made an appointment with Doctor Rostovsky. His verdict was the dental equivalent of life without parole. She would have to have a canine and the incisor beside it extracted and replaced with a bridge, *and* a gold crown to cap a molar that had lost its filling some years ago – months of appointments and thousands of dollars. As soon as she got Dr. Rostovsky's first bill she was in despair. When the second bill arrived she still hadn't paid the first, and Rostovsky's receptionist had become cool, not to say forbidding. The dentist did not accept credit cards. She would need to take out a loan to pay him, and the bank meant to exact some usurious rate of interest. What is one to do in such a case? Is there some annex to a hospital's emergency room where poor people go to have *all* their teeth extracted?

It was at that juncture that his next gift appeared, like a rabbit out of a magician's hat – a deposit into her checking account of $5,000. As inexplicable as it was irresistible. She dared not *ask* the bank how the deposit had been made (by check? in cash? an electronic transfer?), partly for fear that some benevolent computer had erred in her favor, but mostly because she felt that such a question was precisely what she had sworn not to ask. Was his benefaction a direct response to her dental/financial problems, or was $5,000 a one-size-fits-all good deed, like flowers or candy?

Uncannily, it covered Rostovsky's bills with just enough left over for a box of Godiva truffles. She ate the first of them in front of her bathroom mirror. In the only movie of Theda Bara's that Ann had ever seen, the famed vamp had kissed her leading man with a big round chocolate cream poised in her beestung lips. This truffle was no less weirdly delectable.

Her teeth had never been so beautiful. She began, for the first time in almost a decade, to wear lipstick again, and on a whim she went into a department store just to allow the woman in the perfume aisle to give a squirt from her atomizer. She did it for his sake, not her own.

Ann had always envied her friends who were in A.A. or had, in a milder way, assembled some sort of religious faith for themselves. Now she had her own Higher Power – whimsical, protective, and, best of all, unknowable. It was even reliable in an off-and-on way. The presents continued coming, at irregular intervals, but always as though the Giver had had a hot-line right to the neediest niche of her soul. Her nameless benefactor knew just what would soothe her worst aches. German has that wonderful word, *Sehnsucht*, for which "longing" is so imperfect a translation. *Sehnsucht* is an ache for one knows not what – but her knight, uncannily, did know.

He never repeated his taboo-breaking gift of money, nor even approximated it in the (estimated) cost of his future gifts. Some were practical: a Cuisinart; a Burberry raincoat with a matching umbrella; a really convincing forgery of a majolica basin that just barely fit on the underledge of the table beneath the mirror in the hall. Sometimes it would just be a book or a CD. Her favorite among all those was a translation of seven French farces by an author she'd never heard of. She'd been suffering from a cough that absolutely would not let go, and somehow the laughter cured her. Laughter is supposed to be therapeutic, though she'd always hated the idea of sending clowns to hospitals to entertain dying children. Maybe she'd been wrong.

Even more than like having Someone On High this was like having a family. Ann didn't, or hadn't till now. When she'd dropped out of Mount Holyoke her mother had become an iceberg of vindictiveness and hostility, and when her mother died from her own excess of spleen her Aunt Cecilia got the house and the bit of money that was left after all the medical bills from both her parents' deaths. Ann had not wanted the house, but it would have been nice to get a Christmas card from Cecilia. No, Ann's existence had been just about as loveless as Elsa's in the opera once her brother is turned into a swan. She had a job, testing drugs for Pfeil-Findlich, that involved little in the way of bullying or being bullied, only a certain degree of cold-bloodedness *vis-à-vis* the creature comforts of small mammals. The only after-hours liability of the job (aside from the fact that it was a guaranteed conversation stopper) was that she couldn't have pets. You couldn't spend a day avoiding eye contact with mice and then go home to a spaniel. Even other people's cats and dogs and canaries gave her the willies (as she, it often seemed, gave them).

With the presents periodically appearing out of nowhere, like crates parachuting down into the camp of a cargo cult, she knew what it must be like to have relatives who remembered one's birthday or sent get-well cards. She never so much as peeked into the big vase on top of her bookcase, was not even tempted, but she did sometimes fantasize about future presents that she *might* be sent. Her most egregious such fantasy was an engagement ring. It would, of course, have been a diamond of mind-boggling dimensions, beyond, as they say, the dreams of avarice, and she would wear it to work, or at her favorite little bistro on Cedar Avenue, without offering any explanation (supposing she were to be asked for one). Jewelry, however, was the one thing her knight never thought to surprise her with. It was just as well. At her age it would have been embarrassing even to pretend to have become engaged. It was amazing, though, how persistent the fantasy is. And the need to be loved.

The nicest present of all arrived the day before her sixtieth birthday. It was a ticket on an amateur astronomers' cruise off the coast of Iceland to view the impending solar eclipse – not an adventure she would ever have undertaken on her own. She'd never been curious about Iceland, nor taken a cruise, and she had no interest in astronomy. The whole expedition would take a week out of her life. She almost turned in the ticket for a refund, but that seemed like cheating, and when she asked Pfeil-Findlich for the time, they made no difficulties. So there she was, on September 12, on the deck of the forty-passenger *Maid of Antwerp* looking at the serrated coastline of Iceland through the telescope belonging to her table-mates, Professor Arnold Windt and his soon-to-be-ex-wife Mitzy. Through the entire cruise Arnold and Mitzy never left off sparring and sniping at each other and complaining about the food and the weather (the forty passengers never did have so much as a glimpse of the sun or its eclipse). When it came time to escape from the Windts and board the Lufthansa jet that would take her home, Ann was *so* thankful that Fate had spared her the soul-eroding miseries of the married state. She would have been another Mitzy, another Elsa, another Ortrud. There might even have been children.

Her *Sehnsucht* was gone thereafter, and her cruise to view the eclipse was the last gift she was ever bequeathed by her nameless knight. It was as though your psychoanalyst were to tell you, after years of therapy, that you were completely cured and didn't need to see him any more. Now she could live happily ever after.

The Man Who Read a Book

AFTER Jerome Bagley was graduated from Maya Angelou High School in Brooklyn in 1998, he spent the next twelve years either unemployed or attending a variety of vocational and pre-vocational classes at City College and its affiliates. He studied computer programming, hair styling, substance abuse counselling, auto repair and maintenance, cake decorating, and introductory Sanskrit, but none of these efforts ever led to an actual salaried position. Then one day his parole officer, Mona Schuyler, suggested that he look into the possibility of reading books for money, and showed him the ad, in the back pages of *The National Endowment,* that told him where to write in order to find out if he was qualified.

He was! His educational background showed him to be the kind of all-things-considered reader that publishers were looking for. He might well enjoy a career in readership if he were willing to make a strong personal commitment and enlist in the career development programme sponsored by the Yaddo Reading Institute of Boca Raton, Florida. Jerome filled in the Institute's two-page questionnaire and faxed it in, together with his check for $50. The very next day the Institute's Aptitude Profile arrived, and Jerome began answering the Profile's 350 multiple-choice questions. Some answers he was certain he got right: America's Number One Best-Selling Author since 1984 was (c) Stephen King. Tennessee Williams was the author of the immortal 1948 tragedy (a) *A Salesman Named Desire.* Hyperbole was (b) a rare disorder of the lymph nodes. Others he was not so certain of, but he knew enough about test-taking to rule out obvious wrong choices and then flip a coin. In any case, as the Institute's brochure explained, the important thing wasn't getting exactly the right answer. He wasn't a contestant on *Jeopardy*. The important thing was an attitude of confidence, affirmation, and a sheer love of reading.

Jerome mailed in the Aptitude Profile with a check for $200 and waited. But not for long. A week later he got a signed letter from Mr. Yaddo himself, the head of the Institute, congratulating him on his responsiveness, energy, and knack. Mr. Yaddo said that Jerome's Aptitude Profile was absolutely unique according to the Institute's seven-trillion-byte databank, and he personally promised Jerome that he would be hearing from interested publishers in no time at all, publishers who would be paying him top dollar in order to find out what he, JEROME BAGLEY, thought about their books.

His name was written just like that, with every letter a capital letter. Looking at his name in such big letters, it was almost like seeing it on the cover of one of the books he might have to read. Jerome went to Wal-Mart and bought a picture frame the exact same size as the letter, and he hung the letter, in the frame, on the wall behind his dormitory cot, where everyone would see it.

Then he received a letter from a publisher, Alfred Kopf, who had heard about Jerome from Mr. Yaddo and wanted him to read one of the books he'd published and tell him what he thought about it. For this service Alfred Kopf was prepared to pay Jerome $50. A copy of the book Mr. Kopf wanted him to read accompanied his letter. It was the new revised edition of one of their most popular titles, *A Collector's Guide to Plastic Purses*. Jerome didn't know that much about plastic purses, but Mr. Kopf wasn't hiring him for his expertise but for his gut reaction as a Common Reader.

Jerome found himself a quiet area, far from the TV, in the dorm lounge and settled down to read the book then and there. It was incredibly boring, but there were lots of pictures, so it didn't take as much time to read it as he'd originally feared. When he'd finished reading it, he filled out the Official Reader's Report, stating in 200 words or less his own personal opinion that *A Collector's Guide to Plastic Purses* was not a book that most people would want to read, but that it would certainly have an appeal for anyone who collected plastic purses. He was tempted to add that he'd never known anyone who did collect plastic purses and had never even seen a plastic purse like the ones in the book. He didn't want to seem overly negative the first time he worked for Mr. Kopf. For all he knew, the man had already made a big investment in the book and wouldn't be happy to hear what Jerome honestly thought, which was that plastic purses sucked.

A week later Jerome received a check for $50 signed by Mr. Kopf, along with a note from Mr. Kopf's assistant, Betty Kreiner, thanking him for his valuable input. Jerome could hardly believe his good luck. He was employed! Just as the ad had promised, he was earning real money just by reading books!

The very next day he got a phone call from Mr. Yaddo himself, congratulating him on his first success in his career in professional readership. It surprised Jerome a little to think that Mr. Yaddo already knew about the work he'd done for Alfred Kopf, but as the lecturer had explained in his computer programming course, we live in an age when data flows at almost the speed of light, and the data knows, all by itself, where it ought to go. Anyhow, Mr. Yaddo was delighted for Jerome, and wanted to invite him to take part in a seminar that Mr. Yaddo was planning to conduct for a select group of professional readers in his own apartment. The fee for attending the seminar was rather steep, $1,500, but most of it would be paid by a National Endowment Fellowship, if Jerome would take the time to fill out the application Mr. Yaddo would be sending him and return it to the National Endowment Office in Boca Raton, Florida.

"Well, Jerome, what do you think?" Mr. Yaddo asked.

"I don't know," said Jerome. "It's a lot of money."

"It is," Mr. Yaddo agreed. "But faint heart ne'er won fair maid."

"What?" Jerome asked.

"Nothing ventured, nothing gained."

"Yeah," said Jerome.

"This could be your big break, fella," Mr. Yaddo said with great conviction.

"Okay, I guess so, sure."

There was a whirring sound at the other end of the line, and then a different voice announced, "You have been speaking with the simulated intelligence of Yaddo Incorporated of Boca Raton, Florida.

The Corporation stands behind all statements that have been made as being essentially similar to any that Mr. Yaddo himself would have made, were he available. Thank you for your interest and cooperation. And good luck in your new career as a Reader."

Two weeks later Jerome appeared promptly at Mr. Yaddo's apartment, which was in the World Trade Center, and looked more like a class-space than an apartment someone might live in. He was met at the door by a Chinese girl, who introduced herself as Tracy Wu and said she was Mr. Yaddo's protégée, whatever that was. She accepted the copy of *A Collector's Guide to Plastic Purses,* which Jerome had gift-wrapped as a present for Mr. Yaddo, and put it on a table beside other gift-wrapped presents. Then she led him to his seat in the third row of folding chairs that faced a king-size Sony Holo-Man.

"Isn't Mr. Yaddo going to be here in person?" he asked Tracy, before she could go back to the door to welcome the next participant.

"He may or he may not," said Tracy with an enigmatic Oriental smile. "Mr. Yaddo is nothing if not unpredictable. But if he isn't here in person, he will surely be here in spirit. We'll know in just a moment, won't we. Now, please excuse me, duty calls."

Participants continued to arrive for the next half-hour, which gave Jerome time to get acquainted with those sitting on either side of him, who were, just like him, newcomers to the profession of Readership. On his left was Ms. Lorelei Hummell, from Yonkers, a single mom with four children, who intended to specialize in books about Satanism and UFOs. On his right was Studs Liebowitz, a gay plumber with a Mohawk haircut whose chief interest in literature was books about the history of pro wrestling. By a strange coincidence, Studs had also prepared an Official Reader's Report for Alfred Kopf on *A Collector's Guide to Plastic Purses,* so they had something to talk about while they waited for Mr. Yaddo or his simulation to appear. At last, when all the participants had arrived, the Sony Holo-Man luminesced, and there was Mr. Yaddo, in larger-than-life simulation, wearing a five-piece Armani Suit and smoking a large Prestige Brand symbolic cigar, the kind that smells like room deodorant and can't give anyone cancer.

The Yaddo simulation blew a gigantic smoke ring toward the assembled participants, which dissolved into purple fizz as it reached the perceptual boundary of holographic space. It leaned forward and seemed to look at each participant directly in his or her eyes.

"Let's be honest with each other," it said. "Nobody likes to read. Okay?"

There was a murmur of muted dissent and a few cautious chuckles. From the last row of seats, Tracy Wu, Mr. Yaddo's protégée, raised her voice. "Then why are we here, Mr. Yaddo? *We're* all readers."

Ms. Lorelei Hummell nodded vigorously. "I *love* to read," she insisted, turning toward Jerome. "I read all the time. I am an *avaricious* reader. What's he talking about?"

"This is what I'm getting at." It paused. "Got your laptops open?"

"Are we supposed to be taking *notes?"* Studs Liebowitz whispered. "I thought this was going to be more like a party. It's just another damned lecture."

"Reading," said the Yaddo simulation, "is a dying art. It began to die when the movies were invented more than a century ago, and at this point genuine readers are an endangered species, as rare as the white rhinoceros. By readers I mean people who actually sit down a few hours every day with a book in their hands, turning the pages and reading what's printed on each page. It is not a natural activity. It takes training, application, and ambition. And if you want to make a career of it, it also takes connections. Which is why we're all here tonight, to learn to network, to rub shoulders, to earn big bucks."

"Right on!" Studs shouted out.

The Yaddo simulation smiled in Studs's direction.

"As professionals in the book field, we often ask ourselves, why do books exist? What practical purpose do they serve that our computers don't do better? What entertainment can they provide that isn't better provided by the flick of a switch? Maybe these are not the right questions to ask. Maybe we're looking through the wrong end of the telescope. Because the simple fact is that books exist because there is a gigantic industry that is in the business of making books. It is a faltering industry, admittedly, but it's still huge, and lots of jobs depend on it, our own included."

Studs leaned sideways and whispered into Jerome's ear, "I wish he'd cut to the chase and tell us which publishers to contact who want people to read books about pro wrestling. The rest of this is just a lot of crap as far as I'm concerned."

"Fortunately, we are not the first major industry to face such a crisis. When the tobacco industry experienced a similar crisis long ago, the Government stepped in and provided subsidies for tobacco farmers so they could continue producing a product that was less and less in demand. The same was done for breeders of Angora goats and for the Savings and Loan industry. When the publishing crisis loomed, the Government was ready. Thanks to the National Endowment this country now has more writers producing more books in more categories than ever before, and this in despite of the fact that almost no one reads any of them. Fortunately, paper is highly recyclable, and so after most of these books have been warehoused long enough for tax purposes, they can be made into other books, in the same way that tobacco plants can be ploughed back into the soil to grow new tobacco plants."

The Yaddo simulation paused to savour its symbolic cigar. This gave Ms. Lorelei Hummell time enough to raise her hand. "Excuse me, Mr. Yaddo. I have a question."

With a silken shiver of its Armani Suit, the simulation shifted into interactive mode. "Yes, Ms. Hummell?"

"I have read a lot of books. I mean a *lot* of them. So I can't agree with you about no one reads books any more. I have a bookcase *full* of books, mostly about UFOs and Satanic child abuse. So when I joined the Institute I naturally expected that I'd be sent books that related to my own special interest areas. But instead I got this book of *poetry."*

A murmur of sympathy passed through the participants, like the wind stirring a field of wheat.

The Yaddo simulation furrowed its brow. "What were the poems about, Ms. – " It paused as though searching its memory for her name. " – Hummell?"

"They weren't about anything at all in particular that I could see. The weather, sometimes, I guess. And maybe somebody died at some point, but that was never clear. I didn't know that poetry was *supposed* to be about something. If I had, I might not have given the book as high a rating. Anyhow, what I wanted to ask you about – "

"Poetry," declared the simulation, overriding Ms. Hummell, *"isn't* about anything. According to one great poet, it just *is,* period. According to another, it's a real toad in an imaginary garden, and the poet herself says she dislikes it. So it's small wonder if ordinary people dislike it even more. But that's why people are *paid* to read it. Now you tell me you *like* to read books about Satanic child abuse. And so, of course, do millions of other readers. It's one of the few genuinely popular genres left, because it speaks to the fears and curiosity of every parent. But those books don't need a subsidized readership the way poetry does. Does that answer your question, Ms. Hummell?"

"I guess so. Thank you."

"It sounds," Studs stage-whispered, "like we're going to be stuck with plastic purses."

Jerome nodded glumly.

The Yaddo simulation fielded a few more questions from seminar participants dissatisfied with the books they'd had to read, and then it switched tracks and delivered a long speech about the best way to read a book, including practical tips like you should try and sit somewhere where there was no TV and how you should try and set aside the same ten or fifteen minutes each day and make it an absolute rule not to let yourself be interrupted.

Then the seminar was officially over, though everyone was invited by Tracy Wu to have a glass of strawberry-kiwi punch and do some networking.

The punch wasn't free, but Jerome didn't find that out till he'd already asked for a glass and taken a sip. At that point, having forked over five bucks, he felt he had to finish the punch, so he stuck around and introduced himself to some of the other participants, who always wanted to know did he work for a publisher. When he told them he didn't, that was the end of any conversation. They were looking for another book to read, of course, but was that a licence for bad manners?

Finally, just to have some fun, he told the next person who asked that yes, he was an editor at Alfred Kopf.

"An editor! That's wonderful," the man enthused. He was the small, nervous type with a fox terrier haircut and beard, short and bristly, and the same apparent disposition. "They said there'd be editors and publicists here, but you're the first one that *I've* run into. I was beginning to think this whole thing was some kind of con game."

Jerome's was not a naturally suspicious nature, but now that the man had thrown out the possibility, he had to wonder whether he might not be on to something.

"Are you a reader?" Jerome asked. "Are you looking for a new assignment? Is that why you're here?"

"No," said the man with a thin-lipped weaselish smile, "no, I'm something even worse than that – from an editor's point of view. I am a writer."

"You write books?" Jerome marvelled. "The kind that publishers publish?"

"That remains to be seen. Before my novel can be published, I must find an editor who is willing to read it. And I understand, from my correspondence with the Scott Fitzgerald Literary Agency, that to find an editor I must first find an agent, a service that Mr. Fitzgerald offered to perform but only after receiving an initial reading fee that I balked at. For the same price I could publish the book myself in an edition of five hundred copies."

"Hey, would you like *me* to read your book?"

The man regarded Jerome with amazement. "Would you want to?"

Jerome tried to assume the world-weary manner of a professional editor of books, someone who had read dozens all the way through. "Well, like Mr. Yaddo says, no one *wants* to read books. It's a job, isn't it?"

"How much?"

"How much?" Jerome echoed.

"How much do you want to be paid to read my book?"

"Well, I'm not quite sure… I mean I didn't mean to suggest…"

"A thousand dollars?"

"A thousand dollars!"

"One and a half, then. It's all I can afford."

"Well, that's very generous, Mister, um – "

"Swindling. Lucius Swindling." He dropped his paper cup of punch into the trash puppy that had positioned itself by his knee and he offered his hand to Jerome.

Jerome gave the trash puppy his own paper cup, accepted Swindling's hand, and agreed that they had a deal, with two provisos: Swindling must pay him his reading fee in cash and he must deliver the manuscript in person and not Fedex it. It was easier than dealing dope.

Swindling agreed, and they met the next day at noon outside the legendary Union Square Cafe. Two of the tables inside served as the Manhattan office of Alfred Kopf, where its top editors lunched with other top editors and with celebrities wanting to sell their life stories and sex videos to the media. The more labor-intensive divisions of the company's business were based elsewhere, chiefly in Quito, Ecuador.

Jerome counted through the little sheaf of bills and accepted the little envelope containing the disc of Swindling's manuscript.

"You understand," said Jerome, slipping the manuscript into the pocket of the 100% cotton White Collar T-shirt he'd bought specifically for this occasion, "that I can't guarantee you that Kopf will want to *publish* your book. All I can promise is that I will read it."

"Yes, yes. But I do count on your writing me a rejection letter with a few remarks that show you actually read the book and some concrete suggestions for how I might go about re-writing it. A letter like that can make all the difference when the evaluation team at the NEA is going over my application for a revision stipend."

"You had a grant to write your book?" Jerome had all this while been thinking that the Swindling man was an old-fashioned kind of fanatic who wrote books because he wanted to.

"I've *four* grants," Swindling said, and ticked them off: "National Endowment, United Way, Advocates for the Disadvantaged, and a matching grant that went with the Advocates award from Prose Writers in Prison."

Jerome expressed polite surprise. "Gee, you don't look disadvantaged to me."

Swindling glared at him. "I have dyslexia."

"Dyslexia" rang a bell, but very faintly. It was one of those words like "polyunsaturated" that someone had explained to him once, probably in school, but the explanation had come unglued, and now the word was like a disc without a label. It seemed safe to say, "Well, that's too bad," and move on to an exchange of numbers. Jerome coded his phone to take calls from Swindling's and vice versa, and then they said good-bye.

Jerome wondered, as he fingered the roll of bills, whether this was, technically, a white-collar crime, and if so, whether it would have been called something more complicated than just fraud, and counted as a felony or a misdemeanour.

But what the hell, it was a job, and when was the last time he had a job? Swindling wanted a letter of rejection. He'd read his book and give him what he wanted.

It wasn't that easy. If *A Collector's Guide to Plastic Purses* had been a punishment, *The Last of the Leatherstockings* was cruel and unusual. It just about filled the disc and it was almost impossible to tell what it was about. Sometimes it was about a guy called Natty Bummpo, which made you think it might be funny (but it never was), and other times it was about a woman in ancient times called Madame Bovary, and then for a while it was about Swindling himself, who seemed to be some kind of serial killer, which might have been interesting, if he'd got into it, but Jerome figured he'd have made a better serial killer himself. Swindling had no imagination when it came to killing women. Any night on TV you could do better without even switching channels.

About halfway through Swindling's book Jerome had a brainstorm. If it was worth Swindling's while to pay Jerome 1,500 dollars to read his book and reject it, think what *he* must be getting paid to write it! So...

It was a simple thing to copy the disc and then change the name Swindling, each time it occurred, to Bagley, and Lucius to Jerome. The title also had to go, since the NEA's computer probably kept track of things by their titles. While he was deleting the title, Jerome also accidentally lost the first chapter, but that had been the boring part about Natty Bummpo, so getting rid of it was probably an improvement. Once he'd made that conceptual leap – the idea that he could *change* what was on the disc – Jerome was off and running. He downloaded the latest issue of *I'm a Writer* magazine and followed the advice of an article called "How to Write a Book," which was to write about things you know something about.

Jerome tried to think of something he knew anything about. There wasn't that much, but what there was he stuck into the book. He'd studied hair styling, so in all the parts of the book where Madame Bovary appeared she had her hair styled in some new way. It was frosted and braided and teased up into a buffalo and clipped down to elflocks. And where the serial killer was cutting up his victim's bodies, Jerome brought his cake decorating know-how to bear. He sprinkled some choice samples from his introductory Sanskrit course here and there, along with pointers on lubricating the suspension system for an '04 model Toyota Aida and how to deal with idle stop solenoids. The book kept getting longer and longer, and Jerome began to feel the thrill of authorship, as described in *I'm a Writer* magazine.

He retitled the new manuscript *I Iced Madame Bovary* by Jerome N. Bagley. He didn't usually use his middle initial, but somehow, even before he'd printed the manuscript out, it seemed like the sort of name a writer would have: Jerome N. Bagley.

He did not forget that he had an obligation to write a letter to Swindling. "Dear Mr. Swindling," he wrote, on a piece of stationery he'd designed so it looked like it came from the Kopf office at the Union Square Cafe, "Everyone here has been very impressed with your long book, *The Last of the Leather Stockings.* The first chapter shows unmistakable talent, and the character of Natty Bummpo is very interesting and original. However, we do feel that it needs *revision!* Concentrate more on Natty Bummpo and less on Madame Bovary. Maybe get rid of her altogether or give her a name that is more believable. Also, there is too much sex and serial murder. Can't you substitute something in place of that? For instance, plastic purses. At Kopf we are very interested in plastic purses. These are only suggestions, of course. Basically we are very excited about *The Last of the Leather Stockings.* Keep up the good work. Sincerely, Jerome N. Bagley."

A week later, at his regular session with his parole officer, Jerome announced that he had decided to become a writer, and that, in fact, he'd written a book.

"You've written a *book?*" Mona Schuyler marvelled. "What kind of book?"

"Sort of a big one," Jerome replied. He showed her the manuscript, which he'd had printed out on 496 pages of real paper.

She leaned across her desk and lifted up some of the pages to verify that they weren't blank. On every page there were sentences and paragraphs. "I'm amazed," she said. "A book."

"It's about sex," Jerome volunteered. "And killing. Like you'd see on TV, only I've written it all out."

Mona read the title page aloud: *"I Iced Madame Bovary."*

"By Jerome N. Bagley," Jerome pointed out with modest pride.

"It's a novel?"

"Yeah, I suppose so. You can read it if you want to."

Mona shook her head primly. "No, I'm not much of a reader myself. But you know what you should do, don't you?"

He knew, but he wanted to hear it from her. "What should I do?"

"You should apply for a grant."

"How do I do that?"

She explained.

It took most of the money he'd taken from Swindling to print out 40 more copies of the manuscript and Fedex them to the appropriate federal, state and city agencies and to enter it in the different competitions sponsored by publishers and writers' groups.

The first responses were not encouraging. The Great Writers Society thanked him for his contribution but pointed out that only Tentative Members were allowed to compete for the Harold Brodkey Memorial Award for Exceptional Early Promise, and it would cost him $500 to become a Tentative Member. The Authors' Guild, the Fiction Union, and American PEN provided similar disappointments.

And then he won the Pushcart Prize! The news came in a big envelope that announced that JEROME K. BAGLEY was a Pushcart Prize Winner and a contender for the Grand Prize of $100,000 *and* that his book might be optioned by a Major Hollywood Studio. He read through the letter carefully to see if there were any strings attached, and there weren't, except for a coupon that allowed him to purchase, at a substantial discount, 50 copies of the *Pushcart Prize Anthology* in which an excerpt from *I Iced Madame Bovary* was scheduled to appear. The letter was signed by Isaac Pushcart himself.

He was a little miffed that Mr. Pushcart had got his middle initial wrong, and when he returned the coupon he pointed out, in a polite way, that he was Jerome N. Bagley, not Jerome K. But that didn't help. When the 50 copies of the anthology arrived at his dorm, he was still Jerome K. Bagley. It didn't matter. Because there, on page 856 of the Anthology, was the excerpt that he'd written, the chapter in which Jerome Bagley decorates a Lady Baltimore cake with the minced heart and liver of Emma Bovary. The best part of all was the paragraph after "By Jerome K. Bagley" that said that he was a writer to watch out for, and that *I Iced Madame Bovary* was a brilliant contribution to the New Wave Postmodern Splatterpunk Novel, worthy to be compared to the work of Bret Eastern Alice.

Jerome made copies of the letter Mr. Pushcart had sent him and of what it said in the anthology about his brilliant contribution and sent them off to all the places he'd applied to for grants, then he waited for the results. They didn't come at once but when they did Jerome K. Bagley hit the jackpot. The National Endowment for the Arts awarded him a special citation for Writers Living in Dormitories, with an annual stipend for $2,500 renewable for five years. The New York State Council for the Novel offered him a Tenured Fellowship in their programme for bringing artists into homeless shelters. It paid him $8,000 a year, in return for which he was to give intensive workshops in Creative Writing at selected shelters in the Bronx and Queens. And the City of New York awarded him a grant of $5,438.92 so that he could be videotaped by the Department of Parks and Performance Arts while he read passages from *I Iced Madame Bovary,* which would be simultaneously signed for the deaf.

He didn't, in the end, win the Grand Pushcart Prize of $100,000, but by the time he got the bad news about that, he was already at work on his second novel and he'd been elected to the executive board of the New York office of the American Council for Literacy.

What worked for Jerome Bagley could work for you, too, readers! All that's required is an attitude of confidence, affirmation, and a sheer love of reading. So why don't you do what Jerome did and *earn big bucks by reading books!* If you want to know how to get started just mail a self-addressed stamped envelope to the American Council for Literacy, National Endowment of the Arts, Washington, DC and enclose your non-refundable check for $500.

You'll be hearing from us soon.

The First Annual Performance Art Festival at the Slaughter Rock Battlefield

AS THEY DROVE UP along the Delaware, Professor Hatch would keep pointing out objects of interest, mostly having to do with nature. K.C. had no use for nature. He'd had more than enough of it growing up in West Virginia, and the nature here seemed pretty much the same as the nature there, except for the river, and the fact that things weren't as level here so the road had to keep switching directions as it wound around the hills. Otherwise, you saw the usual stuff—trees, tall weeds along the road, some big rocks behind the weeds. According to Professor Hatch there were no towns for miles, just a few scattered convenience stores and filling stations. All the rest was nature.

"Funding," said K.C., lighting another cigarillo from the butt of the last one, "that's been my big problem. I could be doing *incredible* things if I didn't have to be thinking about funding all of the fucking time!"

Professor Hatch nodded sympathetically. "I know," she said. "It's the same here. It's the same everywhere."

"For instance," K.C. went on. "With the blood. I don't use *real* blood in what I do. Human blood, I mean. I buy the blood I use from a slaughterhouse, and I keep it refrigerated. It's *safe!* But then I go to this nowhere museum in Omaha or somewhere like that and, just because Ron Athney was there a couple months earlier and someone got a little blood on them...I mean, hey! is that my fault? I told them Athney uses his own blood, I use *animal* blood. Do animals have AIDS? So, suddenly

I'm not part of their festival, and they want the money back on my air ticket."

"I've had the same sort of thing happen to me," said Professor Hatch, swerving to avoid a road kill.

K.C. swiveled round to see what they'd missed. Raccoon. When he was in the driver's seat K.C. generally tried to connect with the road kill by way of putting his signature on the highway.

"I've had *worse,"* Professor Hatch went on. "I've had the police put chains across the doors of a church to keep my dance troupe from going in."

"No shit," K.C. sympathized. "Blood?"

"No, just nudity. In nineteen-eighty-seven! I can tell you I was depressed for a long time after that. And Alison – she's the co-director of the Festival but at that time she was my dance partner – Alison was traumatized. This lawyer, some official, I don't know, was reading this legal nonsense, and then four policemen started *tearing down our posters!* There were photographers from the newspaper, Alison was in tears, and I myself was frantic. They were destroying my whole life! I will tell you – *that* is the meaning of censorship. When two women cannot dance inside a Unitarian church!"

K.C. tried to imagine Professor Hatch nude, but he couldn't even imagine her with a first name. She wasn't a Miss, or a Mrs., or even a Ms. And he knew better than to ask where she was a Professor, or what she was a Professor of. She liked to talk but she wasn't interested in answering questions, unless they were the kind to keep her moving smoothly along her own private highway.

"This Alison, was she much younger than you back then?"

He'd thought it was a neutral question, but the Professor gave him a dirty look. "She was as much younger than me then as she is now. She was not a minor, if that's what you mean."

"No problem. I just meant they will always use that as a pretext if they can. I know from personal experience: I discovered that I wanted to be a performance artist when I was sixteen, so you could say I was a prodigy. I was working with this group called Early Death. We were more of a rock group really. Anyhow they wouldn't let *us* perform in this club in North Carolina because I was underage."

"North Carolina: that's Jesse Helms, isn't it?"

"I guess so. The blood was a problem there, too. Anyhow, like you say, it's all censorship."

Professor Hatch piloted them through a green tunnel of scenery that veered away from the river to the right. The conversation had fired her up to cruising speed, where she could drive along without feeling she had to keep talking. There was an alert, birdish glint in her eye, and the cords in her neck were stretched tight in a way that K.C. associated with being wired to just the right degree.

He smoked, she drove, the road unrolled in front of them, and then the first sign appeared for Slaughter Rock Battlefield. "There it is!" Professor Hatch said, hitting the brakes. The van skidded past the historical plaque, but she reversed until they were right alongside it.

The plaque said:

> SLAUGHTER ROCK BATTLEFIELD
>
> In this area on August 15, 1780, was fought one of the bloodiest battles of the Revolutionary War. Over 120 militiamen were ambushed and savagely slaughtered by a party of 27 Tories and 60 Iroquois Indians.

"You wouldn't think," said K.C., "that they'd want to advertise what happened – being beat by about half their own number of Indians."

"There's two ways to look at it," said Professor Hatch, as the van lurched off the shoulder and back onto the highway. "You can see it as our militia suffering a sorry defeat – or as the Iroquois enjoying a spectacular victory. The park ground has become very popular with Native Americans. They come from all over the state. But of course that doesn't make for a large overall annual attendance. I've picnicked there on summer weekends when *no one* visited the park all afternoon. As though it weren't *there*. When I made out the applications grant for the Festival, I pointed out that here was one of the finest recreational resources of Sullivan County going completely unused. They were spending thousands of dollars maintaining this hidden treasure, with its wonderful natural amphitheater that no one ever performed in. What a waste! But also, how typical. For there is practically *no* art in Sullivan County.

Of course, for me, and a few friends, that's been a kind of blessing in disguise. You see, New York State's grants programs for the arts are organized county by county. So, if you live in Manhattan, forget it! You could be Judy Chicago herself and you wouldn't get a nickel."

"Judy Chicago?" K.C. asked.

Professor Hatch smiled a Buddhalike smile. "Judy Chicago is the Pablo Picasso of the twentieth century."

K.C. knew he was being condescended to, but he didn't mind. The Slaughter Rock Performance Arts Festival was offering him an honorarium of $250 for his gig, plus bus fare. Plus, most importantly, a chance to be able to show what he could do as a solo artist instead of as part of Early Death. There were critics coming all the way from New York City to see the show – two busloads of them, according to Professor Hatch, who was the driving force behind the Festival. The woman definitely knew her way around the performance art world, so it made sense to suck up to her and listen to what she had to say like she was some kind of guru.

"Sorry," he said, "I didn't mean to interrupt. You were saying about how New York works things county by county."

"Yes. So, it stands to reason, doesn't it, that the counties with the fewest artists will offer the best opportunities? Over the years I've received grants as a choreographer in Allegheny County, and for my poetry in Oswego County. But it was opening the Slaughter Rock Gallery that's been the real godsend, since when you're an institution you can keep reapplying every year. Of course, I still have to do the outreach work, bringing the art to the local communities. There's no escaping that. And it makes sense: it's the people who are paying for our grants with their tax dollars, so it's only fair that there should be something we give back to the communities."

K.C. couldn't resist: "But I thought you said, when we was driving away from the bus station, that we were leaving civilization and that there weren't any real towns up this way."

"There are no towns – but there are communities. What do you think Sullivan County's biggest industry is?"

"I don't know. Timber?"

"It *used* to be tourism. But that was forty years ago. No, corrections is the big employer here."

"Corrections?"

"Actually, adult warehousing of all sorts. There is a federal prison, and three good-sized state prisons – the biggest of them just for teenagers. Plus all sorts and sizes of halfway houses and rehabs tucked away here and there. Including one you may have heard of – Utopia, Incorporated."

"No shit, that's *here?* One of the guys in Early Death got sent there. The last I heard he was still locked up. So what do you do at these places? You go inside the prisons and do your performances there?" In the nude, he was wondering.

"No, much better than that. We offer workshops. In dance. In quilting and poetry. In all the creative arts. It's been a marvelously successful program. There is a genuine *hunger* for the arts among those who have been denied their freedom."

"Believe it," K.C. agreed. "A hunger for *anything*. I know, I been there."

"You were? You didn't mention that on your application." There was something taunting and maternal in her tone of voice that K.C. could relate to.

"I served time in a state home," he said, "around when other kids would be serving their time in sixth or seventh grade. So those records are *sealed* under court orders. But you want to know what I *did,* right? The basic charge was arson and destruction of property."

"Plus ça change," the Professor said, possibly thinking he wouldn't know what she meant.

"You're right," he agreed. *"Plus c'est la même chose.* In terms of the performance art. Though I don't think that would serve as any kind of extenuating circumstance with the family court. For them torching a building is a crime, not an esthetic decision."

"That is the outlook," observed Professor Hatch primly, "of all but a very few. What thin partitions, as they say."

She'd stumped him with that one, as she had with her Judy Chicago, but he wasn't vain about asking to have things explained. How else do you get an education unless you suck up to people who know things you don't? "Okay," he said, "I give up. *What* thin partitions?"

"Dryden," she said. "His *Achitophel:* 'A fiery soul, which working out its way, / Fretted the pigmy body to decay.' Then, a few lines later: 'Great wits are sure to madness near allied, / And thin partitions do their bounds divide.' "

K.C.'s first reaction was to cop a resentment. He was sensitive to remarks about his height relative to anyone else's, and "pigmy body" had to be figured as a slap in the face. But this was not the moment to score one for the home team, so, filing away the slight for future reference, K.C. concentrated on his party manners. "I guess that's like saying genius is right next door to madness." And then, by way of putting a polish on the apple: "Thin partitions: I'll remember that."

Half a cigarillo later, and up a long series of switchbacks, they came to the gate of the Slaughter Rock Battlefield Memorial Park – a pair of four-foot-high pillars of unmortared fieldstone, each bearing a heraldic shield of painted plywood. On the right-hand shield a tomahawk, on the left a musket. Professor Hatch drummed her fingers on the steering wheel while an attendant uniformed in urban camo lowered the chain that barred access to the inner drive. As they passed through the gate, the guard saluted Professor Hatch, a real spit-and-polish heel-clicking salute, which she accepted as carelessly as any five-star general.

After a further steep climb, the road split in two. To the left was Parking, to the right Picnic Grounds. They hung right, passing through another pair of dwarf fieldstone pillars to draw up beside a large Winnebago parked in front of a row of portable toilets. The side of the Winnebago was lettered "Slaughter Rock Gallery – Preserving Sullivan County's Artistic Heritage." Beyond the toilets, scattered among high, thick-boled pines, were some dozen heavy-duty picnic tables and brick barbecues.

At one of the farther tables a small tribe of Mohawks was enjoying a lunch of Kentucky Fried Chicken and keg beer. The Indians waved at Professor Hatch, and she waved back.

"They're not the genuine article, of course," she said. "They're our re-enactors."

"I figured," said K.C.

"There was never any problem getting the young people to volunteer for the Festival once they heard that we'd be re-creating the events of Slaughter Rock. Of course everyone wanted to be on Thayendanegea's side, and not a militiaman."

"No surprise there. Who wouldn't rather dress up like it's Halloween – feathers and war paint and all that? And then, like you said, the Indians were the winners. That bunch over there sure started early."

"We should get started ourselves," said Professor Hatch, unlatching her seat belt and stepping out of the van. "Or at least I should. I'm going to have to leave you here with Alison, while I deal with some of the others. Meanwhile, if we could get your equipment unloaded...."

Professor Hatch opened the rear of the van with a remote, and then stepping away from the van, out of K.C.'s hearing, started talking into a cellular phone.

K.C.'s first concern was for the trunk that Liberty and Justice had been traveling in the whole long way from Camden, New Jersey. They'd never traveled such a distance confined in such a small space, and K.C. had been worried that they might get baked or would suffocate from being stowed at the back end of the luggage compartment on the underside of the bus. He'd wanted to open the trunk back in New York City, when he was changing from Greyhound to Trailways, but there hadn't been time. And when he got out at the crossroad where Professor Hatch was waiting, there wasn't time again. She seemed the kind of person who's always in a hurry, plus she probably was a herpetophobe. Lots of times people will tell you how they think snakes are so cool, the ideal pets and all that, but then you introduce them to Liberty and Justice and they'll go into shock.

They were both dead. He could tell without touching them. Any other time they'd spent some hours in the trunk, being bumped around, they would be hyperactive as soon as the top came off their case. Like as not, one of them would be curled up in position to attack, or might even take a lunge at him, forgetting about the steel mesh or just not giving a fuck. Not this time. They were dead.

K.C. did not believe in stuffing his feelings. When he felt something he expressed it. Any very intense or sudden pain took the form of a scream that started as a low growling, then took a yodel-like two-octave leap into a "Fuck this shit!" of high-octane primal rage. Even in grade school his tantrums had been legendary, but two years of professional experience with Early Death had perfected his native ability, and K.C.'s scream of grief for his two dead rattlesnakes transfixed everyone in hearing distance. Professor Hatch froze. A fat woman, who turned out to be the Professor's dancing partner, Alison, bounded out the door of the Winnebago. The imitation Indians sprinted across the picnic area, zigzagging between the tables, alarmed and excited.

With an instinct for the grand manner, K.C. took up Liberty in one hand and Justice in the other and lifted them over his head and screamed a second, even more artful howl – not as loud but shriller and wonderfully drawn out, with a quaver in it that would stop anyone who heard it in his or her tracks, like a baby's utmost scream. People are hard-wired to respond to that particular sound the way sprinkler systems respond to a fire.

It was Alison who took charge. She was a large, bottom-heavy woman, each thigh the size of an average torso, and she used her weight as a badge of authority. She marched forward, thigh by thigh, and took hold of the limp bodies of the snakes. "No more of this nonsense," Alison told K.C. "Let go."

He let her take the snakes from him and then, grateful as a musician might be for a good segue, went limp himself. Down on his knees with a silent wince of pain as the gravel ground at his kneecaps, then a fetal curl forward so that he could hide his face in his cupped hands and wait for the tears, if any, to begin. He thought of his own naked corpse, with all his friends and family gathered round (a trick he'd learned taking acting lessons at the community college in South Jersey), feeling guilty and regretful. Sure enough, the thought of his own tragic waste, so young and so talented and so thin, released the tears. Not a flood exactly but enough so that when he lifted his head they were there to be seen by the ring of spectators – all wearing Mohawks and war paint and looking amazed.

"Hey, K.C.," said the most elaborately authentic of the Indians, "get a grip, man."

"Jethro? Death Row Jethro?"

Jethro opened his arms invitingly, and, after K.C. had got back on his feet, they performed a solemn male embrace, jeans apart, arms wrapped tight around each other's shoulders.

"It's been a while," Jethro said, disengaging and taking a step backward, "since anybody called me *that.* Here I'm just John." But he grinned in a way that assured K.C. that that was just a lie he had to tell for the sake of Professor Hatch and all the other Indians. This was the familiar wolfish grin of the lyricist and lead singer of Early Death's only song to hit the charts, "Homicidal Maniac."

K.C. wiped away his genuine tears with the cuff of his shirt. "You look a whole lot healthier, man. Compared to two years ago."

"It's holistic," explained Jethro. "You can't deal with just the symptoms alone, like in Western medicine, you have to treat the whole man. Plus, I've been eating a lot of food."

Jethro stroked the area on his thin, jutting chin where his goatee used to be. Without the beard and with his irregularly shaped cranium exposed by the Mohawk, Jethro's face seemed even more like a skull than when he'd been Early Death's lead guitar. The weight he'd put on hadn't altered his basic persona, he was still a living reminder that all men are mortal, some more than others.

"I'm sorry about the snakes," Jethro commiserated, laying thin, fluent fingers on K.C.'s shoulder. "But that doesn't mean you'll be left out of the show. Where there's a problem there's also a solution. Remember when we were in Winston-Salem and the amps got busted up by those rednecks? Wha'd we do? We used those car alarms for back-up and we had a big success. Right? Am I right?"

"Yeah," K.C. conceded sullenly. He didn't like surrendering the drama inherent in his grief for Liberty and Justice, which he probably could have milked for more sympathy, particularly from Professor Hatch and her buddy Alison, who were the impresarios. On the other hand, maybe it wouldn't be such a good idea to come across as too unstrung. Jethro's instincts were right, even if he did sound like he was whistling some limpdick tune by Oscar and Hammerstein: When you walk through deep shit, keep your bootstraps dry, and don't be afraid of the dorks.

In any case, K.C. had a short emotional attention span, and after a primal scream had given his insides a good reaming-out he was usually ready to move on to new feelings. Liberty and Justice were gone now, no changing that, and he'd expressed his grief in a suitable way. Walk on, walk on, like the song says. The whole idea of performance art, as K.C. had come to understand it as a mature artist, was to deliver a gut punch, then step back, go somewhere else where for a while you might seem to be boring, and then when they weren't expecting it, Wham, a kick to the groin. Shock treatment. That was how a good horror movie worked, or a stand-up comic. Make 'em laugh, make 'em barf, keep 'em guessing.

So after being formally introduced to Alison (who was the strict sort of feminist who didn't shake hands with men but just looked at the hand being offered and nodded her head) and to the other Iroquois from Utopia, Incorporated – Keno, Duster, Winthrop, Lou, and Marlene – K.C. settled down with his old pal for a session of lateral thinking. At first Jethro's inspirations were all in the direction of nudity, which was no surprise. Jethro had a big dick, and he'd always been the first to drop his pants at any Early Death concert. And it had worked, since it is a gross-out for everyone, and an inspiration for those who can identify, to see someone so cadaverous also so well-endowed.

K.C. had a hard time diverting Jethro to alternate veins of inspiration, but he persisted. "We got to think of something that will work with that flagpole. The snakes may be out of the act now, but I still got all these ropes and pulleys and the harness. They're a major investment, I can't just scrap them."

"Okay, okay. We're looking at a flagpole. We're looking at you being raised *up* the flagpole."

"Upside-down," K.C. reminded him.

"Right. Up the flagpole, upside-down. Plus, you're in handcuffs?"

"Yeah, but they're gimmicked. I can get them off when I need to."

"I got it!" said Jethro. "What's the most natural thing to send up a flagpole? A flag! We'll burn a fucking flag."

"You think?"

"I know."

"We tried that once at the end of our gig in Durham. It didn't go down so well there, if you remember. Freddy lost two teeth."

"But that was North Carolina, this is New York. We've got two buses of critics coming up from the City, and those dudes will have *no* problem with burning a flag. They're liberals up here, they get off on that kind of thing. It's like you'd be exercising your First Amendment, or the Second, whichever. And it would fit right in with the re-enactments. Better than the snakes would have, if you think about it. Here's a battle that the Indians *won*. This was their land before there was any flags or flagpoles, just fucking trees. And the Professor is very big on the Native American angle, so she'll dig the idea of setting the flag on fire, I can guarantee, besides which it'll give us Mohawks something to do besides scalping our victims. We got a whole lot of Mohawks in the show. Basically, everyone who isn't doing guard duty at the gate is wearing war paint."

"Your whole rehab?" K.C. marveled.

"All of them in the *show,*" Jethro qualified. "Some of them opted out. So they're back at Utopia or decorating the grounds here as fallen heroes. Anyhow, in terms of putting *you* in the line of fire, Old Glory is as good as snakes any time. I like that: the line of *fire?*"

"Yeah yeah, I get it."

"And while the flag is being raised to where you're up there hanging by your heels, we can have Duster play a tape of 'The Star-Spangled Banner.' The Hendrix version. Well?"

"Lemme think about it." K.C. took the last cigarillo from his pack and snapped a wooden match alight with his thumbnail. But instead of lighting the cigarillo he just stared at the quivering yellow flame as it crept up the matchstick toward his fingers. When the heat got too intense, he dropped the match.

"Okay," he said, having thought it over, "I think it'll work. Let's go talk to the Professor."

It was Freddy Beale, Early Death's drummer and resident psychic, who'd originally got K.C. involved with the Tarot. The first time Freddy had read the cards for K.C. he'd told him to pick a card from the deck to be his Significator, and K.C. had picked The Hanged Man. Freddy had objected to his choosing a card from the Major Arcana, but K.C. had never had any doubt in his mind that The Hanged Man had to be his Significator, because his first childhood memory was of his dad dangling him upside-down from a pedestrian bridge while the traffic whizzed by on the highway below. What he was being punished for K.C. couldn't remember, and later his dad would insist that nothing like that had ever happened, that K.C. was either remembering a dream or else making it up. But the physical details were as clear now as though he'd seen it happen on a wide screen with Dolby sound: the perspective lines coming to a V at the upside-down horizon, and the cars hurtling toward him and disappearing with a whoosh and then a semi, sounding its horn like a blast from the last trumpet. Most of all he remembered the way it felt – not at all scary, like his dad had probably intended, but thrilling, like a ferris wheel. Years later, outside St. Louis, riding the big ferris wheel overlooking the Mississippi, K.C. had tried to recapture that sensation by hanging from the safety bar by his knees, trapeze-style, but before he could start spacing out on the visuals, the operator of the ferris wheel had freaked and K.C.'s death-defying ride had wound up in the amusement park's security office, which is not an ideal environment when you're peaking on acid.

This now was the best that upside-down had ever been, thanks in part to the equipment, which was designed for a balanced distribution of weight and minimum chafing, but mostly on account of the view. The flagpole he'd been raised to the top of was thirty feet high and situated at almost the highest point of the amphitheater, with a view in one direction of the tiers of stone benches where the audience would be sitting, and in the other direction across the whole actual battlefield, which was enormous. "Field," however, was not exactly the right term for it, since what K.C. could see was a steep downward vista of trees and rocks and suicidal plummets. From where K.C. was slung in the suspension harness he could see across the leafy treetops to the actual Slaughter Rock the place was named for, which had been decorated by the re-enactors with various dead bodies – very realistically done up, at least from this distance – representing the Yankee militiamen the Iroquois had slaughtered. If he squinted, he could see one corpse that looked like it had been genuinely scalped. Professor Hatch's FX people deserved high points for that one.

Those old Iroquois had been into savagery, no doubt about it. According to Professor Hatch's friend, Alison, who was some kind of expert about the Revolutionary War and Native American torture techniques, the major casualties of the battle had all taken place right underneath that one long ledge of reddish-black rock. As the militiamen had been wounded in different other parts of the mountainside they'd been brought there for medical attention, and then, when everyone else who could had escaped, the Indians had found the field hospital and the 74 wounded men. And that was how the place had got its name of Slaughter Rock. As Alison had pointed out, history isn't always just a lot of names and dates.

Though K.C. was not one to pay much attention to nature and the weather and all such as that, he had to give credit where it was due, and this was shaping up into one beautiful day with big old clouds sailing by underfoot and a wind that kept swinging him round in unexpected ways. He started writing lyrics in his head, which was something he only did when he was in a special mental space. This one looked like it might be a haiku, though he didn't bother counting the syllables the way he would have had to do if he was a formalist-type poet.

Real is the crowd in the bleachers

his haiku began. Then, after one or two false steps, it continued

No less real the clouds
Sailing by my combat boots.

Strictly speaking, the first line wasn't true. There was no crowd in the bleachers at this point, just Jethro and a few other fake Iroquois who were doing Tai Chi exercises on the topmost stone ledges of the amphitheater, so that their half-naked bodies were silhouetted against blue sky and billowing clouds.

Freddy had tried to get K.C. interested in Tai Chi, but for some reason it hadn't clicked. Where was Freddy now? he wondered. The last he'd heard Freddy had been in a shelter for battered women in Biloxi, having finally got himself transsexualized and then married to exactly the wrong guy. Talk about karma. Anyhow, he, or she, was probably still alive, which was one better than Gordon, who'd played rhythm guitar for Early Death – and Russian roulette, once too often. Right on the stage of the 4-H Club Building at the Linnet County Fair. *Those* fans had sure got more than they'd bargained for. And now all those screams and excitement were just so much nostalgia like the snows of yesteryear.

At first it had seemed an amazing coincidence to bump into Jethro this far away from the scenes of their old crimes. But there are no coincidences in real life, there's only networking. Jethro had explained to K.C., while he was being fitted into the suspension harness, how it was all his doing, Jethro's, that K.C. had been contacted to be one of the major acts at the First Annual Performance Art Festival at the Slaughter Rock Battlefield. How Professor Hatch had been skeptical at first but finally caved in when Jethro had explained about K.C.'s act with Liberty and Justice. Never mind that the act had never in fact been performed before a paying audience: it *was* a great idea, even on paper, and Jethro had even been able to dig up a copy of the application to the National Endowment for the Arts that he'd helped K.C. write up just before he, Jethro, had been shipped off to Utopia, Incorporated. Professor Hatch had expressed a respectful admiration but it was her friend Alison, according to Jethro, who had gone bananas. "Darlene," she had said (that being the Professor's Christian name), "we have got to get this boy here. He sounds archetypal." Alison, according to Jethro, was the real decision-maker. Professor Hatch, for all her greater visibility (Alison tended to stay inside the Winnebago), was only following orders most of the time. According to Jethro.

So here K.C. was, by Fate's decree, and Alison's, hanging upside-down from the highest flagpole in Sullivan County in the State of New York, waiting for fame's lightning to strike. K.C. had always known that he was destined to be a celebrity artist on a par with Karen Finley or David Wojnarowicz, transgressing the boundaries, destroying old categories, bringing down the house. It was what his whole life had been pointing toward since even before the accident, so-called, with the kittens in the laundromat when he was only four years old. Back in France there was Rimbaud, and now there was K.C., and who could say for sure which of them would make a bigger dent on the human psyche in the long run? K.C. was bound for glory: he could feel it in the very fillings of his teeth.

A sudden gust of wind twisted K.C. around (his harness had a swivel bolt) so that he was, once again, facing toward Slaughter Rock – and there at long last, on the woodland path leading to the amphitheater, were the critics, off their buses and being herded along by Professor Hatch, who was identifiable even at this distance by her peculiar hairstyle, which looked like a large gray doughnut on top of her head. The critics had stopped to admire the re-enactors, who were brandishing their spears and tomahawks and executing and re-executing the wounded militiamen. The spectacle was given a muted, ballet-like solemnity by the way Alison had choreographed the scene to resemble the clockwork motions of elves in a department store window at Christmastime. Behind and to the sides of the cluster of critics were guards in urban camo, like the one who'd greeted Professor Hatch at the entrance to the park ground.

The wind shifted and K.C. swiveled round so that he could no longer see Slaughter Rock and the arriving critics. His right shoulder struck the flagpole, but he managed to twist his cranium out of harm's way. At just that moment his earphones staticked into life. "K.C., can you hear me? This is Alison."

"Hey, Alison, finally. We've got problems."

"K.C.? K.C., can you hear me? Oh dear. I can see you, with my binoculars, moving your lips. But the sound isn't coming through."

"Come on, don't *do* this to me. I know you can – "

"There's always some glitch, isn't there," Alison went on in a tone of imperturbable sweetness. "Well, we'll muddle through. The show is about to get on the road, and I don't think you could be any more nervous than I am at this point. The things we do for art!"

K.C.'s mike, in the shape of a miniature cobra, was positioned right to the side of his mouth. He did not believe that it wasn't working, but on the chance he *wasn't* being lied to he spoke into the mike with the exaggerated clarity that he'd had to use when he was taking classes to become a TV anchorman, as though his crisp pronunciation might magic away the technical problems. "Alison, we have a problem here.

My good buddy Jethro has decided to play some kind of practical joke. These cuffs he's put on me are not the cuffs I supplied him with. There's no spring, and I cannot get my hands loose. Can you hear this?"

"You're trying to say something, aren't you? But it isn't getting through. The artist's eternal plight!"

"Fuck," said K.C. feelingly.

"I can *hear* Darlene perfectly – she's telling our visitors all about the events leading up to Slaughter Rock, from the perspective of the Iroquois *women* – and I can *see* you, but not vice versa. I would like to be able to fix your mike, but there isn't time now to lower you and do that and get you back up there again, and you do make such a startling first impression. I'm chattering, aren't I? I always get like this before the curtain goes up. Don't you? I call it The Moment. It's not exactly stage *fright,* more a feeling that something unique and terribly important is about to happen. As though – Wait a moment, I'm getting something from Darlene."

The earphones went dead for a while, and K.C. tried to do the same with his thoughts. He was beginning to intuit that something was not right. It wasn't just that Alison seemed flakey. The world is full of flakes, that is a given. But what K.C. was picking up was that the Festival was not the simple scam he'd been expecting, not just an opportunity to give the NEA-funded finger once again to the bourgeoisie, which is to say, to the people who have to pay for their tickets. The organizers of the Festival seemed to have a more ambitious agenda.

Why, for instance, was Jethro, on the top tier of the stone bleachers, firing imaginary bullets in K.C.'s direction from what looked like it might be a real rifle? Jethro would mime taking aim and then, mouthing a *Pow!* inaudible at this distance, he'd jerk the barrel upward. K.C. began to reappraise their relationship. Jethro was a fellow artist, true, and in an ideal world there should be honor among thieves. But Jethro might well be harboring a grudge toward K.C. with respect to how he'd been admitted in to Utopia, Incorporated, under a court-mandated order that allowed him to be detoxed in lieu of serving hard time. The last time K.C. had seen his old friend, on the night he'd freaked, Jethro had been exercising his right to bear arms, and his *Pow!*s then had had real bullets attached, which were aimed at real people, K.C. included.

Sometimes cops are the only solution, but even otherwise rational felons tend to hold a grudge against those who pursue that solution.

A while back, Jethro as part of his ongoing recovery had E-mailed a note to K.C., apologizing for the bullet holes and offering amends, but what if that letter, so sincere and full of honest feeling, did not represent Jethro's final thinking on the matter? What if he was looking for a payback? And what if these new friends of his had agreed, for their own flakey reasons, to help him get even?

Alison came back on line. "It's me again," she said brightly, "and everything is all right, no need to worry. One of our guests was making problems. He wanted to go back to the bus. Which is not exactly possible at this point. But Darlene has things under control. It was the critic from the *Voice,* and we can't very well let *him* miss the show, can we? Good Lord! Especially since the *Times* never showed. Wouldn't you know. After all the promises! Critics!

"Do you know what our major expense has been for this whole event? Catering! I'm not kidding. Each of the buses had to have two cases of champagne. Et cetera. But if we hadn't laid out the money and chartered the buses and *groveled,* there wouldn't be anyone here but us chickens. For a New York critic even Brooklyn is terra incognita, and that has been the story of my life! But not any longer. Somebody has got to draw the line. This far, no farther, stop. Life isn't long enough. Literally."

Alison stopped talking but K.C. could still hear her wheezing breath over his earphones. She sounded like a car that had flooded its engine and couldn't get started.

While Alison was still stomping on the gas pedal, so to speak, the critics began to file into the amphitheater. One of the critics began to make a stink when the guards – who were now serving as ushers – insisted that she had to sit in the area reserved for the press, in the middle of the second and third tiers. She wanted to know why she couldn't sit up in the top tier, since there was no one else in the amphitheater. Unless you counted Jethro, who had finished with his imaginary target practice and settled down into lotus posture, eyes closed, chanting his mantra, which was *Hare Kali, Kali Hare!*

The sound of the argument was drowned out by the opening squawk of the amps and then Hendrix's "Star-Spangled Banner." A procession of local grade-schoolers appeared from out of nowhere, dressed up as little Pilgrim Fathers and Mothers, in cocked hats and bonnets, and trying to sing along with the National Anthem.

Hendrix was faded to allow Alison's much amplified whispery soprano to announce, "From the Benjamin Tusten Elementary School in Fort Tusten, New York, won't you please welcome The Thirteen Colonies."

The critics dutifully applauded as the thirteen children came to attention in front of them. There's nothing like having kids on stage for making an audience settle down and behave, unless it's dogs or horses. The critic who'd wanted to sit higher up had plunked down where she belonged and was paying a bemused, condescending attention to The Thirteen Colonies, who had marched up single file into the bleachers to surround the critics in a loose oval.

Alison began a dramatic reading of Robert Frost's "Mending Wall." "Something there is that doesn't love a wall," etc. As the poem was read, the guards erected, with astonishing rapidity, a real wall of spiraling razor-wire between the children and the critics. As the progress of the wall's construction passed one of the children, he or she would hold aloft a miniature version of Old Glory and announce which of the original thirteen colonies he or she represented. Only little Delaware muffed her line.

"Well, there they are, Darlene," said Alison, unamplified, over the earphones. "Our captive audience. Didn't I tell you?"

"You're right, they just sat there for it," said Professor Hatch. "Amazing."

"It's what they're trained to do, isn't it? No critic will admit to being fazed, or shocked, or disconcerted by anything they might be made to witness. Besides, with that ring of darling children around them, waving flags, and Robert Frost to boot...."

"Which, I must say, you read very well, my dear."

"Thank you. It's a poem I've always loved. I do wish those children could have stayed on for the finale, though."

"Now, we've discussed all that before. *Some* entertainments really are not suitable for the young. In any case, our thirteen darling little colonies are back on their school bus, which must be somewhere along Route 97 by now. And believe me, *cara mia,* they will never forget this night. It will live with them forever."

"Forever is such a lovely word," Alison whispered. "Forever and a day!"

This was followed by a sound that K.C., if he'd heard it over the radio, would have interpreted as a kiss. Did they know he was listening? Would it have mattered?

"K.C., are you still there?" Alison asked, reading his mind. "Oh, I know – what choice do you *have?* But you mustn't think I mean to tease you. I actually have a great deal of respect for your physical courage. That's something I lack entirely. Your friend Jethro says that you are like the boy in the fairy tale who simply could not feel fear, or even embarrassment. I'm just the opposite. Sometimes I simply can't bear to be *looked* at, even by Darlene. So you can imagine what a breakthrough it was for me, with two left feet and ten thumbs, to become a dancer. Every performance I felt I was about to commit suicide. Well, and here we are now, doing just that! So to speak.

"Have you ever had a major medical problem, K.C.? Are you, for instance, HIV-positive?"

K.C. shook his head no.

"No?" She must have been watching from inside the Winnebago, which stood like a dam across the path leading from the parking lot to the amphitheater. "Jethro didn't think you would be. He said you'd get a lobotomy sooner than have sex. The reason I ask is not that I have any anxiety against dealing with Persons with AIDS. It's because it's so hard to explain what I've been through to someone who's never been there. Have you ever heard of Crohn's disease? Not c-r-o-n-e, but C-r-o-h-n. It's what I've got. A medical condition not very well understood. The walls of the intestine thicken, and that can lead to fistulas and abscesses, and that can result in peritonitis. Which is fatal. There's no certain cure. A surgeon may remove one section of the bowel, and then it recurs somewhere else. So...What is one to do? That's what I've had to ask myself. Submit to surgery? That's like telling a woman that since she *must* be raped she might as well relax and enjoy it. I don't think that is a rational solution to the problem. In fact, I don't think rationality itself is a solution. Western medicine treats symptoms, so the essential problem, which is spiritual, remains unsolved. So what *is* the solution? Art! Think about it, K.C. Art."

There was some actual art happening, meanwhile, in the amphitheater, in the form of an old-fashioned square dance, the kind when the men wore little white wigs and the women had big dresses. Apparently, the Festival's budget didn't have room for anything but the most notional wigs and ball gowns, but imagination made up for the lack of funding. The "dancers" – two men and two women – were strapped into wheelchairs and they were being do-si-do'ed and allemanded at high speed by eight of the Iroquois, while, in combination with some jingly super-loud harpsichord music, Professor Hatch spelled out the significance of the event.

"Before the Europeans came to these shores," she boomed out over the amplified harpsichord, "there were no walls. No amber fields of chemically fertilized grain. The dances of the Native Americans were shamanic rituals that united the dancer and her goddess, not geometric diagrams designed to subdue and deform the bodies of women. For the Europeans who came here in their *Niña*s and *Pinta*s and *Mayflower*s this entire continent was one vast woman, whom they would bind with treaties and title deeds and claims of ownership – and then...rape!"

At this cue, the four wheelchairs were equipped with old-fashioned muskets that were supported on tripods connecting to the seats and armrests, so that each weapon would be aiming in the same basic direction as the chair on which it was mounted. The music changed from a square dance to a fife-and-drum version of "Yankee Doodle," and Professor Hatch read the verses of that song at a death-march tempo in her throatiest, most menacing tone of voice, deconstructively repeating some of the phrases, such as "keep it up" and "went to town." To this accompaniment the four miniature armored vehicles converged on the front row of the amphitheater, then tilted back so that the muskets were aimed directly at the critics enclosed within the circle of razorwire.

K.C. had once attended a performance in Louisville of *The Cencis,* a tragedy by the great French schizophrenic Antonin Artaud. At the very beginning of the play, two actors dressed up as soldiers had emptied their bladders into a plastic bucket at the side of the stage. For the remaining four hours of the drama that bucket just sat there, but everyone knew what was going to happen with what was in that bucket before the play was over, just the way you know when you see a gun in Act One that it will be fired before the last curtain.

The difference between the bucket back in Louisville and the muskets here and now was that there was no four-hour wait. Not even four minutes. "Yankee Doodle" came to an end – Professor Hatch was screaming "And with the girls be handy! And with the girls be handy!" – and without anyone having to pull a trigger (they must have been detonated by remote control) the muskets discharged, and the critics went into a state of panic. The muskets had sprayed them with pellets of colored chalk, which, exploding on impact, had turned them into instant living bunting. That was how Indians of India celebrated the holiday of Diwali, as Professor Hatch was trying to explain, but K.C. seemed to be the only one there paying any attention to her text.

One of the women in the critics' enclosure, her clothes and hair red from the chalk, tried to tunnel under the ring of spiraling razor-wire. The wire could not get a purchase on the motorcycle jacket she was wearing, but it did snag into her hair and her blue jeans, despite which she kept crawling forward with her face pressed against the ground until she'd managed to break free of the wire. Then she headed in the direction of the Winnebago and, presumably, the exit. No one set out in pursuit. The Iroquois stood beside the wheelchairs they'd been pushing, and the uniformed guards posted along the upper tier of seats remained where they were, as did the critics, who didn't have that much choice in the matter, after all. Everyone watched as the escaping critic rounded the Winnebago and ran out of sight. Only K.C., from his privileged point of view, saw what happened next, as Duster tackled her to the ground, and Jethro ran her through with a bayonet and then in true Native American style took off her scalp.

"If everyone would kindly return to his or her seat," said Professor Hatch in a schoolmarmish tone of voice, "the performance will continue."

The critics had not actually *left* their seats (with the one significant exception, whose body was being dragged to the parking lot by

Duster), but they'd heard their colleague's screams of protest and of pain and taken them to heart. K.C. wondered if it had begun to dawn on them that they'd been cast as extras in a homemade horror movie. (He assumed that someone was putting all this on videotape.) For that matter, when had *he* copped to the fact? Not till he'd actually seen Jethro scalping the lady behind the Winnebago, really. And yet there was that other scalpee laid out beside Slaughter Rock, which it now seemed safe to assume was not the work of set decorators but a genuine dead body. Whose? Probably someone connected with Utopia, Incorporated – one of the counselors so-called. There was enough free-floating ill will at any rehab to provide the psychic energy necessary for systematic mayhem. Rehabs aren't that much different from prisons, except for the way in a rehab they try and make you say how much you love Big Brother.

"We'll be raising the flag shortly," Alison confided to K.C. over the earphones, "but before we do, I wanted you to know how pleased I am that you've been able to be part of the Festival, K.C. In just a short time you've become very special to me. You have the gift of basic trust, as I do. I've always known that Someone or Something is looking after me. Some call it a Higher Power. Others believe in angels. Darlene has been both to me, especially since the diagnosis. *She* was always the one, before that, who had such crushing depressions. She was the one that had to be rushed to the emergency ward to have her stomach pumped. And my role was the pillar of strength. I'd tell her, 'Darlene, your day will come. Your work *will* be recognized. You mustn't give up now, on the brink of success. Don't turn your anger inwards: *use* it!' Oh dear, our time is so limited, and there's so much to express, to explain, to celebrate! But Jethro and Duster are giving me signals. It's that time."

"The Star-Spangled Banner" kicked in at once, but at a very low volume, as though you were a teenager again listening to forbidden music in your bedroom late at night. Jethro and Duster emerged from behind the Winnebago with a flag the size of a bedsheet. As Jethro and K.C. had mapped it out, the flag had been stiffened at both ends by bamboo rods so that it wouldn't flap around as it was hoisted up the flagpole by the pulley system knotted into K.C.'s braided ponytail. At the base of the pole, they sprayed the flag with gasoline syphoned from the Winnebago's tank, and then, once it had been raised to where the whole length of the flag was lofted up and on display, Jethro flicked his Bic and Duster started hauling on the cord of the pulley.

K.C. knew he was in a desperate situation, but he had had time to think about how best to employ his limited resources. With his hands securely cuffed behind his back (and he had scraped his wrists down to the basic hamburger putting that "securely" to the test), there was no way he would be able to get to the knife inside his belt buckle for some quick assistance. Which ruled out his being able to cut through the pulley's cord or the hank of hair that held it in place. An alternative remained – sit-ups.

K.C. had always wanted washboard abs, and he never finished up any workout without fifty sit-ups on a steep incline. Not full inversion sit-ups, but the principle was the same. He had time for one good try. He turned his head sideways and tightened his gut muscles so his body bent pretzel-wise.

God helped: the double cord of the pulley was hanging down across the front of his ear. With a further twist of his head, he was able to clamp his teeth on both cords, at which point he slowly eased back from his sit-up so that he was hanging back in his original Tarot-inspired position. Directly underneath him, Duster was tugging at the cord of the pulley, each tug a little more vigorous and threatening to the integrity of K.C.'s molars. The burning flag had reached its full First Amendment glory, and K.C. could feel the heat and smell the reek of gasoline.

Duster, who was obviously the kind of person with a low threshold of frustration, gave one final furious jerk to the cord, cracking one of K.C.'s molars but at the same time bringing the burning flag down on himself in a billowing bright extravaganza that could not have been more dramatically satisfying if it had been planned, though K.C. doubted that any of the assembled critics were making such reckonings at this point, for they were being squirted with some flammable fluid by the uniformed guards, who had gathered round the critics at full battalion strength.

"K.C., that was *sensational!* We haven't that much time left to talk, but if you *do* survive, Darlene and I have made tapes that explain everything. The rejections we've encountered as artists over the years. The critical sneers. The assessments of peer panels who never came to a single performance. Basically, it's so simple. I don't understand why no one has thought to do it before. If one is ready to take a big enough risk, and to make real sacrifices, finally, the Establishment can't stop an artist from achieving immortality. Jethro understood that from the first, and so did Darlene in her way. Well, I'm getting signals again. It's closing time."

The charges buried beneath the benches of the critics' enclosure were detonated first, and the critics, guards, the wheelchair square-dancing team, and all superfluous Mohawks were united in a single, kerosene-laced sphere of flame that dissolved all differences between actors and audience, text and context.

The Winnebago went next in a blast that would not have looked meager even in a *Die Hard* sequel.

So was K.C. alone left to tell the tale? In which case what was he looking at in terms of fees from the tabloids, appearances on talk shows, book royalties, and, why not, a TV docudrama? Maybe he might even get to play himself! But no, he had to be realistic. He was too short for a leading role. His best hope was to share credit on the script. Even so, the whole basket of unhatched eggs had to amount to more than a million.

Perhaps it was unseemly to be focused on his performing career at such a moment, with the other victims of the tragedy dismembered by the explosion and still in flames all about the amphitheater, but K.C. had never had strong feelings about other people than himself. In that, according to many of the authorities on the subject, he was not unlike other major artists past and present from Andy Warhol to William Burroughs.

His basket of eggs was not yet out of jeopardy, however, not while Jethro was still alive and, potentially, kicking. The electric motor that powered the winch that had lifted K.C. to the top of the flagpole began to whir, and K.C. found himself descending, a little too quickly for comfort, toward ground level. But a concussion was not what Jethro had in mind, for he braked K.C.'s descent some three feet above the flagstones. K.C. found himself staring into Jethro's beaded loincloth and thinking he was about to be the victim of the most elaborate rape in human history. But that wasn't what Jethro had in mind either, for he started the motor again and raised Jethro up another three feet so that they were eye to eye.

When someone is crazy, or very spaced, the best way to deal with him, according to all the police shows that K.C. had seen on TV, is to pretend he is rational. So that's what he tried to do. "So, what are your plans now, Jethro? I suppose you'll escape through the woods, just like the guys who survived the original battle here."

"I hadn't made any plans actually."

"Oh, come on. You expect me to believe this was all improvisation?"

"I mean, no plans for afterwards. I was supposed to be in the Winnebago with Alison and the Professor. There weren't going to be any survivors. It was going to be like Jim Jones down in South America."

"Well, maybe Fate's decided we're supposed to be survivors. It wouldn't be the first time."

"Fate, huh," said Jethro.

There is something about having an upside-down conversation that is very disconcerting. The other person's eyes are where the mouth should be and they blink in the wrong direction, while the motions that the face makes as it speaks – the lips exposing and concealing the teeth, the glimpses of tongue, the lifting and lowering of the jaw – begin to have the hyper-fleshy look of a Giger alien. Add a Mohawk and war paint and features as naturally Giger-like as Jethro's and the total effect can induce a first-rate sense of alienation or, as they say in the theater, *Entfremdungseffekt.*

"You shouldn't push your luck, Jethro. Even if there aren't any next-door neighbors that close by, there's bound to be some kind of official reaction to those explosions. I wouldn't linger backstage."

"So I should go hide in the woods? Live on berries and mushrooms?"

"If they think you died in the Winnebago, they won't start a manhunt."

"And why would they think that?"

"Cause I could say I saw you go in there right before it blew up."

"And why would you say that?" Upside-down and with the war paint it was hard to know if the expression on Jethro's face was a sneer or a frown of indecision.

"Cause it makes a better story. When it's made for TV. At the end of a story like this you want all the bad guys dead."

"So I'm one of the bad guys, am I?"

The look on Jethro's inverted face was definitely a sneer, and K.C. began to see light at the end of the tunnel.

"You've always been one of the bad guys," K.C. assured him. "One of the worst."

Jethro nodded. "I could take one of the buses the critics came in."

"No," said K.C. "If you do that, they'll know there's someone to look for. What you've got to do is wash that stuff off your face and change into some regular clothes and toss what you're wearing now into the Winnebago while's it's still blazing. Then disappear."

"And leave you to be a witness?"

"Right. But hoist me back up to the top, so I'm hanging up there when the cops get here. It shouldn't be much of a wait."

"I *could* just use your head for a football."

"You could, but if you do that, know what the result will be? When they make the movie about all this, it'll be Susan Sarandon and Geena Davis who are the stars. Whereas, if it's based on *my* version of events, it'll be a movie featuring Death Row Jethro – the first genuine mass murderer ever to be funded by the NEA. Is that reason enough?"

Jethro nodded. The basket of eggs was saved.

Later, hanging from the top of the flagpole, enjoying the scents of the night breeze, K.C. continued casting the movie in his imagination.

THOMAS MICHAEL DISCH was born in Des Moines, Iowa, on February 2, 1940, and grew up in the Minneapolis area, where he attended a succession of Catholic and public schools. At the age of seventeen he moved to New York ("I knew that Manhattan was where I belonged," he later told an interviewer. "A hundred movies told me so, and I believed them") and returned, after serving briefly in the Army, in the late fifties. His interest in literature and theatre led to work as an extra at the Metropolitan Opera (where he played a spear-carrier in *Swan Lake* with Margot Fonteyn and a blackamoor servant in *Don Giovanni*) and in various bookstores and copywriting jobs. In 1962 he wrote a science fiction story, "The Double-Timer," instead of studying for his exams at New York University. When it sold to the magazine *Fantastic*, Disch left school and dedicated himself to writing.

For the next half dozen years Disch concentrated primarily on science fiction, publishing his first novel, *The Genocides*, in 1965, and a half dozen more, including the celebrated *Camp Concentration* and *334* (as well as pseudonymous work in the mystery and gothic genres), over the following decade. By the early seventies Disch was ranging outside the confines of category fiction, publishing short stories in venues such as *Playboy*, *The Transatlantic Review*, and *Antaeus*, and essays and poetry in *The Atlantic Monthly*, *Harper's*, and the *Paris Review*. *On Wings of Song* (1979), considered by many to be his finest work, was his last science fiction novel.

Disch's large and extremely diverse oeuvre includes plays, opera libretti, historical novels, movie and TV novelizations, interactive fiction, anthologies, literary essays, and a considerable amount of theatre criticism. His children's books *The Brave Little Toaster* and *The Brave Little Toaster Goes to Mars* were made into feature films by the Walt Disney Company, for which Disch also wrote story treatments, including one that eventually became *The Lion King*. He served as drama critic for *The Nation* between 1987 and 1993, and in 1990 his verse play "The Cardinal Detoxes" was presented by the RAPP Arts Center in New York, where it caused a controversy after the theatre's landlord, the Roman Catholic Archdiocese of New York, sought to close the production.

Although *The Businessman: A Tale of Terror* sold modestly upon its original appearance, its successor, *The M.D.: A Horror Story*, became a best seller in paperback in 1992. Disch published two more novels in his sequence of Minnesota supernatural thrillers – "a sort of Balzacian *comédie humaine*, with overlapping characters" – in the course of the nineties. In 1996 *The Castle of Indolence: On Poetry, Poets, and Poetasters* was nominated for the National Book Critics Circle Award. Another nonfiction book, *The Dreams Our Stuff Is Made Of: How Science Fiction Conquered the World*, won the Hugo Award.

Following the death of his longtime partner Charles Naylor in 2005, Disch largely withdrew from writing fiction, although he continued to produce poetry, much which can be found on his blog *Endzone* (*tomdisch.livejournal.com*) and in the forthcoming collection *Winter Journey*. He published a novella, *The Voyage of the Proteus: An Eyewitness Account of the End of the World*, in January 2008, with a sequel scheduled for December. His final novel, *The Word of God: or, Holy Writ Rewritten*, composed in the months before Naylor's death, appeared this summer, a few days before Disch died, on July 4, of a self-inflicted gunshot wound.